TWO
VIRGINS

NOVELS BY KAMALA MARKANDAYA

Two Virgins
The Nowhere Man
The Coffer Dams
A Handful of Rice
Possession
A Silence of Desire
Some Inner Fury
Nectar in a Sieve

TWO VIRGINS

A NOVEL by
KAMALA P. Taylor
MARKANDAYA

THE JOHN DAY COMPANY—NEW YORK

The John Day Company, 257 Park Avenue South, New
York, N.Y. 10010

Published on the same day in Canada by Longman
Canada Limited.

Library of Congress Cataloging in Publication Data

Markandaya, Kamala, 1924–
    Two virgins.

    I. Title.
PZ4.M3447Tw3   [PR6063.A642]   823'.9'14   73–4293
ISBN 0–381–98244–0

Printed in the United States of America

TWO
VIRGINS

1

CHINGLEPUT RAN THE only sweetshop in the village. It was static, even moribund, during the monsoon, but in the ten months' dry season it became mobile, trundled around on the little cart Chingleput had decked out himself. No one knew his name, least of all Chingleput; they named him after the town where he was born and bred and grew up, alone, being without parents, and Chingleput agreed that they should. He could do no different. He was three at the time. What is your name? they asked him, and when he did not answer—he was a late developer, did not talk till four—they called him what was written up over the railway platform.

Chingleput grew up more or less on that platform.

3

He sold sweets there, from a tray balanced on his head, to the passengers in the third-class carriages. The old man made the sweets, overnight, in a small cookshop in the town. Chingleput watched him, and learned how, but the old man would not allow him to experiment. He only wanted someone young and sturdy to carry them and sell them as quickly as possible, before flies and ants could make fretwork of the sweet glossy surfaces. He kept nine-tenths of the gross profits for himself. When the one-tenth net had added up, Chingleput left the old man and the railway station and began to trade on his own. He was a good sweetmeat and pastry cook. The roasted nuts in his *ladus* stayed crunchy to the end, and the sugar he drew up on the ends of his tin prongs came up as fine, people said, as maiden's hair.

But the machines were better. They spun sugar finer, faster, than he with his prongs. They roasted nuts by the barrelful. The town was full of machines.

Chingleput bundled up his spare shirt and cooking vessels and implements in his sleeping mat, said goodbye to Chingleput Station. There was hardly anyone else to say goodbye to. He walked to the village and set up there, under a banyan tree. His bright charcoal *sigri*, and the quality of his sweet-making, soon brought him customers. In no time at all he was done with the tree, moved into a cookshop of his own. He built it himself, with a baked earth floor and a corrugated-iron roof, and sacking at the sides to save his ribs when the wind got up. There was a brick burner in one corner and a stone slab for a counter.

Chingleput called all the boys "young brother," and all the girls "little sister." They were his good custom-

4

ers. He called Saroja Saroja because her mother sold him buffalo milk for his extra-special fried milk sweet. As far back as Saroja could remember, she could remember Chingleput sitting in his sweetshop cooking sweets. Some of the time he sold them over the counter, done up in small newspaper cones; but most times he loaded all his stock on a cart and hauled it through the village and did a good trade. Not good enough, though, to buy a bullock. Or so Chingleput said. He put himself between the shafts and padded his forearms where the wood abraded. He didn't want the bullock eating up his nine-tenths of the profits, he told Saroja, and himself back to the old one-tenth. He preferred sweating to that. He preferred anything to that, he told her with great force, and she saw it had made a scratch on his soul. But she wished he would get a bullock when she saw the sweat running in rivers down his naked back, especially in April and May, when the sun turned white by noon. He told her he was used to it, all that cooking, and the perpetual fires he had had to keep burning for the old man. He told her a good many things, and if she listened well he opened the glass box in which his special sweets were kept and popped one into her mouth.

Saroja liked listening to Chingleput, in the mornings, while he was cooking and she could watch, before he tacked himself up to his cart. In the evenings she watched Manikkam rounding up his three cows to milk them. There was a fourth, but it was barren. Manikkam wanted to sell it to the butcher, old and scraggy though the cow was and only dogs could have chewed through the gristle, but his wife wouldn't let him. She was a good Hindu, she told him, and never would consent to cow slaughter, but the real thing was she was too fond of the old scraggy cow. Saroja knew, because she had seen Manikkam's wife stroking the cow, and bathing its udders which were cracked and yellow, and rubbing coconut fat into the splits. Should I grudge her a mouthful of grass? Manikkam's wife would ask, after all the milk that has flowed from her these past years? Manikkam's wife understood about milk the way Chingleput understood about tithes, because she was a wet nurse. She could not have other women's babies for them, but she suckled them at the same time as her own. When the women in the big houses had babies they sent for Manikkam's wife, if she happened to have had one too. They sent *jutkas* to summon her, and she climbed in with her own infant because without it, she said, the milk wouldn't flow. The women, she told Saroja, used her because they did not want to spoil the shape of their breasts, which suckling did. They wanted to keep them firm and round for their husbands. Saroja wondered, if she had a husband, if she would put him or her baby first. She was certain she would never give away her milk to another woman's baby. Sell it, Manikkam's wife corrected her, and her eyes became a narrow: I *sell* it, dear. Besides, she said, it flows, see how it flows: and she opened her bodice and squeezed the nipple between finger and thumb so that Saroja could see the bluish-white milk spurt. She did not press hard, Saroja noticed. She did not have to press at all sometimes—the milk squirted out in five or six thin jets of its own accord when her baby cried. Saroja thought it was wonderful. Manikkam's wife did not. She was used to it

6

with all the babies she had had and the others that she suckled. She was glad of the money, though.

Sometimes the dry cow doddered over into Appa's acre. This was not difficult to do because the only thing in its way was an old clump or two of prickly pear. Appa planted the prickly pear to protect the crops in his acre. Amma said What crops, the only crops there are are in your imagination. But Appa said all the same it was his land and Manikkam's cattle should not stray over it, and he planted some more prickly pear. Amma sniffed and said it was no good to man or beast. Saroja could not agree with her mother, because she had seen the dhobi's donkey nibbling at the cactus. The donkey had white circles round its eyes like eye shadow, and velvety lips, but its tongue and palate must have been tough to tackle the bristly cactus. Saroja liked the prickly pear too, for its bright yellow flowers and its red fruit, but her fingers were soft and often got badly pricked even when the boys helped her get at them. Saroja loved the pulp, which was sticky and very sweet and delicious, but you had to be careful on account of the prickles buried in it, which could leave a nasty rasp on the tongue. It was hardly worth eating the fruit, there was so little left after you had picked all the prickles out.

Manikkam didn't care about his cows wandering on to Appa's acre. He put up bamboo palings around his own crops and sucked his teeth while Appa complained about his ground being trampled over. His cows must eat, he said. Did Appa, or Amma, or Saroja, or the boys, eat grass? he wanted to know. That was all Appa grew, and it was a long time since anyone had eaten grass, not

7

since the time of the sahibs. Why grudge animals, he said, what men didn't want? and he rounded up his cows and led them home to milk them. They would have gone anyway, Saroja often saw them crossing the boundary at sundown; but it appeased Appa to have them driven off his land, which Manikkam knew.

The land was a gift from the government, Appa told Saroja. Appa had been a fighter for freedom—not like some, he said, bootlickers, who had fawned upon the sahibs for crumbs from their table. When their time ended, those who had fought for the freedom of India were rewarded. Sometimes he told them this, and sometimes he said it was because he had given his all. Amma said he had lost all through his own folly. The ancestral home was stuffed full of freedom-fight leaflets which he had printed. He should have distributed them too, but he hadn't got round to it. When the British Tommies found them they simply set fire to the whole lot, not being finicky about what caught light, and the house went up as well. So did the printing press and every stick of furniture bar four chairs.

When the Tommies had gone, and the Civil Service as well, and the new government was in, there was nothing Appa could think of to do. He hung around, and one day the resettlement officer asked him was he a small farmer, because land grants were being made to the landless. Appa said yes, he believed he could be anything he turned his hand to, so he got his acre of land. Appa said it wasn't like that at all, it was twisting the truth to say it was, and Amma must have learned from the British who were adepts at it. The British had called him a terrorist, though everyone—even they—

8

knew he was fighting for freedom, and if that wasn't double-talk, what was? Appa wished Rangu was there to tell them what was what. Rangu was dead, though; he had died after being taken to the police thana for interrogation: beaten up, some said, but no one really knew because he had simply collapsed and died without ever speaking.

Rangu had been Appa's best friend. They went everywhere together and shared everything they had and did their freedom work together, which was like a blood bond. Whenever Appa spoke of Rangu, which was often, a fondness came into his voice; sometimes it went husky and cracked, though it was so long ago. He and Rangu had planned to be partners in some enterprise or other when the struggle was over. Appa said they would have had lakhs by now, would have been rolling in the stuff only Rangu had gone and died.

They scattered Rangu's ashes in the river which ran at the bottom of the field. The boys could remember Appa going down there afterwards, walking along its banks in the evening. They said it was to speak to Rangu's spirit, to wring from it what Rangu's lips had not had time to reveal, because he came back stumbling and mumbling and they caught snatches of what he was saying before Amma could whisk him away. Saroja could not remember, she had not even been born, but all the same she was a little afraid of that stretch of the river, never would go down on her own, save by full light.

A lot of ashes got scattered in the river. It was handier than the Ganges, for which one had to traipse up north, or even the waters of Kaveri, for which one went south, which were also holy. Some people would, though. Appa called them fanatics, said which river carried your ashes did not matter, they all went down to the sea and eventually into fishes' bellies; but Amma said fishes didn't eat ashes and told Saroja not to pay too much attention to her father. She had been to Varanasi and bathed in the sacred river. In fulfillment of a vow, she told Saroja, which her mother, Saroja's granny, had made. Its terms she would never disclose, but Saroja guessed it was to do with having babies, because Amma always began by saying it was before the boys were born. Appa said, guffawing, he had turned his energies to creation after the struggle was over, it had nothing to do with the vow, but Amma said tartly What about the years in between, then, when your energies were spilling over for nothing?

The river had a name of its own but after Rangu it became Rangu's River, although it took a lot of people away besides him. When the river was in spate the ashes were rushed along, but when it shrank to a trickle the current was barely enough to shift them. Saroja watched them, gray and cindery and floating lazily by, and wondered who they had been. Sometimes she knew, which made it more interesting, but sometimes it made her quite sad, made her afraid for her Amma. Although, of course, her soul was quite safe, Saroja knew you couldn't destroy the soul, but she loved her mother's body as well.

Amma's body was soft and brown and smelled of the sandalwood paste she used. It came as a powder in a tissue-paper packet which the Sikh hawker brought. He came once or twice a year, carrying a suitcase in

which were a good many things besides sandal powder. There were carved wooden toys and hair slides
and hair nets, and cream and jars of pomade and
sprinkler bottles of rose water. Saroja loved it when
he sat down and threw open the lid of the treasure
case, but she was a little afraid of the Sikh, who was
burly and bearded, totally unlike anyone she knew.
He wore his beard trapped like a bird in a hair net;
and below his pink turban his eyes were black and
piercing. Altogether he looked like an eagle, that
might seize you in its talons and bear you away.
Amma laughed when Saroja told of her fears. He was
a human being like them, she said. Appa said all India
was one now, and they must learn to live as one. It
was a British stratagem, he said, to divide the people
up and set them one against another in order to rule
them, and they must never make that mistake again.
Amma said Can't you ever forget the British, you've
got them on the brain? But Appa said Remember
Rangu!; and Aunt Alamelu, who was Amma's wid-
owed sister, told of some Sikhs who had knifed some
Hindus in some train during the great exodus and left
them on the carriage floor weltering in their own
blood. Appa said How do you know, were you there?
You should not keep these vile stories circulating; but
Aunt Alamelu sniffed and said Brother, you are a wise
and educated man and you never forget what the British did, so why should we forget the iniquity of our
own people, which is an indelible stain on us as their
crimes are on them? Saroja wanted to ask if the Sikh
hawker was one of their own people, he looked so different, but she guessed if she did her elders would bark

at her and vent on her head the ill will they obviously felt for each other in moments like these, so she did not.

Later Amma brought out her lacquered wooden box and picked about in it as she did when she needed to regain her composure. She got out the packet of sandal-wood powder and poured some into her palm and worked it into a paste with water and rubbed the paste into her arms, slowly, in little circles. The skin when she finished was golden-brown from her wrists to where the sleeves of her bodice ended. Elsewhere it was the color of dark honey, except for the creases in the bend of her elbow and the root of her neck which were purple like grapeskin. Saroja had never seen her mother all over, all at once, but she had seen her bare from the waist up when she was oiling her hair, and bare from the waist down when she stood on a plank and washed between her legs. She was careless about closing the bathroom door when only the girls were about. Lalitha said Saroja should not look at their mother when she was like that, but Saroja didn't see why not, she liked Amma's body, which was plump and soft and as com-forting as a cushion, especially when you had one of those miserable spells.

Appa's body was hard. Saroja could feel the bones through his shirt when he hoisted her onto his shoul-ders, but it was only a remembered feel because he did not pick her up like that any more. She was too big now, he said. The boys sometimes did, though, when they came to visit. They whirled her up and said How you've grown!, which they had loathed when they had it said to them, but she supposed they'd forgotten because they were fully grown men and would not grow any more. When you're grown up there's only one way left—downward, said Aunt Alamelu, but Amma said not to be so depressing. Amma was a good deal younger.

Appa was also younger than Aunt Alamelu, but although she was older, Aunt Alamelu tried hard not to cross him. She didn't have the status. You didn't have status if you hadn't a husband, and if you had no father like Chingleput it was almost as bad. Appa said Nonsense, it's only a question of money and men happen to earn the money in society as it is at present organized. But the women knew better.

Lalitha had status. She had no husband yet, but everyone could see when she did she would have more than her fair proportion. There was no lack of emissaries. The young men's mothers sent them, and the women came and spoke to Amma and pinched Lalitha's cheek, and Lalitha was demure, pressed her delicate feet together and cast down her eyes to show off her lashes, which were long and lustrous. Saroja knew it was for show because Lalitha told her. It was a pity, she said, that Saroja had such an insignificant fringe, since a lot could be done with sweeping eyelashes. She gave Saroja some of her scented castor oil and Saroja rubbed it in but her lashes never grew thick and smudgy like Lalitha's, which didn't really surprise her, Lalitha's lashes were quite phenomenal. It is a pity, some people are pretty, some people are plain, said Lalitha, examining herself languidly in her hand mirror. Saroja knew which she was, but she had become used to being plain. Secretly she hoped one day she would turn out beautiful, like a butterfly bursting out of a chrysalis, perhaps when she was older.

Lalitha, though, had not had to burst out of anything, she had always been beautiful. A prettier newborn babe I never set eyes upon before or since, Appa said in his boastful moods, but Amma said All our babies were beautiful, not a flaw or blemish on any of them, why do you have to make a difference between them? But Appa couldn't help it, Lalitha was his favorite because she was pretty and pert in the same way that Manikkam's wife favored the old cow above the others because it was decrepit and helpless. There were always reasons, Appa said, and Saroja knew it was true.

Lalitha went to the school where Miss Mendoza taught. Older people remembered it had once been called the Mission High School but it was now called Three Kings School and Miss Mendoza told Appa it was better than the state school because of the artistic opportunities it offered its pupils. She told Amma it developed the character of the girls, especially the moral side. Amma was a bit dubious, because Miss Mendoza was a Christian, although an Indian, and she didn't want Lalitha taking up curious religions, but Appa said Think about the opportunities. So they transferred Lalitha to Three Kings School and she learned moral science, and how to dance around a bamboo pole which Miss Mendoza said was a maypole. There was a fee to pay for these privileges, whereas the state school was free. Appa said it was money well spent. Amma agreed, but only when she saw Lalitha dancing round the maypole.

They all went, Amma and Saroja and Aunt Alamelu,

and the other mothers and aunts, and even fathers like Appa who had plenty of free time, to the school concert to which Miss Mendoza had invited them. She was fond of organizing events like this, and the parents said How good it is for our girls, it brings them out. Saroja thought they must mean the way sunshine brought buds into flower, because the girls looked very like a bunch of flowers, very grown up in their saris whereas usually they wore skirts and blouses. They all wore different colors, and the dancers had ribbons to match. Lalitha was dressed in rose-pink, and pink ribbons fluttered from her waist as she took little dancing steps around the maypole, which was painted in rainbow stripes. As she danced, and the girls danced, the ribbons which dangled from the pole were woven into pretty patterns. Saroja had not seen anything so pretty. She clapped hard and wished the state school taught maypole dancing, and felt quite ashamed when Aunt Alamelu said loudly maypole, beanpole, bamboopole bunk. In the *jutka* going home Appa was cool toward Aunt Alamelu. He said how some people could spoil anything, but Saroja did not think anything had been spoiled. She hugged her knees tightly, and rested her chin on them, and thought of the entrancing ribbons and Lalitha dancing round with them. She was glad she had such a beautiful sister.

On Appa's land grew a tamarind tree. It was a very old, spreading tree, with a gnarled trunk which both Saroja's arms could not girdle. Amma was always asking Appa to chop it down. Nothing, she said, would grow in its shade, its shade was not like that of the neem tree, it was a malign shade. Aunt Alamelu corroborated; it gave off airs that heated the blood, she said, it was not good for the health. All our trunk roads, Appa informed her, are lined with tamarind trees, under which travelers take their rest and do they all fall ill like flies? Yes, and who planted those trees, said Aunt Alamelu: it was an edict of the British, and you know what ninnies the British were, but you show me any traveler from these parts resting under a tamarind tree! Appa said What nonsense, but Saroja could see he was in a dilemma because he often told them what ninnies the British were, ignoring the ancient wisdom of the country they were supposed to rule. The next time they were on a trunk road, going to a fair, she kept a lookout and saw that Aunt Alamelu was right because the travelers who were resting had all chosen the shade of banyan trees. The tamarind trees were full of monkeys.

The boys liked the tamarind tree that grew on Appa's land, and so did Saroja. It was good for climbing, and there was a rope suspended from the topmost branch from which, if you were fearless, you could swing right up, right up over the tilting fields with the sky and the horizon tumbling about you. Amma kept saying Chop it down, and at first they were afraid Appa might have a bout of energy and do it. After a time, though, they saw it was just a habit Amma had got into, because really she was quite fond of the tree, which yielded enormous quantities of tamarind for her pickles and for sale. Saroja liked the taste, which was sweet-sour. Chingleput called it outstanding, always came to Amma to beg for some of her piquant tamarind for his recipes. He told Saroja the leaves were even better: the leaves when young, so young that they were still furled up at the base. When she tried them her jaws ached and the saliva ran, but both were nice feelings; she agreed with Chingleput that they did taste better than tamarind pulp.

The spring rains washed the leaves and that was the best time to eat them. The worst time was when the hot winds blew. They swirled the soil off the land and wafted it up and the leaves became coated and gritty with dust. You could wash them of course, but it didn't make much difference, the dust was embedded, it got embedded into everything, even your hair which was black took on reddish undertones. Amma said it was the most terrible time of the year, but she said that of the monsoon too, and the season when mango flies swarmed, and the time when the monkeys arrived.

The monkeys came when the trees were fruiting, and the papayas ripening, and the gourds fattening nicely on Manikkam's wife's vegetable patch. No one knew where they came from. There were no monkeys for miles around until these times when the influx began. Whole families came. You could see the grizzled elders, and babies clutching the underfur of their mothers' bellies. They stripped the tamarind tree. Appa rigged up a contraption of gongs, but it did no good, only woke them all when the wind got up at night. Manikkam came and he and the boys stoned the monkeys. Amma supervised, crying Be careful, be careful! because she didn't want to hurt any of them, only to scare them off her tamarind. A baby was hit; it fell to the ground, crying like a human infant, tears running down its face. The mother clung to the branch above, chattering and making faces at them, but too frightened to come down.

They were too afraid of her to approach the baby monkey. It was badly hurt, Saroja could see, and crying, and she felt anguished for it; in the midst of her anguish she was wondering if a baby monkey's cries would start Manikkam's wife's milk spurting and she stole a look but it wasn't, the bodice was dry.

While they were hovering Aunt Alamelu came out and told them of a similar incident in which the second cousin of a friend had had an eye plucked out by the mother monkey. Appa shut her up with a look. He said we must all go away, the mother will know how to deal with the situation.

In the morning the mother monkey was gone together with the rest of the tribe. Only the baby was left, still where it had fallen, and Saroja could see dried blood on its fur. Amma took it in. She sighed and said Haven't I enough of my own? What crime have I committed in past lives to bring me a monkey infant at my age? But Aunt Alamelu instead of sympathizing with her said, grimly, it is your punishment for stoning these poor harmless creatures. They quarreled. Amma was bitter and ferocious, unlike her usual self; Saroja could tell she felt quite bad about it, having seen the star-shaped hole the stone had made in the baby's thigh.

On her way to school Saroja stopped off to tell Chingleput about the baby monkey. He said it ought to have been left to die as its mother intended when she abandoned it, because the tribe would never accept a cripple, not properly, that is, though it might manage to tolerate one. Saroja was horrified, until she remembered Chingleput had a crippled foot, and concluded he must know. She asked if Chingleput's mother had intended him to die when she abandoned him as he had told her she had done. He said probably, but he didn't hold it against her, society was the criminal. Saroja thought about society and wondered what it was. Appa and Chingleput often blamed it, and now the boys were beginning. Appa said at least it was in their power to mend society now they had the vote, whereas in his time they had been powerless, not having any vote worth speaking of. He said being helpless like that was the worst kind of feeling, and they the future generation must never allow themselves to fall into alien hands again. Saroja was determined never to fall into such hands, even if it was not too clear what they might be.

What she was definitely and dreadfully afraid of was falling into Lachu's hands. Lachu did nothing all day long but sit by the roadside stretching out his hands to the girls on their way to school. Sometimes he lurked behind bushes, and this was worse than knowing he was there and coming up slowly to him and getting past as quickly as you could, because he could get hold of you, haul you into the bushes before you could whisk by, before you could run fleeter than any deer you had heard tell of to the school compound, which immediately assumed the aspects of a haven. His hands were terrible; they were puffy and fat and they looked like a bunch of bananas. Jaya said what terrible things those fingers could do if they reached up under your skirts. Saroja closed up her thighs and asked what exactly, but Jaya only said it was not to be described. Jaya's eyes shone when she told; she was older than Saroja, but in the same class.

Saroja could not interpret that sheen. It disturbed her, made her feel she was missing out.

Amma and the other mothers said it was scandalous. They made up a deputation and they called on the police sub-inspector in the police station which was the bottom half of a grain store. The sub-inspector said he knew, he knew, wasn't he a father himself? but you couldn't put away a man who was innocent and a man was innocent until he was found guilty, that was the law, and where was their evidence? The mothers went away. They called the law an ass, said everyone knew about Lachu, and what crimes must be committed before their daughters were protected? but they had no evidence to offer because none of the girls would testify.

The girls were too terrified to, because Lachu told them he was a madman, and madmen were the children of God. If you tell on me, he said, God will make you a goat in your next incarnation, you will be chopped up to make goat curry by Muslim butchers. Secretly the mothers were glad the girls would not testify, they did not want it shouted in the courts what had been done to their daughters. Especially Amma, who had been walking with Saroja, and both had seen Lalitha flicking her lashes at Lachu. What if? said Lalitha, and tossed her head; he is a simple man, he wouldn't harm a fly, he just dallies with girls, didn't Krishna dally with girls? Krishna was a personification of God, cried Amma, are you daring to compare him with this gutter lout? Who said I was, I'm only saying, said Lalitha, but she shut up, put her mouth in the shape of a rosebud and lowered her eyes when she saw Amma's wrath, which was turning her cheekbones purple. Watch it, said Amma, just you watch it, my girl; and you could tell the rage she was in from the way she marched on with her sandals slapping up against her soles.

It's her coming out in me she doesn't like, Lalitha told Saroja. Saroja didn't know what she meant, but she knew she was scratching at the edge of a mystery from the way Aunt Alamelu clapped a hand over her mouth when she asked her, then removed it and told Saroja not to pay any attention to Lalitha's rubbish. Saroja paid attention when she was told to, and even more when she was told not to because she had discovered you learned more that way, and mostly they were the more interesting things.

Saroja asked Lalitha if Amma had dallied with Lachu. Are you mad? asked Lalitha scornfully, and added that Amma was too ancient to dally with anyone. So Saroja asked if Lalitha had dallied with Lachu, but Lalitha said Mind your business, and turned her back on the charpoy.

Saroja listened to the crows. She often did when Lalitha would not talk to her, turned so that the cot strings bounced and showed her back. The crows roosted in the tamarind tree. They nested there. It was disastrous for the nests when the monkeys were around, but when the monkeys had gone the crows came back. It was their country: the monkeys were itinerants. A plague on them both, said Amma. Saroja was of a different opinion. It lulled her to listen to their sleepy cawings and rustlings at night, whereas Amma said it kept her awake. Except the night Appa rigged up the gongs against the monkeys. He called them gongs; they were more like wind chimes, being hollow metal tubes suspended from a string which the least rustle of wind set off. He was cunning, did it before the monkeys came. That night the crows were shocked into silence, but everyone else felt jolted when the wind got up. It didn't stave off the monkeys either. Another of your father's fancies, one might have known, said Amma.

All day the crows flew round, looking for food. They had very bright beady eyes, could spot a grain of rice a mile away. They had the corn off the cobs before Manikkam could get round to netting his crop. When he parted the floss to feel if the milk was filling out the kernels he found each cob as stark as a lingam. Appa was amused when Manikkam told him; it was the kind of thing that more often happened to him. He laughed immoderately, offending Manikkam, but Manikkam had the last laugh because when it came to hoisting the beam Appa had intended for the buffalo shed it was so light both men keeled over. Appa had left it lying around too long: white ants had eaten away the interior. Manikkam was convulsed; he liked being one up on Appa, who was an educated man whereas he, Manikkam said, was only a humble cultivator. Appa was quite put out, said That's what's wrong with this country. Amma wanted to know what other country he had in mind for comparison, considering he'd never been out of India, but Appa said he could read, couldn't he? and only the dimmest didn't know the wisdom of ages was to be found in books. Books, fooks, said Amma, didn't you read in your books only to buy a teakwood beam, never this softwood rubbish? Appa said no he hadn't, he had relied on that idiot carpenter Kannan, but next

22

time he would consult his books, then there wouldn't be such disasters.

The eaten-up beam lay around for weeks. It kept its shape, but it was crumbling and hollow inside. White ants scuttled in and out of the tunnels, with wood crumbs in their jaws. Saroja knew they ate wood, but it never ceased to surprise her. People will eat anything, said Amma. Saroja knew she was thinking of one of two things that narked her: either that Muslims actually ate cow's flesh, or that in famine times during the British raj people ate grass. Saroja often heard her elders talk about this—she could see from the way they told it that this cut, too, was past healing. She wondered how the British could have been so cruel, but Appa said it wasn't deliberate cruelty, it was just they were too superior to go round and see how the poor people were faring. Like the people in the big houses? Saroja wanted to know, but Appa said no, that is quite different, they are our own people. Besides, he said, there has been a green revolution since those days, we are growing enough to feed ourselves. First I heard of it, said Amma, meaning Appa's land, and flounced out of the room to show what she thought of his efforts.

What does she expect, you are an educated man, one can't have everything, said Anand, who was second cousin to the departed Rangu. He was a crony of Appa's, took his side in any argument and vice versa. Amma tolerated him, because Rangu was the people's hero, not just Appa's. She didn't care, though, for the way Anand took advantage. Saroja heard her muttering it was only rubbed-off glory, but she never said it out loud. In women's company, the two girls and Amma,

Aunt Alamelu was more forthright, called Anand a scrounger. Appa overheard, stalked in and asked the company out loud what one called women who had their board and lodging laid free in their laps like a gift. It's the blood tie, Brother, said Aunt Alamelu with dignity, but you could see she was hurt. She had nothing, no husband or children, and she lived with them for nothing. Her only contribution was cooking vessels, and even these were wearing out, if you held them up you could see light coming through their bottoms. They had to go for tin linings twice each year to save them all succumbing to lead poisoning. Amma said Appa ought to be ashamed, and he was, he was nice to Aunt Alamelu the rest of the day, but he was a man, he could not grovel and apologize to her.

In the night Appa and Amma quarreled, each saying false and terrible things about the other's scrounger. Saroja was dreadfully frightened, she always was when Amma and Appa hissed at each other like this, but Lalitha said not to be a baby, they were only working themselves up and it would all end in the same old way. When Saroja heard the charpoy creaking away she knew Lalitha was right, her parents were making love. They made love quietly to start with, but then it got frenzied, the cot strings twanged although they were only made of rope and the wooden frame groaned. One of the charpoy legs was loose, it groaned most fearfully. Sometimes Amma would hiss that she could bear it no longer and they would bounce off onto the floor. Saroja knew she ought to be pleased her parents' quarrels ended in love-making and in a way she was. In another way, though, it disturbed her, made her thighs flutter

24

and her inner lips moist; she longed to know what it was like for Amma, who was constructed like her, same openings only larger, Manikkam's wife told her, because of the babies pushing out, not to mention what was pushed in.

Why don't you find out? said Lalitha. She had pebbles collected from Rangu's River, shaped like lingams, smooth as anything. She showed Saroja how, got to moaning working herself on the stone, and quite shameless, showing her thighs and crotch and even her little wick. But Saroja ran off, she didn't want to try, she was frightened to in case the pebble got lodged, got in the way of babies which were more important than anything else a woman must have.

Lalitha called Saroja a sissy, a baby, a mooncalf, an ice cube. Miss Mendoza made ice cubes in her refrigerator, and Lalitha brought some home in a thermos flask for Saroja. She often brought things for Saroja, said nice things to her when she was in a giving mood, called her sweetness and pet and combed her hair, running it through her fingers and saying it was like silk. Saroja adored her sister in these moods, boasted about her to the girls at school. There was no refrigerator in her school, only a mud pot with a tap to hold drinking water. The more refined girls called it a goglet. It wasn't half as much fun as a refrigerator. You couldn't make ice in it, or jewel-colored jellies like Miss Mendoza did, using little packets of pink and yellow powder. Hoofs and horns boiled up, said Aunt, sniffing disparagingly at what Lalitha had brought home, but Saroja could only smell delicious sherbety smells. It was a nasty thought, though, took some of the taste from the jellies.

It's barbaric, not having a fridge, said Lalitha. Saroja thought she must mean the school, she couldn't imagine them ever being able to afford a fridge at home, but Lalitha said everyone in the city had a fridge. She didn't specify which city. Amma said Just listen to Miss Millionaire, and since when had Lalitha become a film star, only film stars could afford such luxuries. Lalitha said it wasn't a luxury, it was a necessity in a tropical country, and she didn't like fishing insects out of the curd, which having a fridge would avoid. She said to Saroja, afterwards, it was pathetic the ignorance their parents were steeped in. Amma had something to say too, afterwards: she told Appa that Miss Mendoza was putting notions into madam's head. Appa said notions were good things in anyone's head, the bad thing was having it rattle through emptiness, but Amma said Don't go riding your hobby horse, remember it is your daughter. Appa said he always bore it in mind, and Saroja knew it was true. She knew Lalitha was borne in Appa's mind more frequently than Saroja, from the number of times he brought home presents for her but forgot about Saroja. She didn't hold it against Lalitha, she understood Lalitha was nicer to give things to, being so beautiful and graceful, and with such winsome ways as well. She tried to copy Lalitha. Lalitha said Imitation is the best kind of flattery, but she said it kindly, took Saroja's face in her hands and said You're not bad, not bad at all, little waif.

Lalitha was brave, braver than Saroja. If you dared her she would walk past the well that was haunted, which Saroja would not, especially at dusk. A ghost walked there, wearing widow's weeds, which people said was not its entitlement seeing it was a woman who had not bothered to wed before getting herself with child. The weeds dripped, people said, you could see the drops trickling down off the white cotton sari although when you looked at the ground there was nothing. Nor could you see where the ghost went; it walked thrice round the well and vanished. Some said it gave a piercing cry before it melted away, others heard an almighty splash. It made Saroja very sad to think of the crying woman, and especially the child inside her, but she was also terribly afraid of the ghost. She had never seen it, though on a misty morning there were shapes. Once she had run home gasping and howling though wild elephants wouldn't have dragged from her what she had seen. She wasn't certain herself, because of the vapors looped around the well, which was located in a hollow. When it rained it was worst: steam came off the earth and hung in wraiths, clung smoking to the ropes and made them ghostly. The pulley squeaked horribly. No one would oil it, it was no one's responsibility, being a communal well. The farmers' wives used it, but not Amma, nor any of the landowners in the big houses, having their own piped water. There was a standpipe too, but you had to walk to the outskirts of the market for that.

See what education does for you, said Appa, it makes you clamor for your rights, where would you be without me? In my own home, said Amma, you conferred no favors taking me from it, at least we never had to traipse to the well on account of the tap running dry,

27

which is what befalls here every other day. *Every* day, Brother, amended Aunt Alamelu, you must clamor at the municipality for your rights, my feet are practically on fire running up and down with water pots. No one asks you to, said Appa, sourly, but Aunt Alamelu said, I am eating your salt, Brother, I must help must I not, and cast her eyes down. She knew it made Appa furious, and Saroja often wondered why she did it, because when Appa was furious he could be very mean.

Anand was Appa's upholder and champion. Amma's was Aunt Alamelu. Aunt Alamelu had no one to uphold her except, occasionally, Amma. Occasionally, mutely, she appealed to Saroja. She sat cross-legged on the mat with her feet on her thighs, in the lotus position, which displayed her soles. Her soles were yellow, unlike Saroja's, which were buttermilk colored, and there were cracks in them like fissures in the earth in the hot weather. Aunt Alamelu rubbed coconut oil into the cracks, moaning. Saroja felt sorry for her, felt her own soles smart although her feet never felt hot and sore the way Aunt Alamelu said hers did after walking backwards and forwards from the well. She wanted to help but Aunt Alamelu said No, the child of the house must not sully her hands; besides, I must learn to bear my ills. Appa was getting restless. He was trying to read, but her keening got in the way. He closed his book with a snap and said the joint family system is outdated, an anachronism, it has outlived its usefulness. Aunt Alamelu closed her eyes and rocked. I know, Brother, I know, she said, just tell me to go and I will, I know I have outlived my usefulness.

Where will you go, no one will touch you with a bargepole, said Appa.

Ah yes, that too I know, croaked Aunt Alamelu, but what matter, I am only a widow, less than the dust, so do not torment yourself about my fate, Brother, and she pulled her sari over her head like the poor widow that she was. Go then, I'm not stopping you, you meddling old bag, cried Appa. He was shouting, and his hair had become electric, wiry and flying away from his head. Aunt Alamelu got up, tottering a little. She rolled up her mat and made a small bundle of her belongings, and touched Saroja's eyes with her knuckles and kissed her knuckles and said Sweet child, don't wear out your eyes crying for your old aunt, God will take care of her. But Saroja could not help it, she sobbed and cried seeing Aunt Alamelu totter down the path with her bundle although Lalitha reassured her, said not to be silly and everyone knew Aunt would be back before nightfall. Lalitha was sensible; she always remembered how things ended, but Saroja could never be sure, she was very much afraid one day the hobbling figure would be lost from sight, departed forever along the twisting path.

Amma had gone to the temple. She was more religious than Appa, went more often. On her way back she met Aunt Alamelu, who had not got very far. Amma was carrying a coconut, betel leaves and *ladus*, all consecrated food, but she insisted on taking up Aunt Alamelu's burden as well. Saroja saw them coming up the path and was in two states of mind: relieved that Aunt Alamelu was back, although of course God would have taken care of her, and terrified because there would now be a row. She ran and hid in the storeroom, between the sacks of rustling grain which would absorb the worst of the noise.

Lalitha stayed where she was. She was playing *palangoli* with cowrie shells and she kept on, Saroja could hear the cowries clicking away for quite a long time, until the shouting began. There was always a period of deadly calm, in which Amma and Appa could hear the polite insults they were exchanging, before they really began to let fly at each other. It could go on for hours if Anand and Aunt Alamelu were there, which they were. Saroja closed her eyes and stopped up her ears, she often thought flaps over earholes were specially invented, divine contraptions to shut off what you didn't want to hear, since as far as she could tell there was no other earthly reason for them. The boys said Idiot, no, they have a physical function, but Saroja stuck to her opinion. Sometimes it worked and sometimes it didn't. Sometimes nothing could stop the outside penetrating in, and when it did it was best to open your eyes and see what was going on, otherwise imagination would spin monsters out of the muffled sounds that came thudding in.

Saroja opened her eyes and stretched up over the grain sacks and saw it was the coconut which was cracked. She had feared it was a skull. It lay in a corner and leaked, coconut milk lay in a puddle on the floor, wetting the shell's coarse beard and Aunt Alamelu's sleeping mat. Appa had thrown it. He still had his hand out and was staring at it as if it were some heinous thing, which Amma was saying it was. A consecrated coconut, she was screaming, and had he no respect for anything, not anything at all, neither God nor man?

Saroja crouched down again between the sacks, trembling. She knew it was a terrible thing to do, laying

30

violent hands on God's gift. Even Lalitha had stopped clicking cowries. Even Anand and Aunt Alamelu were silent. Saroja tried to listen to the crows, which were cawing outside, but she could not. She tried to black out the vision of Appa, but she could not. She went on seeing him standing there, rigid, with his hand which had done the blasphemous thing held out stiffly, and her heart was knocking and swelling, threatening to burst with the sorrow she was feeling for him. So she let it out, she had to, and it came out in a great wail, the wail was so shattering she clapped her hand over her mouth but not before everyone had been galvanized into activities on her behalf.

Aunt Alamelu had some Amrutanjan. She unknotted her bundle and took out the jar and rubbed the balm into Saroja's temples. Saroja wanted to be cool more than anything, whereas the balm made her burn, being invaluable for chest complaints, but she bore it because she knew her aunt meant well. Amma crushed cloves, mixed it in milk with sugar, and brought it to Saroja. She did it ostentatiously, but she forbore from saying see what you have done to your own child, which Saroja had been fearing she would. Appa did nothing, it was a woman's situation, but he looked as if he wished he could. Later he consulted the women and they told him, so he took off for the temple. The priest there said to return the next day, after spending the night in re-penting. Appa wasn't too pleased but he did it, sat up till all hours and went back in the morning to the tem-ple, and traversed its precincts thrice in bare feet with his head bowed and carrying a coconut in his hands in atonement for what he had done. Lalitha told Saroja, having learned it from Appa, who confided it to her. She told it reproachfully, implying it was Saroja's fault, but Saroja flared up and reminded her that Appa had broken the coconut before she began to wail, which Lalitha conceded. She was solicitous, though, toward Appa, and Amma was solicitous for Saroja, so for days there was a rift in the family.

It took half an hour to walk round the precincts of the temple. Saroja knew because she and Lalitha had paced it to settle a bet and Lalitha had won, so many paces she had said and she was right, Saroja had had to surrender the necklace of coral-colored pierced pods she had rashly betted on. People were always surrendering things in the temple, not to each other but to God. The priests took them in his name. Mostly it was fruit, flowers, coconuts, honey and milk which they laid at God's feet, which Saroja considered beautiful and proper. Sometimes it was necklaces: garlands of roses and jasmine and rosemary, gold chains, necklaces set with rubies and diamonds, which the priests hung round God's neck. Appa said the priests took it for themselves afterwards, but Amma said Is there no limit to your apostasy? Appa said it was Amma's gullibility that had no limits, but Saroja knew Amma was not as gullible as Appa, who believed whatever Anand told him and would have destituted his family for Anand's sake only he was prevented. Besides, she had seen the jewelry. It was kept in the temple's treasury, and you could view it once a year, and at festival times it was taken out again and placed on God, and Saroja could see a lot of it was there, though of course they could not pile it all on.

Amma said, thoughtfully, that naturally some things had to be sold to maintain the temple, and to feed the poor, and of course the priests had to live too. Some living, fat living, said Lalitha. It came out of her pat, which made Amma suspect it was not her at all. She wormed and whittled away until she had it out of Lalitha that it was Miss Mendoza. That three-rupee convert, said Amma in a rage, although really she respected Miss Mendoza, who was a Bachelor of Arts. She was a spinster, but the Bachelor took away some of the shame of that. Anand said one should not indict Miss Mendoza for her ancestors' actions, they had had a pretty lean time and ought not to be blamed for changing their religion for three rupees apiece. It might have been Appa himself speaking, said Amma, sourly. Some people she knew, she said, would sell their souls for less, and she looked Anand up and down in a way that would have pulverized anyone else, but Anand being poor was robust.

Chingleput said if you were poor you learned to be robust, and if you didn't learn fast you were done for. Do you mean dead? Saroja wanted to know. As good as, confirmed Chingleput, and his eyes were glittery and hard like stones in his face. Saroja knew she and her family were poor, her mother often told her, but not poor as Chingleput had been, or poor like the beggars who sat in a long row and held out their begging bowls to you as you approached the temple. Some people were too respectable to beg, though they were very poor too, instead they came and queued for a free meal which the priests handed out once daily. When the rains failed, or the monsoon flooded the fields, the queues grew longer, stretched halfway round the temple and met up with the queues in front of the mobile food vans the government sent. Appa told his daughters to observe the change: when he was their age the only thing the government sent was the tax collector. Amma demurred. She could remember a grain depot being opened, she said, and one must give the devil his due, but Appa said she must be thinking of the time the hungry populace had stormed an Army store and appropriated it. Their memories brought them into harmony. Saroja could see that whatever it was they had shared in the past had drawn them close together, it was an enduring bond however much they scuffled and squabbled about other things.

The other time the temple grew congested was during epidemics of smallpox and typhoid. When they began Chingleput stopped going to the town, he trundled his cart to the precincts of the temple and did a brisk trade there instead. He could have done with another pair of hands then, but the trouble was he didn't trust anyone sufficiently. Except Saroja, he told her, and Saroja understood it was true, understood there had to be someone even if it was one as feeble as herself.

You could be enriched during an epidemic, like Chingleput and God and his priests in the temple, although of course God was above worldly riches, besides having an infinity of his own; or you could be impoverished, like Manikkam and his wife, whose baby contracted smallpox. No one would buy their milk for fear. Manikkam's wife had intended to have him vaccinated, but she had not got round to it and he was covered from head to foot in blisters, it didn't spare even his wick.

The blisters were full of watery stuff and Saroja knew if so much as a drop got on your skin you were done for too, but she had to peek at the baby to see how he was getting on. He cried a lot and his mother cried too; she put him down on a cloth in the shade and went off, weeping, to see to the cows.

Saroja wished she could pick up the baby and comfort him, it was awful watching him lie there and cry, but Amma would not let her go near. No one would go near except the doctor from the clinic. The milk from the cows lay about in pots and pails and went sour, a curdled smell hung over Manikkam's land. Appa said Fools, milk doesn't carry smallpox, but he was nervous, supervised the scalding of vessels in which he brought home the milk, and hovered round Amma when she boiled it, insisting on its frothing up thrice. Aunt Alamelu said Brother, it is Fate, how can you guard against that, was it not Fate that took my husband so early in life? but Appa turned a furious purple and said No, it wasn't, it was the lack of a little elementary care that took him, plus an absence of sense which was characteristic of his generation. Aunt Alamelu said As you will, Brother, and compressed her lips. Her husband had died of the cholera.

Manikkam's wife could not go to the temple but she sent an emissary pledging a silver bangle to God in return for her child's life. Saroja thought a child's life was priceless, but she could see that was as high as poor Manikkam's wife could go. People were always promising something in return for something, usually their children's health, there was a lot of dialogue with God. Sometimes they could not keep their promises, but they went to any lengths to try. It was a dreadful sin, Saroja knew, not to keep your promise to God. She kept her own modest for that reason.

In Miss Mendoza's church people gave candles. You could see them flickering in the evening, and the melted wax flowing like slow tears down the slippery columns. It was very moving. In the crypt were what the richer people gave. You could not see the crypt from the windows, Lalitha had to describe it for Saroja. She said rich people gave objects of silver and gold, which were kept in a glass case. What sort of objects, Saroja wanted to know. Hearts, Lalitha said, and looked at her sideways, her odd look. Hands, she said, and livers and legs and kidneys and breasts and male tools, it depended which part of the body had been cured by divine intervention. Saroja was consumed with curiosity to see the crypt but she could not, not being a Christian. Lalitha was covered by Miss Mendoza's mantle. Appa said anyone could go into a church; but only Christians did. He said by law anyone could go into a temple, even those who cleaned the public latrines, but only a few of them did, by way of a gesture. When they did you could see they weren't too happy, Saroja felt sorry for them huddling together for strength and everyone else shrinking away as if they were polluted, which they were not, only dirty and smelling from not having a bath, but she could not help shrinking too, it was the nature of the work they did, it created mental images, which was off-putting.

When the baby died Saroja cried for him, but Lalitha said one ought to be glad really, because he had suffered so much and now it was ended. She could be quite hard like that. Saroja wanted to know if she were suffering would she prefer to die or go on living and suffering, but Lalitha would not answer, screwed up her eyes and said That depends. There was a fear in her eyes which Saroja interpreted.

Appa interpreted too. He said kindly there was no need to worry, they had all been vaccinated. They pulled up their sleeves to show the nurse at the health center the marks on their arms, but Lalitha had to lift her skirts because the marks were high on her thigh. She had been done there to avoid disfiguring her arms, which were shapely and beautiful. Lalitha blushed when she showed her marks, not from having to lift her skirts but because of the compliments she was paid. A lovely girl, the nurse said, such wise parents to have had her vaccinated, her lovely skin would never be pitted and scarred. Lalitha was afraid of that. She was not afraid of anything, not even the ghost which rose from the well, but she was terrified of that, she would rather have died than have her beauty spoiled. Even the vaccination marks did not reassure her, or Appa, or the nurse. She went around with her face drawn, railing at people who started epidemics and so did Appa. They were much in harmony, even more so than usual, at such times.

Manikkam's baby was burned and his ashes were thrown in the river. Saroja did not see the burning, but she sat on the bank and waited for the ashes to come down and speculated on what the spirit was doing bereft of its home. She hoped it would soon find a nice abode, perhaps enter the new baby Manikkam's wife was making, but she thought perhaps it was too late for that, she had seen it moving the folds of its mother's sari and no doubt another spirit was already in occupation. She wished nevertheless it could have been born to someone like Manikkam's wife and have a splendid mother like her, because it had been a nice baby, a nice spirit had dwelt in it and the body had been bonny too, except at the end, when it had looked awful. At night for a week while the worry was strong she said a little prayer to this effect. Lalitha asked what she was praying for but Saroja wouldn't tell, although she knew Lalitha was good at guessing.

Lalitha said Miss Mendoza said souls did not enter other bodies. They went straight up to heaven, or down into hell, or were cooped up in purgatory which was an in-between place for doing penance in, but none of this happened until resurrection on the day of the last judgment. At this time a bugle call sounded which woke the dead, who heaved off their tombstones and rose up from their graves. It made Saroja shiver to think of it, she visualized a skeleton with bits of flesh and hair clinging to it like the man they dug up who everyone kept saying had been poisoned by his wife until the police were forced to act. After Lalitha told her she hated going past the cemetery where Muslims buried their dead, and what with this and avoiding Rangu's River by night her wanderings got a bit restricted.

A lot of things got chucked in the river besides ashes. People flung tins and bottles in it, and bits of broken mud pots, and the wheels and chains of ancient bicycles past redemption even by the blacksmith. The dhobi's donkey went in it too, after it had died. The dhobi was too weak to bury it, he was recovering from the smallpox. The carcass lay about for days, exuding a vile smell and attracting blowflies and vultures. At night jackals came. The vultures went for the eyes, and what fat there was, there wasn't much, it was a thin donkey and its legs had become bowed from the weight of the bundles the dhobi piled on its back. The jackals took the rest, fought for it, at night you could hear them snapping and tearing at the flesh. The skeleton was left, picked clean; the bones were white and glary under the sun, in moonlight they gleamed and you could imagine eyeballs glimmering in the empty sockets. What you couldn't imagine was velvety lips on those jaws, nibbling at Appa's prickly pear.

Appa said What a country, not even an efficient disposal system. Then he wrestled with himself and took the blame, because he could not have brought himself to deal with the corpse. Then he halved it, blamed the British, who had not even organized a sanitary system in two hundred years of rule, and blamed people like himself who were so squeamish they could not do it. Amma said the pariahs should do it, it was their job, they were used to handling filth, but nowadays they were getting above themselves. Appa said Remember what Gandhiji taught, they are the children of God, why should they do all the unpleasant jobs, but Aunt Alamelu cried out It is their karma, their fate, Brother!, which rendered him speechless.

In the end the dhobi dealt with his donkey. He rose from his sickbed and gathered up the bones and tottered to the river and flung them in. He could not toss far enough, he was too weak; some of the bones got stuck in the sludge at the edges, he had to squelch in and

39

poke about with a stick to release them. Saroja watched, she had no school. School had been closed for the duration of the epidemic, which left time for these absorbing activities.

The dhobi wanted to borrow from Appa to buy another donkey, but Manikkam got in first. He was broke too, all that unsold milk and another baby on the way. Appa lent him money and said it was the last time if he did not go to the family planning and stop these umpteen babies, and Manikkam said yes, he must, but clearly he was afraid. Lalitha told Saroja he was afraid in case he lost his virility, without which he could not make babies. Saroja said she thought that was the object of the exercise, but Lalitha said in a superior way there was more to it than that but she obviously was too young to understand. Saroja made up her mind to ask Jaya when school reopened.

Manikkam's wife came round to thank Amma for the loan and to bring her a basket of jasmine buds she had picked. Amma went rigid, but she managed to be gracious, accepted the thanks and the jasmine and smiled. When Appa came in she said how she didn't have a decent sari to her back and showed him holes in the one she was wearing. Appa was wary, didn't cotton on immediately, but knew there was something. Plenty of money to throw around, said Amma, tight-lipped, but for his own wife nothing, not even a new sari once a year at Deepavali. Appa knew then. He jingled the small coin in his pocket and said it was the only decent thing to do, Manikkam had not had a handful of rice in the place, and he bolted. Amma told her daughters to witness how they lived, on the edge of a precipice, she said. She sat down cross-legged and looped raffia round her big toe and began to string the jasmine buds together, not being one to waste anything. Now and then she wet the raffia with water, to save breaking or bruising the stalks. It was soothing, after the alarming picture she had painted.

Appa was the unofficial moneylender, known as a soft touch for miles around. He didn't charge any interest, was delighted merely to get his own money back. Perumal did. He charged a rate which made people sullen when they mentioned it, but they had no option but to go to him if they wanted a loan. There was no one else, except the co-operative bank, but the bank was choosy, laid down condition this and condition that whereas Perumal obliged all and sundry. He would take anything they had for security. There were brass and copper vessels on the shelves in his office, farm implements, sacks of rice. He kept gold and silver trinkets in his safe. At night he pulled down the shutters and fastened the grille and counted his day's takings. The boys told Saroja and Lalitha and the four of them went down to see. They peeped through the chinks in the shutters and saw Perumal hunched over his table, counting. Saroja had not seen so many notes in her life. The boys were angry, swore, and said it was damnable one man having that much while others were starving. If it wasn't Appa preaching it was one of the boys. They were not around much, though: they were the first batch of Amma's children and were away earning their living. When Appa preached Amma said good luck to him, he's a shrewd hardworking man, and they took her meaning that Appa wasn't, having no notes to count. If

41

the boys said it, though, she agreed, said bad cess to Perumal and the flesh-eating likes of him. Saroja thought it over and recognized Amma was right, those who went to Perumal ended up with very little flesh on their bones. The worry, Aunt Alamelu said. She told them she had never borrowed a rupee from anyone in her whole life and set up the fact as a shining example in front of them. Aunt Alamelu had plenty of flesh. It was flabby and flopped over her waist like dewlaps when she sat down. She had no waistline to speak of. Perumal was the same. He had flesh all round him like rubber tires, and his breasts were like a woman's.

Perumal paid the police to keep an eye on him. There was often a constable or two sauntering past the premises. They caught them peeping once, swung their fists ominously and ordered them off. The boys stood up to it. It's a free country, they said, you uniformed bullies aren't running the country any more. They didn't know, they got it all from Appa, from echoes Rangu had left behind.

Perumal paid the Kallars too. He paid them to refrain from robbing him. All the rich people did, they had to keep their wealth. In the big houses they did it another way, employing Kallars as nightwatchmen, paying them fat wages. No Kallar would rob a house with a Kallar watchman. No Kallar would bother to rob a house like Saroja's for that matter, which was a distinct relief. It made Saroja feel burdened to think of Perumal hunched up over his money, paying out left and right to preserve it. The boys said it was a burden they wouldn't mind assuming, but Saroja could not believe them though she respected their opinion.

Chingleput did well, if not as well as Perumal. He wouldn't pay anyone, though, neither the police nor the Kallars—blood money he called it. They left him alone all the same. The boys said It's the only way, you've got to stand up to the thugs of society. Appa applauded them, told everyone what fine sons he had. Chingleput admired them too, but he did not come out loud with it, you could never have told what he thought but for the way he looked at them, up and down and up and down with his eyes all soft and respectful. He was a quiet man. He carried his earnings about on his person, in a cummerbund he wore all through the seasons. There were pockets stitched into it, which Saroja saw when he took off his shirt to rub down his shoulders which sometimes got swollen from trundling the cart around. Chingleput did not mind that Saroja saw. He did not mind anything that Saroja saw. Saroja did not either, it was ordinary and natural, but it frightened her to look at what Lachu deliberately displayed, besides he seemed to foam when he showed it. He can't help himself, said Chingleput. There's no reason to be afraid of him, there's no need to go near him either, he said. He was gentle with Saroja, as Appa sometimes was. Chingleput was about Appa's age.

Saroja tried to look at Lachu differently, but she could not, she thought him grotesque. All men are, said Lalitha, but they are lovely too: you'll find out. She could be very provoking to Saroja, looking at her sideways and with the tip of her pink tongue playing about her lips. Saroja ran off. She had better things to do. She had to go to school. In the evening Manikkam's wife

43

had promised to show her the new calf which had begun to be born.

In the evening the hawker was there. His beard was bushier than ever, in between the hair his mouth was as red as a flower. Amma had spread a mat in the court-yard and they were both sitting on it with the suitcase open between them. Saroja postponed the calf and squatted down to inspect the contents. Do you want anything? Select anything you want, said Amma. She was smiling. She smelled very fresh and there were roses in her hair. It was so unusual to be invited to select that Saroja took her time. Haven't you finished yet? said Amma, if you don't hurry up the calf will be dead, it has been ailing since morning. Saroja was torn. She closed her eyes and tossed a coin in her mind, it came down with the three lions uppermost, which meant she had to pick the little wooden handcart like the one Chingleput pulled instead of the mirror with the pink frame which she also wanted. The hawker presented it to her with a flourish. He added a doll in a matchbox as a present. Pretty child, he said; his voice sounded false. Saroja took the cart and the matchbox and put them away in her own special cardboard box before going over to Manikkam's. There were so many children there, one of them would certainly have broken her treasures.

The calf was dead. It had died that afternoon, soon after being born. The cow stood near, sniffing the corpse and lowing. It had big, mournful eyes. Manik-kam's wife looked very sad too, her eyes were mournful to match. What will you do? Saroja asked, being fearful on her account. Manikkam's wife said she didn't know, she had banked on the calf to retrieve their fortune. Then she saw Saroja's face and said Never mind, at least we shall have the milk to sell. Saroja was surprised; she knew when babies died their mother's milk dried up, but Manikkam's wife said no, they would stuff the calf and the cow would be deceived by the smell into thinking it was alive and the milk would continue to flow. Saroja looked at the cow and did not think it could be as stupid as that, but she believed Manikkam's wife, who knew about these things in a way Saroja did not. Appa did not, either. He had planted a papaya tree once and railed at it for not bearing fruit until Manikkam's wife told him it was a male tree. She did it kindly, understanding an educated man could not be expected to know these earthy things, being rightly concerned with higher matters. Appa had mixed feelings about the subject. He said All knowledge is good, it cannot be anything but, but you could tell he thought it unseemly the kind of knowledge his children got from Manikkam's wife and the like.

We have come down in the world, said Amma, associating with all and sundry, what do you expect? Saroja was glad about associating, she would have hated to be like her second cousin Usha, who was hardly ever allowed out alone and did not even go to school but was taught at home to save her from mixing. Saroja thought this extreme. She would have hated to be cut off from Jaya, and from Chingleput and Manikkam's wife, it would have made her life dull and uninteresting.

She asked Manikkam's wife if she could watch while the calf was stuffed, but Manikkam's wife said No, no, it is not a pretty sight and at your age you should only see pretty sights like birth, which is miraculous, it turns your thoughts to God. Saroja was cross, called Manikkam's wife Gangamma, which was her name but she loathed it, would not allow anyone to call her that, Saroja would not have known it was but Appa had filled in a form for the two of them. You call me that I'll tan your behind, said Manikkam's wife, so Saroja picked up her skirts as if not willing to be contaminated one minute longer with the dust of Manikkam's household and marched home.

Amma was still sitting with the hawker in the courtyard but now the suitcase was not between them. She had moved round and Saroja could see if the hawker's hand strayed ever so little it would touch her. Her face was hectic and secret, like Lalitha's when she came back from watching Lachu, but when she saw Saroja it changed, became sullen and heavy so that Saroja knew she was the cause, just as the hawker was the cause of the color in Amma's cheekbones. Have you seen the calf? Amma wanted to know, Isn't there anything else you can find to do? and she sighed, said children are such a tie, forever under your feet, using her second tone, which was resigned, the first one intended for Saroja had been exasperated and shrill.

Saroja went in. She felt miserable, but Aunt Alamelu had returned, which cheered her up. Ordinarily it would not have made much difference. Saroja brought out her little wooden cart to show her but Aunt Alamelu would not admire it. A bit of flashy trash just like him, she said, transferring her disapproval to the cart, which Saroja could not do, for it was a pretty thing, there were even small models of fruit and vegetables inside it. But their feelings against the hawker united them, they sat side by side on the mat chopping coriander and onions, and now and then Aunt Alamelu got up to relieve her eyes, which were watering, she said, but really to show her disapproval by staring out from the doorway. She had a piercing stare. Appa said it could bore through metal, but of course he was prejudiced.

The hawker persevered, but he could not hold out. His lips drooped and his eyes grew melancholy, he could no longer use them to flash bold looks at Amma. Saroja could see that Amma was trying to rally him, and failing. Sadly he began to pack away the pretty articles he had taken out to display to Amma, sadly closed the lid of his suitcase. Saroja wanted to dash out for a last look, it would be months before he came their way again, but prudence held her back. She gazed at the melancholy Sikh instead, and felt rather sorry for him, and when she felt sorry he ceased to be quite the stranger he had been and became human, someone who could be hurt like herself. All the same she knew he was not one of them, when he came round again he would be strange once more and she along with everyone else would wonder and speculate about him and his beard, the bangle at his wrist, and what besides hair he kept in his turban.

When Amma came in she was quite put out, her nostrils and chin were quivering as if she was going to cry but it wasn't that, it was rage. Can't one be allowed to choose a few toilet articles, she cried, advancing on Aunt Alamelu, without having you behave like a basilisk? Is there some rule, some law, some interdict that

47

forbids even such innocent pleasures? Aunt Alamelu
retreated. She stood behind Saroja and put her hands on
her shoulders and said, I am only thinking of you and
your children, is it not my duty as an older woman,
who will advise you if I do not, I who have only your
best interests at heart? You, said Amma, will advise me
when I ask you to and not one moment before, and as
to old, yes, you are old, you are past it, you would give
your eyes for a man to look at you but no man will,
which is what irks you, makes you act like a malevolent
she-devil. Amma was gasping; her chest was going up
and down and her sari had begun to slip from her
shoulder. Saroja watched, fascinated; laid bets with herself as to how long the muslin could last, could cling to
the rock of shoulder before it was dislodged by the gale.
In between she sampled the tempest within her, the
turmoil that sent her first to Amma's side, then remembered Amma's impatience and ferried her over to Aunt
Alamelu, then recalled the hawker's melancholy eyes
and set her spinning again. She concluded the best
thing to do in the circumstances would be to steal away,
but Aunt Alamelu's hands were grasping her shoulders, her fingers were trembling but firm, were holding
her firmly as if she was some kind of bulwark which she
was not.

Above her head wicked words flew.

When Appa appeared she would have run to him,
run and flung herself into his arms but she was not sure,
not being Lalitha. Appa was not sure either. He was
staring at Aunt Alamelu, staring at Amma, at her
breasts which were popping out of her bodice as if he
had never seen them before. He was not used to them

48

like that, in broad daylight, without a cover on, and neither was Saroja. It was better for both when Amma remembered to pull up her sari, it was a sign of returning to normality. But she was still quivering. Appa had to ask twice before she could tell him, she was so speechless, then it came out in a spate. See, she said, and showed him a packet of saffron she had bought, though she concealed the other things; See this, I bought it today from a hawker, he had a fine selection, I took my time selecting, is that a crime? But there are people in this world who would wreck even these simple pleasures. Under an open sky, she told him, right out in the open, and my own child present, but there are those who see evil even in innocence. She would not name Aunt Alamelu, though it was clear whom she meant. Appa took her side, said how much damage suspicion and rumor could do. He did not name Aunt Alamelu either, or remind her of her position, but his presence reminded her, she said not a word in defense. Perhaps it was having both of them against her, Aunt Alamelu was more used to having them go at her one at a time, she could have coped with that.

Appa expanded, in the absence of interruptions. He made a little speech, said how narrow-mindedness was the curse of India, and urbane intercourse between men and women a mark of civilization. It made Saroja feel uneasy, she kept remembering the looks that Amma and the hawker had exchanged, and tendrils of her hair brushing against him as they bent over his suitcase. It made her feel worse when Amma rounded on Appa, reminded him of his daughters and of the dangers of too-free association between the sexes which he was advocating, which brought Aunt Alamelu back on her side. There was a lot of flux, a shifting of positions which Saroja found unsettling. She crept away, out of the house to the tamarind tree and swung on the rope swing, high up and swooping down, and the tumbling world became the proper one, she was glad she had it apart from the one made by her elders.

In the morning on the way to school Lalitha was avid to know what had happened. She had missed it through having to stay late for a music lesson. She was learning to play the flute; Miss Mendoza had arranged it, she had organized a group and a man teacher called Mr. Jacobs taught them. Saroja would have liked to learn the flute too, but there was not enough money to go round. Appa's eyes slithered away when he explained it to her, he said perhaps when she was Lalitha's age, but Saroja knew he was only saying it to make her feel better, or possibly not to feel so bad himself.

Saroja told Lalitha about the row, but she would not divulge all the details. Lalitha pressed her, she was curious to know how Amma had erred but Saroja would not explain, in any case she could not because what happened between men and women was so subtle, so full of half hints and mysteries you could never tell how you knew what you knew. Lalitha got in a huff. She said there was no need to be told about anything, she knew all about dalliance, which was true. Saroja considered inventing something to tell her, but resolved to do so later, when she needed information from Lalitha for which it could be bartered.

They bartered things at school. Bits of gossip counted as things and could be exchanged for something you needed, usually pencils and rubbers, which were forever getting nicked. You had to be on guard against inventions though, you could lose on the deal by believing nonsense. On the other hand, if you invented and were found out you were honor bound to give back what you had got in exchange.

Sometimes the girls invented blockbusters which no one could possibly believe unless you were a bit feeble, like Nalini. Nalini's head was too big for her body, it wobbled about on her neck, which was long and limp. It reminded you of a cobra, until you saw her eyes, which were soft and misty. Saroja thought she must suffer a lot to have eyes that looked like that. On the other hand, cobras suffered a lot too, stuffed into stuffy baskets and their poison teeth pulled out one by one, but their eyes remained lustrous.

Everyone said Nalini had water on the brain.

Nalini said so too, which made her a lot of friends. At the end of each year if you didn't pass the exams you stayed in the same class, but with Nalini she was passed anyhow, the teachers didn't want her subjected to a whole batch of new classmates. The old ones protected her. You couldn't be sure about the new, one bad lead could turn the entire class into a pack of savages. Saroja could see what a perilous existence Nalini led.

Jaya told Nalini her mother was pregnant, just to test how far she could go with Nalini. Jaya's mind was on things like that, she was the oldest girl in the class and developing fast. The girls were all giggling. Nalini's mother was a widow of ten years' standing, a short dumpy woman shaped like two round pots, without any cleavage visible in front or behind. She came in

51

Amma's category of a woman no man would look at, and she was too respectable to look at any man either. But Nalini believed Jaya. She was overjoyed by the news, she was an only child and sold on the idea of a brother or sister. Jaya stopped her rushing off at once to congratulate her mother, she must have been a bit scared even then at what she had started and extracted a promise from Nalini not to tell anyone. But Nalini forgot. Perhaps she was too brimming over. She told all the neighbors. All the mothers of the girls heard. Amma asked Saroja if it was true. Saroja said no. Amma said Nalini seemed to think it was and she ought to know. Saroja felt uncomfortable. She wriggled unhappily, and her hands grew hot and sticky, but she could not tell about Jaya. No one wanted to be a tell-tale.

The whole village was scandalized, was in uproar.

When Nalini's mother heard she marched down to the school. She had Nalini in tow. They were met by Miss Krishnan, the Head. The girls heard her say she intended to get to the bottom of it before the day was out. The door closed on the three of them. Jaya was scared then, all right. Her face was pinched, it looked discolored and was splotched like a croton.

In the middle of the lesson Jaya was sent for. As she went out she put on a show, swaggered a little and grinned, but it wasn't convincing. She came out the same way, but her eyes were swollen and red. So were her knuckles. At school if you were really bad you were given two raps with a ruler on the knuckles. Saroja knew Nalini's mother had been wronged; its full gravity she only realized later though, because it had been a joke, and there had been all that giggling. Aunt

Alamelu went very solemn and said it was a terrible thing to happen to a woman. A woman's good name is her most precious possession, she told Saroja and Lalitha.

I thought it was her virtue, said Lalitha.

The two are the same, Aunt Alamelu told her, but Lalitha would not agree. She said Nalini's mother's virtue was intact but it hadn't helped, she had lost her good name just the same. Aunt Alamelu sighed and said You are right, poor woman, a terrible, an irreparable thing has been done to her. Saroja felt queasy again, there were spiders in her stomach because she knew they were all in it, the whole class not only Jaya even if Jaya had been the one to think it up, but Appa said Aunt Alamelu was talking nonsense since in nine months at the utmost Nalini's mother's good name would be restored to her. Aunt Alamelu put on her worldly-wise face and said, True, Brother, true, but when mud is slung a little always sticks. Dirt never sticks to a clean surface, said Appa, and he explained that what he had in mind was minds. Saroja could see Aunt Alamelu wanted to let fly, but she had her status which pinned her down. So she looked pious and folded her hands together and said In an ideal world, Brother, it would indeed be as you say, what a pity it is we do not live in such a world!

Saroja mused about an ideal world, what it was like, and about the world Amma and Appa lived in, and about the one the boys inhabited now that they had left the village for town for good. She did not need to think about her own, which was secret, and separate, and chugged along quietly beside her ready for her to step into when she wanted. Sometimes it wasn't beside her, it was inside, she and it became a round perfect orb which nothing from outside could penetrate. Appa said when Saroja was off he could shout himself blue in the face but she wouldn't hear, but the reality of it was she did hear, only what she heard did not concern her in her world, it ran off her like raindrops off the waxy petals of oleander. The shape of the orb would have spoiled, if it hadn't, would have got twisted or warped, and lost its perfection if the outside had got in.

Saroja could not quite visualize the kind of world a town was. It was not that she hadn't been to a town, she had, she and her family had once gone to the wedding of a relative in a town. It was just that she could not realize it in the way that living in the village was realized. The boys said town was all right. They said it was a case of every man for himself. It was a bit of a thieves' kitchen, they said sometimes. You have to have your wits about you, they told Saroja. Saroja could see that having your wits about you took something away, took away the dew which was a softener, put on a lacquer instead which when you looked closer you saw was the beginning of blight. The boys' faces were hard, in a way no one's in the village was, even faces that were twice their age.

When the boys came home they brought presents. They forgot about time going by, bought incongruous gifts. They bought Saroja a yellow paper kite with a six-foot tail which she managed to sail at first attempt. Lalitha's kite was green, with silvery streamers. She couldn't get it off the ground. She pouted, asked what she was supposed to do with the thing, run about in the fields like a demented child? Later she was vindictive, trampled on the kite until the green tissue paper tore. Later still she was sorry, wept tears on the tattered remains and said she couldn't understand how she could be so horrid to her own brothers. She wept for Saroja too, apologized for calling her a demented child. Saroja said she didn't mind, which wasn't true.

There were bikes the year after. The boys bought them second-hand and did them up and rode them home. Bikes, said Aunt Alamelu, it is scandalous, what do girls want bicycles for? She was behind the times, definitely, even Saroja thought so whereas to Lalitha she was positively antediluvian, which was a word she had learned from Miss Mendoza.

One of the bikes was a lady's bicycle, the other had a rod, you had to cock a leg over to get on the saddle, which was difficult to do in a skirt. The boys said Have which one you like to the girls; they were like Appa, expert in passing on problems. Lalitha was generous; she said You choose, I have lots of things—meaning the flute and such, which Appa bought her; so Saroja chose the lady's bicycle. It was beautiful in her eyes, Chingleput taught her to ride and she learned in a day. Appa paid Manikkam's son to teach Lalitha. He had to run along the path holding the saddle and the handlebar to steady her while she pedaled and each time his hand touched her behind she blushed and fell off. It took Lalitha a fortnight to learn. She was not very good even then. She could dance and sing beautifully, she was better at these things than Saroja, but Saroja could bicycle better.

In Saroja's opinion Lalitha neglected her bike. She

55

did not clean the spokes or oil the chain, and the tires were as flat as pancakes. Sometimes she forgot to bring it in when it rained. It stood out and got soaked and dried out again under the sun and the Manikkam children watched it with hungry eyes for none of them had a bike, not one of that numerous brood. Saroja could not bear to contemplate Lalitha's neglect. She adopted the incipient ruin and cleaned and polished it until it shone. In the end they exchanged bicycles in the hope that Lalitha would handle the lady's model better, which she did, but only marginally. Saroja rode the bike with the rod. She sat the smaller Manikkam children on the rod and soared with them down the path. Aunt Alamelu said Remember they are the milkman's children, they are not our class of people. She was kind to them in her own way, which was distant.

Saroja's bike was a Raleigh. So were most of the bicycles in the village. Appa said they dated from the time India had been forced to buy British goods. A captive market, he said, for British rubbish. The boys demurred, said Raleighs weren't rubbish. They weren't pro-British, but they weren't snarled up by memories either. They conceded it was wrong, though, to be tied to Britain, to have to buy British because of the terms of the government loan. They became very close talking about it, at times like these Appa and the boys were very close indeed. It made Saroja shiver to think of the times when men were not, when they opened their mouths and tore each other up. Men are like that, Aunt Alamelu said: that is why creation has been entrusted to women. Saroja liked the thought, it made her feel good, but Lalitha sniffed and said creation was given to men too, which stopped Aunt Alamelu dead in her tracks, stopped her from going on cozily about nestlings and nests, which she had been about to do. Saroja knew because she often listened to Aunt to oblige her. Lalitha would not, unless it was something she was interested in; she was too impatient. Life is too short, she told Saroja, but Saroja could not think of life like that, it seemed to her more like a shining ribbon, yards and yards of it coming abundantly off a heavenly blue spool.

How the days fly, Amma took to saying. She usually said it at Deepavali, and when new years and birthdays came round, but now that the date for Miss Mendoza's visit was fixed she said it almost every day. It drove Aunt Alamelu frantic. She said she knew she was getting older minute by minute, but was there any need to be constantly reminded? She was quite caustic, the truth of the matter was she disapproved of Miss Mendoza's ways, which were modern. Cosmopolitan, said Lalitha, who knew a lot of words like that, used them when she was in the mood to disparage village life, which was often. Westernized, Appa backed her up, he liked Indians to be Westernized, which advanced them into the big world instead of remaining static in a backwater. Amma was ambivalent; she admired Miss Mendoza for the way she ran her school, and all the lovely things she taught Lalitha, but she would not have wanted her daughters to be unmarried teachers like her. Saroja wouldn't have wanted that either. She wanted lots of lovely cuddly babies, and, as Appa said, the way society was organized you had to be married for that. A peasant's ambition, Lalitha called it, but

Saroja did not feel herself demeaned by that, there were lots of qualities to peasants that she greatly admired.

Everything, Lalitha told Amma, must be just so: Miss Mendoza has high standards. And haven't we? said Amma, bridling; why, the place is so clean you could eat off the floor! That's just it, said Lalitha, moodily, and she told how Miss Mendoza was used to sitting in chairs at tables, and eating with forks and spoons. Yes, and see what it's done for her, cried Aunt; she's the laughing-stock of the village! which was not wholly true since a good many people respected her, but not wholly false either because people did snicker seeing her sitting and eating in solitary state in her bungalow, which was small but see-through in the modern manner. She had a chokra who served up the dishes, and he laughed at her too, behind her back, and said how anyone could tell she was not born to it. He meant himself, he had worked for a European family and knew who was born to it and who wasn't, but a lot of people in the village couldn't have told, not having worked for Europeans, and Europeans being as rare on the ground as Sikhs.

After weeks of Lalitha saying how things must be just so, and Amma repeating herself about how the days flew, it got to be quite a strain and you could tell everyone was a bit fed up with Miss Mendoza's forthcoming visit. No one would admit it. Appa kept on about what an honor it was, and Lalitha dropped hints, told how many other girls had invited Miss Mendoza but she was the only one favored. Saroja understood Lalitha was a favorite, which wasn't surprising, Lalitha was very charming, she could be the most charming person in the world when she tried.

58

On the morning—it was a Sunday of course, Miss Mendoza was busy the other six days of the week—Appa set out the cane chairs in the courtyard and Amma spread her best mat, the one made of finest rushes with a flower design in each corner that she had brought out for the hawker, so that Miss Mendoza could take her choice. The chairs dated from the Rangu era and had been rescued from the house that burned down. There were only four left and all four were scorched, some middling and some badly, and Amma and Lalitha worked themselves into a lather trying to arrange them so that Miss Mendoza would take the one they were certain wouldn't give way.

Aunt Alamelu said What a fuss over one woman, she would like to know was it a maharani they were entertaining, would someone enlighten her? and she threatened not to stir from the kitchen which as Saroja knew was an empty threat because this fate was already decreed for her, there being only four chairs. She wondered what was to become of herself, because Lalitha had already warned her she would not tolerate any squeezing-up on the same chair which normally she did not mind. It will crush my clothes, she told Saroja, one seeks to appear flower-fresh at all times, and she surveyed Saroja, who tended to look crumpled most of the time. Saroja secretly resolved to be flower-fresh too, she scrubbed her face till it shone and painstakingly wound jasmine and rosemary into her plait, but there was no doubt about it, it all happened effortlessly for Lalitha.

They were all flower-fresh the morning Miss Mendoza came, but she more so than any of them. There were flowers in her hair, and patterning her sari, and

59

there were rosettes on her shoes which were high-heeled. Saroja saw them as Miss Mendoza held up the hem of her sari to step out of her *jutka*, she was speculating on how anyone could walk on stilts that high when Lalitha hissed at her to come away from the window, said she must have peasants' blood in her to behave like that. Saroja didn't care, she watched Miss Mendoza's pointed toe quavering on the footboard of the *jutka*, which was bouncing, it had a springy little pony attached to it, and Miss Mendoza's stricken expression as she held onto the jutka-wallah's shoulder, which was grubby.

Appa had gone out to meet her. He was standing quite near, but of course he couldn't grab her even when she tottered, it wouldn't have been seemly. Instead he took the blame for her imbalance upon himself, said how disgraceful the path was and he really must see to it, at which Amma twisted her lips, though only slightly because of guests being present, having heard it all many times before. Miss Mendoza said Not at all, was ever so polite as she tittuped along, with Amma on one side and Lalitha on the other and Appa who had been tutored by Lalitha behaving like a contortionist, somehow walking backwards and sideways at the same time in order not to turn his back on the ladies. Saroja thought it silly, ladies were quite used to seeing backs, and anyway how else were you supposed to lead the way unless you were some kind of crab?

When they came to the courtyard Aunt Alamelu kept grimly to the kitchen but Saroja emerged, stood outside to welcome the party as bidden but feeling awkward, feeling like a palm tree sprouted in a patch of watermelons except she could tell she wasn't the only one, Appa and Amma were not having it easy either, which helped.

Please be scated, said Appa; he said it uncertainly, and his eyeballs were frantic, swiveling madly between the mat and the chairs which would have been the two choices except that the way they had got round to standing meant Miss Mendoza would get the worst of the lot which they had schemed so hard to avoid. Please take a chair, said Lalitha, and was adroit, whisking away the disgraceful chair, propelling the sound one forward. Saroja had to envy her, had to admit by comparison she was a peasant, with stiff wooden limbs. She wondered if it was going to Miss Mendoza's school that made the difference, or if it all came naturally to Lalitha, who was so gifted; she concluded it must be a bit of both.

So gifted, Miss Mendoza was saying, a child in the round: which was puzzling, even Amma and Appa were looking strained, since Lalitha was anything but round, she was slender and tall like a lily, she even refused the superlative sweetmeats Chingleput sent home for fear of putting on fat. In Saroja's school the girls wanted to be rounded and curvy, like goddesses in pictures, but in Lalitha's they were crazy for slimness, the fashion was to be skinny everywhere except for breasts. Most of them didn't have much of breasts anyway, being in the beginning stages.

There are a number of careers open to girls like her, Miss Mendoza was saying. Have you thought of a career? she wanted to know, fixing her eyes which were beady but brilliant on Appa and Amma in turn. Saroja

61

could tell Amma hadn't, she was sharing a chair with her, squashed up close to her soft body which catered for men and children, and the way her flesh baulked it was clear she considered that more than sufficient.

Appa cleared his throat. He said young women these days did go in for careers, and he brought out that, yes, his daughter might have one too. What had she in mind? he asked Miss Mendoza, and nothing was more clear than that his was quite blank.

Teaching, said Miss Mendoza, which made Amma stiffen. Or nursing, she said, which turned Amma to stone, some kind of glittering rock which you felt would draw blood if you so much as touched it. So no one attempted to move except Miss Mendoza, who was courageous, who said bravely that in England where she had done her training it was a respectable occupation, but Amma said Not for any daughter of mine, in tones that would have shriveled anyone. Miss Mendoza, however, far from shriveling seemed to be expanding, seemed to be putting out petals of enthusiasm for Appa and Amma. How right you are, she cried, what admirable parents to seek to get away from the dreary and the conventional in the interests of an exceptional daughter! Then she whirled on Lalitha, flung both arms up and wide as if she were supporting a vast globe and said The world is your oyster, my dear, which made Saroja uncomfortable but Lalitha was looking solemn, her lustrous eyes were popping.

When Aunt Alamelu marched out with the tea arranged on a wooden lacquer tray as ordered by Amma they were all in harmony which made her grimmer than ever. This is my sister-in-law, Appa said gloomily, there were inflections in his voice that apologized for her manner though Miss Mendoza was pretending not to notice it. Aunt Alamelu however did not intend to pretend anything, she banged the tray down without speaking and strode back into the kitchen.

When she had gone Appa launched into a discourse on the drawbacks of the joint family system which was boring since they had heard it all before. Miss Mendoza, however, hadn't, not from Appa anyway. She was entirely understanding, nodded and said absolutely, and how she agreed with him. Saroja wondered how she could judge, living as she did with no family joint or otherwise, but supposed it had been her state when young. She could not easily, however, imagine Miss Mendoza being young, she seemed permanently stuck in her present age-groove, having changed not at all since their first meeting the day of the maypole dance. Jaya said she dyed her hair, but Lalitha said Trust you, ignoramus, it's hair spray she uses which modern ladies use, it's not at all the same thing. Saroja examined the reddish glints in Miss Mendoza's hair and concluded that must be what hair spray did to black hair. She couldn't be certain, though, because dust had the same effect; on the other hand it wasn't likely to be dust, it wasn't the high season for it even if Amma, in the strung-up state she had worked herself into before the visit, had insisted on sprinkling the courtyard with woodash and water to keep specks of dust down.

In the middle of this debate, before she could come to any decision, Lalitha kicked her hard on the ankle, so Saroja transferred her attention. She gazed at Amma instead, and at Appa, and at the bottom of his chair

63

where the cane had unraveled and hung in a shaming spiral, but there was no doubt about it, Miss Mendoza was most magnetic. She crooked her little finger, Saroja noticed, when she drank her tea, it did not touch the tumbler, and after every sip she dabbed her lips with a lacy handkerchief that she took from her purse. Saroja watched her out of the corner of her eye, to improve herself, she excused it in her mind, but her mind threw it out, it knew the real thing was it was interesting. Later, to rebut her mind, she tried to copy Miss Mendoza, but her little finger was obstinate, refused to curl, stuck out as it was used to doing, and she hadn't a handkerchief to dab with, even Amma hadn't, she used the end of her sari but not for need, for show, since the way she ate and drank there was never anything to mop up. Appa however had a pocket handkerchief, he knew about such things from the days before coming down in the world.

When Miss Mendoza had gone Lalitha said The world is my oyster, in the dreaming tones which came over her when she spoke about what she couldn't see properly, only glimpse in flashes. She said it again at night, when they were lying on their charpoys.

What is an oyster? Saroja wanted to know. She remembered reading about them but not what she had read. She had never seen one. She had never seen the sea, in whose depths, she recalled, they were found. It was cozy lying on her charpoy imagining the seabed studded with oysters, like precious gems set in gold. She resolved to check her imaginary picture with Chingleput, who had seen the sea. Chingleput town was near the sea, he had told her, only a few miles from the

64

ocean, which was wondrous. Lalitha said oysters were found in riverbeds too. Saroja asked if she meant Rangu's River and Lalitha said Probably, but Saroja, who had explored it pretty thoroughly, told her the only things to be found there were snails, and toads in the rainy season. Lalitha said You must go at night, you will see them then, shining through the water, but Saroja could not contemplate going to the river at night, not for oysters, not for anything. They shine, said Lalitha, inside and out, and sometimes when you open them you come upon a pearl. Her eyes were smoky; Saroja could tell she was thinking about the world which was her oyster; she very much hoped that when her sister came to opening it it would yield her a pearl.

2

AMMA KEPT THE buffalo to provide milk and curds for her family. If one relied on that milkman, she said, with scorn, from time to time, one would long since have given up the ghost. She meant Manikkam, whose supplies tended to be erratic, depending on his cows. In good years he had three cows, one milking and two in calf, and the milking cow's calf would gambol around with a muzzle on—nothing damped its spirits, not even the muzzle it wore all day long—to stop it drinking the milk Manikkam had to sell. If the calf wasn't sturdy it died, and Manikkam would stuff the skin and carry it about on his shoulders during his rounds and the cow's milk would continue to flow as Manikkam's wife had explained it would but never abundantly, the milk never gushed richly the way it did when the cow felt the calf's wet sucking mouth.

Saroja felt it was wrong, felt the calf had an entitlement to its mother's milk, but the boys said What entitlements, the way society is organized there are no entitlements. Which society, Saroja wanted to know, not being sure if it was the same Appa often found fault with. Society generally, they replied, but especially Western society, which is a spreading thing, one cannot escape it, and they told her about things which were done in the West which made what Manikkam did seem a lot less heinous. They told her about calves. They were taken from their mothers, they said, within hours after they were born, before they could even stand properly, and put in wooden crates so small that they could not turn round, could not even turn to lick themselves clean. The whole of their lives, the boys said, beasts were tethered, never saw sunlight or ate grass but were kept in sheds until led out to slaughter, and the cattle were forcibly fed on corn. What for, Saroja wanted to know, it seemed to her like a wicked madness, but they told her it wasn't, it was done for money, the farmers were organized to make as much money as they could, which was best done in this way.

Saroja tried to imagine these farmers, she wondered if they enjoyed the money they made, she knew in their place she could not have done. It made her think about the West, which was full of rich countries like England and America, and to speculate how rich one had to be before one stopped wanting to be richer. She thought if this was the way society was organized she would prefer it to be reorganized, which made Amma cry Not you too! She asked Saroja to inform her how Manikkam could earn his livelihood if he allowed the calves to drink all the milk and Saroja had to concede he could not, but what he did seemed more allowable than the other because he was a poor man which was evident from the state of his ribs. But she still considered his calves had rights too, every living thing had its rights and it was wrong to deprive them entirely.

Amma said Saroja took after her father. She sighed and said all her children took after him, it was a lucky thing none of that strain ran in her line otherwise by now they would all be sitting in a *chatram* depending for their food on charity. Saroja could see she was really imagining life in a poorhouse, she looked downright miserable, but Lalitha said at least they took after their mother for looks which cheered her up although it wasn't strictly true, because no one knew where Lalitha got her looks from, they were much more spectacular than Amma's.

When Lalitha was born, Amma told them, her weight in milk had been distributed to friends and relatives, it had been a gala occasion. Lalitha yawned to show she was tired of hearing the story and said what a waste of milk and Saroja agreed, although sneakingly she wished it could have been done at her birth too. At her birth the buffalo had been dry, and there had not been enough money to buy milk from Manikkam. There were other festivities, Amma told her, held her close to her squashy body and said her youngest was very precious to her which Saroja liked to think was true.

It was Saroja and Lalitha's job to look after the buffalo. They took turns at it, week and week about, unless Lalitha had something special, like when she had to practice her dancing for fetes at her school, or her flute, which she played in concerts. Saroja had spates of busyness too, like caring for the new baby at Manikkam's, which was small and ailing but as pretty as a little doll, but she was better at managing, she could fit things in whereas Lalitha was rushed, she had so many things to do, she told everyone, she didn't know how she was going to get through them all. It took her an hour to bathe and braid her hair in the morning, which amazed Saroja, she could not make out how anyone could spend that much time peeking and prinking, which was what Lalitha did, but Lalitha told her she would soon be doing the same, wait and see, told her she was pretty, told her she was sweetness itself and would she mind attending to the buffalo seeing how little time she had. Mostly Saroja did not mind; sometimes she did, rebelled and said it was not fair and told her sister so, but Lalitha had a way with her, she could usually get round Saroja, she was good at getting round people.

Saroja's gift was for getting round babies and buffaloes. The Manikkam baby moaned at its parents, but it gurgled and smiled at her, Manikkam's wife said it was miraculous. The buffalo followed where she led, it would even heave itself out of the river though it loved water, was fanatical about it even if it was only a small rainwater puddle, but it turned stubborn with Lalitha, stood with its horns lowered, and nothing would shift it. It made Lalitha cry, made her knot the leading rope and thump the beast with it, but it did not feel much, its hide was too thick.

It was dreadful when it rained, both of them dreaded the monsoon rains when it was their job to bring the buffalo in and tether it in its stall, but of the two of them Lalitha hated it most. She could not get round Saroja so easily then, because Saroja was afraid. She was afraid of Rangu's River which in the monsoon became one with the raging sheets of rain, of the wind which howled the way Rangu was reputed to have howled when the police were beating him up, whose echoes people said still rose from the river. Lalitha called her a coward, stamped on the ground on which the first heavy drops were falling while Saroja shivered, would not budge, could not.

Lalitha wept. She screamed and said she was not turning out, not for the buffalo, not for anything, it could stay put and survive as best it could and all was on Saroja's head. Saroja knew it was not, it was not her turn, but she knew nothing could survive a monsoon storm if it chose to be vicious. She and Lalitha went down to the river together, welded together under Manikkam's umbrella, which being made of palm leaves withstood gales better than Appa's, which was a city umbrella, a black cotton affair that turned itself inside out at the least provocation.

The buffalo was wallowing in the river, nibbling at water weeds, up to its hocks in water. Lalitha was impatient, called it a stupid animal, but it was not, it was a water buffalo, it enjoyed its natural element. When she advanced it retreated, she had to stand behind Saroja, who was not feeling brave, who was praying for the twilight to last while she got the bridle over its horns and around its neck. They had to drag the beast back, step by step. It was reluctant to leave, which made Saroja conclude the storm would not be as bad as she feared, because the buffalo usually knew, would come in of its own accord if it was going to be dramatic. It wanted a soaking first, though. In the process they were both soaked, and the river whose banks were like a bog because no one bothered to maintain them sucked at their heels, sucked and sucked with hideous gulps, their legs were covered in mud right up to the knees.

This *dump*, said Lalitha. She was furious. She stood in the buffalo's stall which Appa had never finished reroofing and tore off her clothes which were sodden and flung them in a heap. Stood there naked, without a stitch, and her body spattered and blotched with mud splashed up from the river and the muddy rain which dripped through the ragged thatch. Her eyes were burning. This *hole*, she said, she shouted above the storm so as to startle the buffalo, and ran out as she was which Saroja would not have done, not even in the dark but it was not, it was golden and black between the twilight that was ending and the storm that was brewing up among the dark rolling clouds.

Lalitha was shrieking out there in the rain, calling to Saroja to come out and enjoy it. She was mercuric, the way her moods changed was quicksilver. Saroja wanted to join her, be with her in her joyous mood which was infectious, but she had the buffalo on her hands. It had to be tethered before it yielded once again to the call of water, responded to the joyous calls Lalitha was making. There were rings in the floor to tether it, but they were rusty, they got blocked from disuse between one season's rains and another, Saroja's nails were breaking trying to get the rope through, trying to hold the beast, which was jibbing in its wish to join Lalitha outside. Saroja wished Lalitha would help her, would stop bawling at least, she called to her but when Lalitha came in she did nothing. Stood there dripping, and watched. Her body was wet and golden. Her hair was streaming.

Look at me, said Lalitha.

Saroja had been looking, out of slits, her eyes had turned shifty.

Look, said Lalitha, and tilted up Saroja's face which wanted to turn anywhere except where it was bidden but was mesmerized.

Look, said Lalitha, and ran her hands down her body, down the length of it, touching its secret places. Her nipples were rubbery, perked up when her fingers passed. She knelt with her knees together beside the rustling hay, parted her knees to reveal the cleft which was wet. Her whole body was wet and shining and slippery.

It's lovely, said Lalitha. She was laughing. Her limbs were bold and free, they did not seem to mind what they did, were capable of anything. Saroja did not know if she meant her body was lovely, or felt lovely, or was full of lovely sensations from what she was doing to it. She concluded it must be all three, which surprised her, she had not connected lovely sensations with the groans Appa and Amma let out when they were doing bodily things to each other.

Try it, said Lalitha. She lifted Saroja's skirt and reached up and touched her the way Jaya said Lachu had done. Jaya had closed her thighs and run off, she didn't want his finger exploring, but Saroja did, she wanted to find out, she opened her legs to allow Lalitha and felt sensations but they weren't wild, she knew they weren't like what Lalitha felt.

When you're older, Lalitha said. Saroja believed her, because Lalitha knew so much, a great deal more than anyone else whom Saroja knew, it came naturally to Lalitha, she got it the miraculous way animals did, from within her. Besides, she wanted to believe her sister. When she was older she wanted to look the way Lalitha did, which was glowing, as if candles were burning under her skin.

*　　*　　*

In the morning the sun came out. Aunt Alamelu said not to be deceived. She said to mark her words, the monsoon was not far behind, which everyone knew because there were always these preliminary downpours. Lalitha begged her not to be so depressing which made Aunt sniff, made her inquire what made madam so blithe? Lalitha said Wouldn't you like to know? and executed a little dance around her old aunt to cheer her up, she said. Aunt Alamelu wasn't cheered, she was suspicious. She said Lalitha was full of fizz, she resembled the poisonous stuff that Bundi sold, which was a dangerous state for maidens to be in. Lalitha didn't care. She was in a shimmering mood. She washed out her clothes of the

73

night before and draped them over the rosemary bush to dry.

The rosemary bush was frequently festooned with Lalitha's clothes, it gave them a bouquet, she said. Smell, she translated for Saroja's benefit. Lavender was better than rosemary, she told her. Miss Mendoza had a friend in England who sent her dried lavender which wasn't a specialty of India. She put it among her clothes, which made her smell the way she did. Saroja thought she smelled musty but Lalitha said this was because she hadn't acquired a taste for refined smells. She told how, once, Miss Mendoza's dried lavender had been seized by a Customs man who mistook it for bhang. She thought it funny how anyone, let alone a Customs man, could mistake one for the other. So did Saroja. She had seen the dried-up lavender clinging like burrs to Miss Mendoza's blouse whereas bhang was altogether different, especially the smell, which was in a different class. Appa said there was nothing funny about bhang. He modified that and said bhang was one thing, but it could lead to opium, which was entirely another matter. He told them the opium trade was a vile trade that the British had engaged in to line their own pockets, had gone to war to protect this commerce. Not in India, Anand corrected him, that had been done in China, and not by the British alone, by a European gang. India, China, are not all men brothers? Appa wanted to know. He said how the wheel had come full circle, now it was Europe that was frantic to stamp out the trade. Amma said If you sow dragon's teeth, meaningly. Aunt Alamelu said she didn't profess to know much about such things, but to her mind opium was no worse than what Bundi concocted and sold, which made Appa inquire was she simple.

Manikkam took bhang. It was a trial to his wife because when he was high she could not get at him for his shortcomings. Nothing could get at him then. Saroja had an idea that that was his reason, when things got bad he didn't want to know, you could see him ferreting around the town for money to buy bhang. She figured it was his escape, like the orb she carried within her which was a sanctum into which she could retreat, but Chingleput said no, hers was formed out of strength, whereas Manikkam's was a bolthole created of weakness. Saroja could not agree; she said in his place she would do the same, but Chingleput said no one with moral fiber would. On some issues, like this one, he coincided with Aunt Alamelu. It was rare, but when it happened she remembered the gap in their ages which otherwise she did not think about at all.

When Manikkam was high his eyes became dreaming, he lay on the haybales in his cows' byre, because his wife would not let him in the house, and told wonderful, rambling stories. They were like the universe, without beginning or end, and when you listened to them you felt you were being allowed a glimpse of what the universe was about. Afterwards, though, you couldn't pin it down, for the life of you you couldn't say what you had seen, the inability made you restless, you were yearning for something, you didn't know what, only that it was infinitely beautiful and desirable, that you had been shut out from. Afterwards was bad for Manikkam too. He shriveled up, it was like watching cut vines withering under the sun. Sometimes he had rigors.

Manikkam's wife raved when Manikkam's eyes began dreaming. She accused Perumal of lending her husband the money to ride to hell on, but everyone knew Perumal wouldn't, he was too wary, he knew Manikkam, demanded security from him before allowing so much as a peep in at his outermost shutters, and Manikkam had none, even his sickle was mortgaged. When Manikkam's wife got demented, at her wits' end with a sick baby or a recalcitrant cow, she even turned on Appa, accused him of lending money which he certainly did but never to buy bhang. Appa got indignant. His innocence lent him strength, he yelled at her to clear off and let him have some peace. Partly he was innocent and partly he was afraid Amma would start on him. Amma totally disapproved of his loans which were tantamount to gifts, told him charity began at home but he was not to be cured of his penchant.

It created a coldness between Manikkam's wife and Amma. Manikkam's wife said how anyone could see when her husband was headed for the bhang, it was incumbent on folk not to speed him on his way. Amma said There's gratitude for you. Manikkam's wife said her gratitude was boundless for what they had received in the past, all she was saying was discretion should be exercised. Amma asked her was she trying to teach her betters; she had notions about the proper place of a milkman's wife which she aired. Manikkam's wife became nasty. Betters, she said, Amma and Appa might well be, she wasn't going to dispute that point, but there were certain things affecting their daughters.

Such as, Amma wanted to know; she was hard and cold, like an ice cube. Certain goings-on at night, said Manikkam's wife, but she would not like to specify because of not seeing clearly in all that rain. She was looking hard at Lalitha as she spoke, and at Saroja, who was frozen, but Lalitha was cool, she was cool and brazen at the same time. A ghost, she said, was what Manikkam's wife had seen, the ghost of a naked dancing woman which she and Saroja had both seen, been frightened by, taken refuge from in the buffalo's stall. Manikkam's wife was jolted; you could see she was trying to cling to her legitimate suspicions but pale about the gills and wavering, and shuddering, no match at all for Lalitha.

When Manikkam's wife had departed Amma said, Saroja too? raising an eyebrow, and Lalitha said yes, Saroja had seen it too, replying for Saroja, who could not utter, who kept her eyelids firmly down, a chisel could not have levered them up to make revelations.

* * *

You have to be quick, Lalitha told Saroja; you have to seize your opportunity before it passes you by, you have to be quick with your answers if you want to get anywhere.

It is an art, said Lalitha, which either you have or you haven't. Saroja knew she hadn't, she knew she was slow, she was often compared with Lalitha on this score and found wanting. She went on pitching horseshoes, neither too fast nor too slow because that was the best way to get them around the nail.

The boys had implanted the nail, it was the axle pin from a bullock cart, in a tree stump on the site earmarked for the new grain store Amma wanted which Appa had never finally shelved and never finally built. The shoes were cast from the hooves of the little *jutka* ponies, they were small and worn and had square holes in them from the special nails the blacksmith said were necessary. The blacksmith was a kindly man, would always oblige with a horseshoe, or weld the seam in a leaky vessel. Aunt Alamelu's vessels were forever developing leaks. She sent Saroja down to the blacksmith's to have them mended, with a pot of curd or some of her chutney done up in a strip of banana leaf by way of payment. Saroja did not mind, quite liked it in fact, liked the patient little ponies and the fire gilding up under the puff of bellows, liked everything except the smell of charred hoof and the weary look of the ponies which were overworked. Some of them were worked to death, they died in the shafts, simply fell down and could not rise again. The drivers got panicky then, their livelihood being tied up with the ponies, whipped the poor beasts until passers-by got angry and restrained them.

Amma said Muslims were worst for this kind of thing, being flesh-eaters they were callous of animals' feelings, but Lalitha said Europeans were flesh-eaters too, yet they were very kind to animals, Miss Mendoza had told her so, having seen for herself in England. The boys said Yes, maybe on the surface, the cruelties they inflict are hidden and unspeakable and on a vast scale, since everything they do has to be on this scale for profit motives, and the people prefer not to know what goes on, it would turn their stomachs. Europeans are great eaters, the boys said, eat four times as much as we do, they wouldn't let anything stand in the way of their eating, certainly not animals suffering. Appa respected his sons' opinions, he sided with them about profit motives, but you could see he was torn, he wanted to agree with them and at the same time with Lalitha and the two were incompatible. So he deflected the subject, said that Muslims, Europeans and Hindus could be equally callous about animals and there was good and bad in all, it was wrong to discriminate against any minority in their midst. Discriminate, cried Amma, what is the matter with you, where is the discrimination, are we all not living peacefully together as Gandhiji said we should? Show me where there is one iota of discrimination, she challenged him, so that Appa finding himself at odds on all sides fled.

The blacksmith was in love with his work, you could tell from the way he honed and hammered at the shoe until it conformed to the shape he had made for it in his mind. He said so himself, in between bouts of coughing due to the coal fumes which his wife claimed brought up bits of his lungs. He told Saroja no one could turn out work like he did, which Saroja believed, even the terrible rents in her aunt's cooking vessels were beaten out and mended so skillfully you would never have known them from new but for the shine on the welding. No machine, he said, could be fashioned to do what he did, he was not afraid of machines usurping him which was the great fear of the weavers in the village.

It was Chingleput's fear too. It was buried deep from his years of being in the village but sometimes he would dig it up and exhibit it to Saroja, she thought he did it because he enjoyed frightening himself. She always said a prayer though, just in case, asked God not to allow machines into their village which would destroy Chingleput and his skills. She kept her prayers secret, however, because of Appa and the boys who were progressives. They often said machines were the answers to the country's problems.

Are you listening? Lalitha wanted to know. She watched the horseshoe spinning round on the nail where Saroja had triumphantly pitched it and called it a childish game. Saroja said she didn't mind if it was; she was cheerful from having made that surpassing cast. She said she had been listening, which was true, though Lalitha's observations had had to share with the thoughts that were tracking through her mind. She was adept at this. It often flummoxed her teachers, who suspected she hadn't been paying attention and tried to catch her out. What specific opportunity, she asked Lalitha, did she have in mind that ought to be seized? The opportunity to become a film star, said Lalitha. A what? asked Saroja, and stopped her pitching, interrupted a throw which she was certain would have been another winner. A film star, said Lalitha, a film actress, a personality of the cinema, no less. Her eyes were starry and serious at the same time so that Saroja could see she was in earnest, wasn't daydreaming as she frequently did, which was the first thought that had flitted through her mind.

It was my dancing, said Lalitha. It caught his eye, she

said, it took his fancy, he asked Miss Mendoza who I was.

Who? said Saroja. She was dumbstruck but she brought it out.

The film director, said Lalitha. She was bubbling, but suppressed. Saroja had the impression she was near to popping, like the bottles of liquor Bundi sold; when the corks were loosened they flew right off, one of them had struck Bundi in the eye, which Aunt Alamelu said was his right deserts. He was not blinded, though; even Aunt Alamelu would not have wanted that.

Lalitha told Appa and Amma. She had to, to get their cooperation, without it she could not have seized her opportunity. No one was clear what that was, not even Lalitha. A film star, she said, a film actress, a chance to be in a film: she whittled it down to fit the reality which would eventually have to be conceded. Appa said We must see. He said One must have the full facts of the matter to enable one to come to the right decision. Not in this world, said Amma, in this world it is not possible to have the full truths on any subject. It was clear they were talking for the sake of it, to save face in front of their children by refusing to admit the subject was wholly outside their scope and experience. Appa said the Indian film industry was the second biggest in the world. He said it gave employment to two million people. His brow was furrowed, he paced the courtyard with his hands locked behind his back and it was as plain as anything could be that these were not the facts that were needed; what they wanted was another kind of information and not all his books could help to provide it.

Aunt Alamelu heard. She was grinding dhal for chutney, but she halted the grinding stone to get an earful. That is the trouble, said Lalitha, this hole, this dump, there is no privacy for *anything!* Amma said Where is the need for privacy? It is a family matter, she said with dignity, best discussed within the family circle, of which your aunt is a member.

Aunt Alamelu was preening herself, her features were set in a righteous mold. She often issued reminders, when Appa was absent, of her blood entitlements, her place in the family, but she preferred Amma to do it for her, it carried more weight.

You want to be what? she cried. Are my ears deceiving me, can I be hearing aright? She smelled of dhal and the green chillies she had been crushing, it was a formidable smell. You heard, said Lalitha. She was insolent, stuck out her lower lip and glared at Aunt Alamelu but it was wasted, it glanced off the hide she had developed, which rivaled Chingleput's. You, a respectable girl, a girl from a respected family, cried Aunt Alamelu, you want to be a nautch girl, a devadasi such as no one in our line not for twenty generations has ever descended to being, is that your ambition? A film star, said Lalitha, these days girls from respectable families act in films, can I help it if an old fossil like you hasn't heard? She was pale. Aunt Alamelu was fuming. You need not tell me, she cried, I know what is going on these days, these days young people think they know best, they have no respect for their elders, they have no respect for anything except their own willful ways, in my day do you think a respectable girl would have dared to speak as you do?

I respect what is worthy of respect! cried Lalitha, echoing the boys.

There were a lot more exchanges, all about respect, before Appa managed to stop them. He had to bellow to do it, they were already shouting and he had to shout them down, there was quite a commotion. Manikkam's tottering hut was half an acre away but they all came swarming out, they ran out eagerly as far as the prickly pear hedge which was the boundary to their land and stood there with their ears flapping. Appa was put out. He said they had no respect for their betters, which was unusual for him since he was all for an equal society, often spoke up against class and caste with which he said the whole world was riddled. It emphasized for Saroja the nature and extent of the emergency.

Amma agreed with Appa. They left the verandah, where proceedings had been conducted, and retreated into the house. Amma closed the door and unrolled the *thatees* at the windows, which made the place stifling. There were more agreements between her and Appa; their disagreements were for theories, Saroja had discovered, when it came to practical matters they nearly always closed ranks.

*   *   *

SAROJA was sent to bring home the Mysore *pak* which Chingleput had promised to make. She rode pellmell, with the tin box clattering on the bicycle carrier to which it was strapped and the wind slashing at her face.

On the return trip it was a tail wind, she used her brakes on the slopes and cycled sedately skirting the potholes so as not to break up the Mysore *pak*. This was difficult because Chingleput's sweetmeats were feather-light and crumbly, but she managed, delivered it intact into Amma's hands.

Amma took out the glistening squares, complimented Saroja on the care she had taken. Saroja was offhand, said it was nothing, though it had been, the potholes were like moon craters, of which she had seen pictures in the magazine Miss Subramaniam passed round the class. She watched Amma, who was making *vadais* in curd. These were her specialty. The *vadais* were crisp and the curd sauce she made was rich and creamy. Saroja's saliva was running. She licked her lips and felt glad the film director was coming, otherwise she would have had to wait for a festival to sample such festive food. The nearest festival lay months away. In other ways it was terrible, worse than the day Miss Mendoza came. Miss Mendoza was coming too, but her importance waned, became secondary to that of the film man.

This one-horse town, this backward place, this out-post of civilization, moaned Lalitha.

She sat immobilized by the green crushed leaves she had smeared on her palms and harped upon the absence of a fridge. She watched Aunt Alamelu squeezing limes for the cordial and described how an extractor worked, its speed, its efficiency. Aunt Alamelu said if God had wanted men to be machines he would have embedded wires in their limbs. She said hands were best, which made her look at Lalitha's, whose palms were now the palest, most delicate shade of vermilion. Temptress's palms, Aunt said, she exploded, after gazing with some intensity. In her mother's day, she stated, only loose women stained their palms, dancing girls and such like. And brides, said Amma. Yes, brides, said Aunt Alamelu, and nubile girls awaiting their suitors—no, not suitors, that no doubt was tomorrow's shameless fashion, suitors' intermediaries—and would someone tell her what was this film director, a bridegroom, a suitor, an intermediary? A man, said Lalitha in a suffering way, with whom it was intended to converse; such conversation, she said, between men and women was a mark of their civilization, which shut Aunt Alamelu up, she recognized the sentiment as Appa's. Everyone knew, though, it was only temporary, she would be a nuisance if she possibly could, and Appa was frowning, the way he did when he had to issue demeaning orders but he did it in the end, forbade her to stir one inch out of the kitchen and strode out to see what Kannan was up to.

Kannan had delivered the bench which Appa had ordered. Its balance was wrong, Kannan had come with his saw to make reparations on site. He was not the best carpenter, when he had finished the bench had two legs on the ground and two off it, no one could have sat on it with assurance. Kannan said it was the uneven ground, suggested wedges to counteract the deficiency. Appa defended his ground, insisted it was the bench that needed perfecting. Perfection was not within Kannan's power but he began to saw, chips and sawdust were flying.

Amma came out, she saw the courtyard she had

cleaned, it looked like a carpenter's shop. For heaven's sake, she cried. She said any more sawing and they might as well sit on the ground, which was true, the bench wasn't far off it as it was. Appa said she was right. They glared at Kannan, who was huffed. He leaned on his saw and asked what should he do, would they make up their minds? Appa said he could tell him with pleasure but he didn't, he couldn't afford to, he had a problem on his hands because of the shortage of chairs. He said Just leave. Kannan said Glad to. He shouldered his saw and left the bench, which was now balanced on three legs: they contacted the earth but it was a tenuous contact, and intermittent. The fourth leg was off the ground entirely.

In the kitchen Aunt Alamelu was lamenting the puncturing of one of her cooking vessels. She told Saroja to rush it down to the blacksmith. Saroja said it was too far, she was too tired, she wouldn't. She didn't want to miss the film director's arrival. Use another, Amma said shortly. One must use the correct vessel, each has its allotted function, said Aunt. Hidebound, that is your trouble, said Amma: What are we discussing, cooking pots or some world-shaking topic?

On the floor there was an oily pool, made by the leaky vessel, which was spreading. If it touches my clothes I am ruined, shrieked Lalitha. She was in the next room, holding her sari bunched up in her hand, and screeching.

Saroja went out, to cool off. She stood by the tamarind tree, under the vast lattice of its branches, and wondered why they could not be like the tree, which achieved so much, such a majestic result, without any fuss, in utter silence as far as she could tell. A silence of the heavenly spheres, her teacher had said, a phrase which appealed to Saroja. She was a small mousy woman, Miss Subramaniam, a devout Hindu who asked them to pray before and after each lesson. She lived a noisy existence in a house full of relatives, but she often said surprising, peaceful things. Saroja wished she could hear this heavenly silence, had an inkling if she did it would be here under the tamarind tree, but Lalitha was calling. She was in some dire need as you could tell from the metallic thread in her tone. Saroja ran in to help.

It's the hem, cried Lalitha, I can feel it isn't straight, it's hanging like a dog's tongue, I *know* I look ridiculous! She was twisting herself, twisting and maneuvering the hand mirror to give her the view she wanted but it was inadequate. The way we live is *primitive*, said Lalitha. She told of cheval glasses that civilized ladies had, that were an indispensable part of their toilet, in which they could see themselves from top to toe and so emerge well dressed. Saroja squatted down, she played the part of the cheval glass that was missing, told of lapses and shortcomings while Lalitha pirouetted, asked anxiously where the border of her sari fell if she swirled, if she stood still, if she stood so, she had a number of poses. The length has to be right, she told Saroja, just cover the bottom half of the heel, that is the fashion. Saroja arranged the folds of the sari, she tugged and pulled as she was bidden until Lalitha was satisfied. Sweetness, said Lalitha. She was radiant, flower-fresh. Saroja sat back on her heels and surveyed her; she thought the world of her sister, she could not imagine the film man not thinking so too, but she said a little prayer just in case.

*　*　*

The film director came in a car. It was left at the bottom of the field because of the rutted path and the party walked. It was a party of four, and it walked in the shape of an arrow with the film director in front and his assistant and Miss Mendoza behind and far behind trailing them the driver of the car. In the car Miss Mendoza had been in front; Saroja had seen her sitting up straight with a scarf over her hair, which was short, and arranged in scrolls. She had on sky-blue shoes which matched her parasol and the border of her sari, Saroja thought them very fashionable though the heels were not very high, not as high as before, perhaps because Miss Mendoza remembered the state of the path. The film director's shoes were two-colored: tan and white, in symmetrical patches, but the white was anything but, being covered in dust. So was the director, or so he claimed; he kept flicking at his coat with his handkerchief, said it had been a dusty ride.

Appa said it was the dust season, apologized as if it were his doing, then he overdid it, said he would have changed it for his honored guests had he been able and emitted a nervous titter for this extravagance. Lalitha shot him a glance, she had issued a general warning not to gush, under guise of instructing Saroja she had described it to them as the worst social sin. Appa glanced right back, the visit had exhilarated him; he said he was always ready to listen to the young and added roguishly that the older generation had a trick or two to teach the young, did Mr. Gupta not agree?

Mr. Gupta was the film director, everyone seemed intent on getting his agreement. No one bothered too much about Devraj, his assistant. Devraj was secondary, like Miss Mendoza in present company. He wore white trousers and a flowing white cotton shirt over them, whereas Mr. Gupta had on a cream silk suit with a handkerchief to match peeping out of his top pocket. The silk was not good for mopping. It did not absorb, it streaked the sweat over his face, which looked greenish and smooth as if it had been sandpapered. There was even some powdery residue, it resembled what Kannan left on the surfaces of timber after rubbing them down.

Mr. Gupta was accommodating; he agreed with Appa though he was not the same generation. He was middling, older than Devraj but a lot younger than Appa, although his polish made it difficult to bear this in mind. He said Appa was right, the young indeed had a good deal to learn from the old, but as an educated man he would know the converse was also true. Appa said absolutely, that was very true. He grew expansive, passed the lime drinks round himself. Have a *nimbu-pani*, he said, bringing out one of the only three words of any northern language he knew. The others were *chup* (Be quiet!) and *jaldi* (Be quick!), he had picked them up, during his years of internment as a freedom fighter, from the English jail superintendent whose total repertoire they had been. Lalitha was growing restive, in case he launched into an account of those days, which he was very apt to do. Besides, she wanted to bring the talk round to her, her part in the film, but she could not interrupt.

Amma was cool and flustered in turn, she too had in mind the purpose of the visit. She invited Mr. Gupta to partake of some sweetmeats, asked him in the next breath what were his intentions? Intentions? said Mr. Gupta. He choked over his *nimbu-pani* and had to be thumped on the back before he could speak again. His intention, he said, was to make a documentary. No one knew what a documentary was. No one would confess. Miss Mendoza interpreted the silence. She said it would show life as it was, be a microcosm of village living. Mr. Gupta said that was it, in a nutshell. He said he had been looking round for some time, he thought their village would do. He had never thought, he said, to see English dancing in a village; it was truly fantastic, it had really riveted his attention.

Miss Mendoza simpered, she took it as a compliment. We like to give our girls total opportunity, total experience, she said. Some are able to take advantage, she said in a vibrant voice; they are, shall we say, gifted. Her brilliant gaze was beamed straight on Lalitha. One of our most promising pupils, she cried, that is why, Mr. Gupta, I have not hesitated to bring her to your attention! Her hand was laid on his sleeve. Mr. Gupta looked at Lalitha, who was doing her eye act. Delighted, delighted, he murmured abstractedly, then suddenly became brisk, said crisply what he could use was some good folk dancing, or a spirited Indian solo. Lalitha was startled, she forgot to act. Her face fell, she didn't know much Indian dancing, it was not a specialty of her school, in Miss Mendoza's school English dancing was the specialty. Then she rallied, got her bold look back and claimed that that too was in her scope, well within her competence. Good, said Mr. Gupta, he seemed to take more notice of her than he had been doing. In that case, he said, he could use her, definitely. Amma was looking slightly dizzy. In what way? she inquired. In the documentary, explained Mr. Gupta patiently, which he proposed to make.

No one was very clear, even now, what that was. It seemed to be bits and pieces taken from here and there and put together like the mosaic panels on the doors of the Muslim mosque. Mr. Gupta called them shots. He said there would be shots of the village pond, and of the weavers' quarters, and a wedding and a funeral as well. Amma, who knew what went on, said neither was in the offing; there was no pond either, the villagers used the river or the wells. Mr. Gupta said these were little difficulties to be got over. He turned to Appa and said he might use the whole set-up, meaning Appa's house and field and Appa himself, as typifying village living. Appa didn't look too pleased, he didn't regard himself as a typical villager, he suggested that Manikkam might more suitably serve as typical. Yes, said Mr. Gupta, Manikkam should be included too, his style of living, his farm, his homestead, which made Amma exclaim, she could not see what he could see in that unlovely hovel. It was not lovely in Saroja's sight either, but she was beginning to have a glimmering. She saw the documentary would be like the panels, the mosaic was made up of gilt and enamel but it was the plain marble chips laid between which brought out the color, made the panels beautiful. At least she hoped so, she wanted the film to be beautiful, she would not have wanted her sister to take part in anything that was ugly.

* * *

THERE was another little difficulty to be got over, actually it wasn't little, it was the monsoon which had been limbering up, which as anticipated broke in due season. What did I say? exclaimed Aunt Alamelu, did I not warn you it would not be long? She said this every year, as if signs were vouchsafed her alone, which was tedious because everyone knew, you would have known if you were blind from the sullenness that hung in the air.

It made the cattle restive. They plunged about the field, not feeding or drinking, they even lost their fondness for ruminating. Their turds stank; plopped down green and loose, lay on the ground without drying, attracting hordes of blowflies. Manikkam's wife groaned, said disconsolately her best source of fuel was done for, allowed Manikkam to scrape up the mess for his crops. It was always a contest between them as to who got the dung. The milk went sour in no time. Manikkam blamed the oil cake that the government store distributed when grazing was sparse. Manikkam's wife swore it was the thunder. She got her husband up, sent him off on his rounds even when the rain was pelting down so as to get the milk sold before it could turn.

Manikkam had his palm-leaf cuirass and hood, he tucked up his dhoti round his waist and drove his beasts before him. The beasts had nothing, they drooped their heads and went forth as if bound for the Muslim butchery. When it rained really hard, the raindrops thumping down upon their flanks, they vaulted over the prickly pear supposed to protect Appa's land and took shelter under the tamarind tree. Appa said it was the silliest thing to do, because trees attract lightning. He said it with relish. Each time he did Amma said Remember they are fellow creatures, they have feelings the same as you, and Aunt Alamelu said Holy Mother Cow. They were sisters, and had similar opinions, but they did not always chime one hundred percent together.

When the monsoon was imminent Amma cleared the window sills where prized possessions were kept. There were Appa's books and pamphlets, and framed pictures of Brahma the Creator and the Goddess Saraswathi, and pottery busts of Gandhi and Nehru and Mrs. Gandhi, and a model of the Taj Mahal made out of pith, and a framed certificate Lalitha had been awarded for her music and dancing. Amma wiped them all, damp was already breeding green on their surfaces, and put them away in her tin trunk. She got out the trestles which Kannan had made, hoisted the rice sacks onto them in case the grain store got flooded. She hauled the charpoys and chairs off the courtyard and piled them on the verandah, right at the end where the rain wouldn't reach them even when slanted by gales.

She developed her virtuous look doing these things, it spoke volumes for seeing to essentials in good time.

It irked Appa. He stood about in the chaos and complained. He knew chaos was inevitable, but that didn't stop him. He said Sufficient unto the day, which he had picked up from Lalitha, which made Amma snap None of your Christian riddles here, this is a Hindu household. Normally she was tolerant, it was the humidity, and Appa, getting on her nerves. Appa, who was not immune, said Everything in good time, and he stood around some more, to show her. It was like a red rag to Amma, she got out pots and pans, lined them up pointedly under where the drips in the ceiling came. Appa took a look, pretended not to see. He signaled to Anand, who was lurking in the storeroom out of Amma's sight, and the two of them sloped off down the path carrying their sandals in a rope sling in the direction of the coffee shop. No one wore sandals coming or going, in the monsoon the path was like a quagmire and the potholes were mud traps.

In the grounds of Miss Mendoza's school Mr. Gupta and his men were putting up tents. Miss Mendoza had given permission, the school vacation having begun. Lalitha took Saroja down to see; she was privileged to do this, being as it were bespoken. Amma was suspicious, but she let them go. Aunt Alamelu tilted the balance, she was muttering disapprovingly in the background, until Amma said brusquely it was right out in the open, what possible harm could there be, no doubt remembering her own persecution.

Miss Mendoza had come down too, to watch. She was wearing boots, which she called Wellingtons, said how useful they were. She had brought them with her all the way from England. The patent was cracked, crinkly all over like an old enamel pot. She had stuffed her sari into the tops, which in Saroja's estimation made her look ridiculous, but Mr. Gupta took one look and said How sensible. He was squelching about in his two-tone shoes, you wouldn't have guessed they were except from having seen them in their original state, and casting dark glances at the sky, which was rolling with monsoon cloud. The monsoon, he said, he had known about that, he hadn't been born in India for nothing: reality, though, that was altogether a different matter, that really got him. One is down to grass roots here, he said, mystifyingly, there wasn't a grass shoot to be seen, only acres of churned-up mud. Mr. Gupta had been educated in England.

Miss Mendoza sympathized. She cast up her eyes as he was doing and said What terrible weather we are having. Mr. Gupta agreed. He said in a suffering way What a country!, which made Saroja wonder if he meant the whole of India, or the country as opposed to the city he hailed from. Terrible, terrible, murmured Miss Mendoza; it was getting to be like a duet between the two of them. Agreed, Mr. Gupta said, but in his job one carried on regardless. He called it a trade. Miss Mendoza would not allow it. You are too modest, she declared, it is a craft, a creative vocation. While they were arguing it began to pour in earnest, and Mr. Gupta and his men retreated into their tents. No one at all could have carried on, raindrops the size of coins were smacking down, and there were sudden shattering gusts of wind.

Half the village had turned up to watch. Normally they wouldn't have ventured out so close to the rains, but they couldn't resist the filming. When the downpour began, though, not even the hardy ones wanted to linger, they ran, they fled, it was like watching an army in rout. Saroja was minded to join them, she was getting horribly wet, but she was joined to Lalitha, who was standing by Miss Mendoza. Miss Mendoza was in a dilemma. She could not enter a tent with so many men, it would not have been seemly, even Mr. Gupta, who was modern, coming from a city as he did, did not dare to invite her. Girls, girls, she cried, and dashed up the steps of the school clutching a hand of each of them. Her boots were taking in water. The schoolhouse was locked. The three of them stood, a triptych, under the eaves which fended off the worst.

Overhead lightning crackled. It was forked and ripped up the sky. Saroja thought of Amma, whom lightning terrified, who went round when it was like this, the storm at its height, covering up all the reflecting surfaces, which she said gave back the lightning, tempted catastrophe. Superstition, Appa called it. Amma paid no attention. She covered the brass vessels, and Lalitha's hand mirror, and the sliver of mirror Appa used for shaving which, being nailed, she could not turn to the wall, and even masked the window panes with oblongs of gunny. It made the house terrible, the rooms looming, and muffled, and shadows in corners, you couldn't breathe properly until it was over. Besides, it took away the pleasure, you were shut in, you couldn't watch the rain outside, the shining lances and spears that sprang into being by the thousand when lightning flickered.

Under the eaves Miss Mendoza was crossing herself.

She touched her forehead and her heart and her shoulders, said Mother of God preserve us. It was clear she was superstitious, in the way Appa said Amma was. It was also extreme because the storm was not bad as storms went, it was already blowing over, there were frills of light showing where the sun was pushing out from under the clouds. Quirky, said Miss Mendoza. She was wet to the bone. She folded away her parasol, which had not stood up to the test, and went squelching down the steps to meet Mr. Gupta, who was emerging from his tent.

Saroja and Lalitha followed behind. They were soaked too, but the earth was steaming, was delectable, was giving off tender vapors and odors. Lovely, said Saroja, she could not resist, she was taking deep breaths, and gulping, it was the way it affected her. Child of the soil, said Miss Mendoza, with inflections, but Lalitha, who was a child of grace, could not resist it either. Lovely, she said. She was radiant, she was dazzling, the raindrops in her hair were sparkling and her form was sculptured. She looked the way she had that time in the gloaming she had danced around naked, with the sun and the rain playing on her body. Mr. Gupta's attention was riveted, he could not pluck his eyes off her. Lovely indeed, he said, he said it indulgently, like the city man he was to the village girl which was Lalitha, but there was nothing like indulgence in his eyes. His eyes were like Lachu's, they ran away with what was inside him.

                          *   *   *

THE quirky weather went on. It grew worse, in the
monsoon pattern. The worst season, said Manikkam, it
exhausted him, there was more to do now than during
the sowing, or the reaping, or the calving. Water ran
down his back, sweat and rain mingled. He had been
clearing the trenches which drained his land, which silt
had blocked up. They got blocked every year by the
mud washed down by the rains. His banana grove was
also in urgent need of attention; the stems were swoon-
ing over fallen stakes, would snap at the next squall, the
leaves were already hanging like tattered banners.

    Manikkam's wife agreed it was the worst season. She
had little fuel, she said, she walked for miles to gather
barely a half-bundle of firewood which wouldn't keep
a decent fire going. Everything was wet, she said dis-
gusted: her clothes, herself, her children, there was no
way she could think of to dry them. And the children,
she said, and moaned a little and told Saroja, who had
been sent round for milk, how tiring it was having
them all day under her feet. You'll find out, she said,
there's so much to do you're never finished. Saroja
picked up the milk and pelted back. She knew she
would never be like that, she was a different class, Amma's class, which had its own sufferings but never
touched Manikkam's, whose brand was basic, it scraped
the very marrow of his bones. Besides, as Appa said, it
was the children that did it. Saroja would have chil-

dren, of course, but they would be planned, like Amma's, they would come one at a time whenever she wanted her arms filled with cuddly baby, not swarm tiresomely around her skirts in dozens. How it was done she was not sure, but it would be revealed.

Everything, said Lalitha, was revealed in time. She veiled her eyes and intimated such revelations were already in her keeping. Saroja said she could wait. She reminded Lalitha it was her turn to attend to the buffalo, which was bellowing accusingly, but Lalitha said In this? Are you out of your mind? so Saroja called her *mundi*, obstinate, as Amma did, and flounced off on her own, knowing that Lalitha would not budge.

The buffalo was hungry, pretended it was starving. It wanted its hay, it had nothing to do all day but think of eating. It was dry, being between calves, but its appetite never flagged. Amma said it was greedy, it knew what kind of house it had, whereas Manikkam's cows were easier to manage, they were complaisant, they accepted being hungry never having known anything else. It appalled Appa. He called it immoral, a pernicious doctrine, but Amma said she wasn't advocating anything, certainly not hunger, she was only pointing out its horrible effects. They often came together like this, beginning from different points in the compass.

The hay was in a truss, suspended from a beam to keep it off the floor, which was damp. It was covered in plastic sheets to save it from the drips. If the hay got wet it went moldy, gave the buffalo cramps in its belly. It never had the sense to keep off the moldy food, ate it up heartily and roared all night. It ate plastic as well. You had to be nippy getting the bale down and gouging out

99

forkfuls before the buffalo could get at the sheets. The truss was lowered by a pulley that Appa had fixed. It squeaked dreadfully. Saroja had to grit her teeth when she worked it, she worked it gingerly to mitigate the terrible squeaking but was hampered by the impatient buffalo. It snuffled at her skirts. It put down its muzzle and rasped her bare heels with its rough tongue. It nudged her, it thumped its hoofs on the floor and carried away by the sounds, it forgot its strength and shoved her face-first into the descending bale. Burrs were embedded in her hair, sharp against her skin. Hideous, hideous beast, wailed Saroja. She was crying. Water was running down her back, streaking her cheeks, sweat and tears mingled. She could hardly bear to finish, only the thought of having to come out again spurred her on. When she was done she banged the door to vent her feelings and fled.

There's nothing to do, said Lalitha. She piled her tresses on her head in a new style and invited Saroja to judge it since she seemed to have nothing better to do. She questioned further while Saroja mulled, asked her what on earth she found to do all day long. Plenty, said Saroja, but she didn't go into it. After her dealings with the buffalo she could not do battle again, peace was essential. She considered the hair style and said it suited Lalitha, which it did. Most things did, which encouraged her to go to extremes, she knew she could get away with more than most people. Lalitha had already lost interest. She was listless. She let her hair tumble down and said It's so wet, it's so humid, it's impossible to do anything. She sounded like Mr. Gupta.

It's impossible, Mr. Gupta told Appa. His car was

lodged in a quagmire, he walked up, skirting the field. He wasn't getting cooperation, he said. This climate, he said. One would carry on regardless, only no one was ever available, he said, when wanted. He meant the villagers. Lalitha was always available, she intimated, nothing would hold her when the film unit was ready to use her services.

Film unit was the correct name, Saroja learned from Lalitha, for Mr. Gupta and his gloomy men. The unit popped in and out like demented squirrels, out at the first glimpse of sun, in at the first drop of rain. It is heartbreaking, hopeless, said Mr. Gupta. It has wrecked my schedule, he said in a wrecked voice. Water kept running down his face. It seemed to Saroja he couldn't have known much about the country to come at this season, subject himself to such torments. It seemed miraculous to her any work was done at all, there were so many starts and stops, but Lalitha said More credit to Mr. Gupta. It's the equipment, she told Saroja, it's so expensive, he can't take risks with it, the cameras alone cost a fortune besides being irreplaceable because of the foreign currency situation. She knew a great deal about Mr. Gupta and his unit from hanging around as much as she did, though not as much as she would have liked because of Amma's and Aunt Alamelu's strictures. Mr. Gupta filled in the gaps during visits. He was as frequent a visitor as Anand but he didn't get short shrift being, Saroja supposed, who he was, though it could also have been because he wasn't a scrounger. Anand was; his excuse was his joblessness, but still it griped Amma.

Mr. Gupta hardly ever came without bearing presents for Appa and Amma and Aunt, for Lalitha and Saroja. Saroja suspected his largesse to her was to do with her accompanying Lalitha, who wasn't permitted to go off alone. It pleased her all the same, it wasn't easy having Lalitha singled out for the favors all the time. Sweetness, said Lalitha: sugar-doll, sugar-sweet, sugar-candy. Whom do you mean? asked Aunt Alamelu. She knew who was meant, she often accepted gifts herself from Mr. Gupta—grudgingly, and hinting she was incorruptible. Why, said Lalitha, I meant these dainties and delicacies, what else should I mean, did you have some *person* in mind?

These Delhi wallahs, said Chingleput. It was his moribund time. He could not drag his cart through the morass the village became, and it was hardly worth lighting the huge fires under his cauldrons for the few who still squelched round for his sweetmeats. Bombay, said Saroja, going by the box on which BOMBAY A-I HULVA COMPANY was printed. It was a present from Mr. Gupta which Devraj had handed to her. He said he hoped she would like it, his eyes were brown and soft when he spoke to her. Mr. Gupta was busy distributing to Lalitha but he turned round and said You will, you will, Bombay hulva is in a class by itself. I am not a Bombay man myself, he told them, but I refuse to be prejudiced and parochial, I like to believe I am a citizen of the world.

Do you like it? said Saroja to Chingleput. She hoped he would, she did not often bring him things, it was usually the other way round. Very pretty, said Chingleput, meaning the silver-leaf on the surface, which you could eat. The taste, said Saroja, for that had importance too, although it tended to fade compared with the joyous surprise of eatable silver-leaf. Very nice, said Chingleput. Excellent, he conceded, although done by machine. Machines are easier, said Saroja, going by what Lalitha said. No doubt, said Chingleput, in a pinched way, which made Saroja wonder what had made her say that, made her sorry she had spoken, knowing as she did his hatred of machines. So she laid her hand on his sleeve, which was clean and white though not as white as Devraj's shirts, which were of another quality, to show she had meant no harm, and they finished the hulva between them.

When they were done Chingleput took the box from her hands, it was empty except for its fancy packing, examined it closely and asked her if he could keep it. Saroja was surprised, she thought she had detected a dislike of Bombay and Delhi wallahs and anything to do with them, but Chingleput asked did you have to like someone before you learned from them? Saroja admitted he had a point, but she also felt it was easier if you did, Lalitha would not have learned as fast as she had unless she liked Mr. Gupta.

Appa called Chingleput a shrewd man, said all he needed was a little capital to have a thriving business. He knew a good many people with the same lack, often spoke in this vein. It irritated Amma. She inquired where was his thriving business, what had he done with the capital he had undoubtedly had? It was her stock question. Appa had stock answers too. They had perfected their dialogues over the years. He said it was a matter of timing, asked Mr. Gupta would he not agree it was a case of opportunity and capital coinciding? Mr.

Gupta did. He said capital was indispensable. He told them it had taken him two years to finance his present venture but now he could not move, he was stuck, it was ruinous. Appa sympathized. He called him a charming man. Aunt Alamelu said he didn't seem to be in any hurry to move, but why should he? Appa's house had become his home away from home. Amma was charitable, said it must be awful camping in a tent, houses were a lot more comfortable. Aunt said it wasn't comfort he was after, it was something else. Be plain, Appa invited. His brows were knit together, black as a thundercloud. Your daughter, said Aunt, she didn't have to make it plain which one she meant; he's after your daughter. She spoke right out, you could see her feelings had carried her away beyond the bounds of respect she owed Appa.

Lalitha's face was flaming. Shameless, she cried, how could you say such shameful things! It's you that's shameless, said Aunt Alamelu grimly, you're throwing yourself at him, you're so full of this film star nonsense you can't see you're only making yourself cheap to him, even if he says you're wonderful. Lies, lies! cried Lalitha. She pulled herself together and said, loftily, I'm an artist, you have no conception of artistic affinity, which is what lies between us, you can see only evil in the most beautiful things. She was distressed, there were tears on her lashes, it brought Appa onto her side though clearly the allegations perturbed him. That will do, he said in his head-of-household voice, which earned him silence to be heard in. It is your upbringing, he went on, to Aunt Alamelu, whose bosom was heaving. He spoke heavily, with pain, saturating her with the depth of his understanding. It is the dismal paucity of your education, he said, that must be blamed for your limited horizons. Aunt Alamelu said no more, but she could be very vocal with her shoulders, one of which she hitched up to show her disdain. The thing was she was up against an expert: Lalitha had eloquence even in her silences.

* * *

WHEN the monsoon was over the film unit began working again. They filmed the village market, and the funeral of a young man who had obligingly died before his time, and the beggars who queued at the temple, and the monkeys that were plaguing the countryside. They filmed the grain distribution center, and the school with Miss Mendoza standing welcomingly on the top step, and would have filmed Perumal and his money-lending premises only he slammed down the shutters.

There were several shots of Lalitha. She danced one of the Indian dances she had been assiduously practicing, and posed gracefully beside the well to which she hardly ever went, and there was to have been a picture of her tending the buffalo, but Lalitha refused, said it would render her a cowgirl, which she was far from being, it was only her family's upper-class hankering for rich milk that brought buffaloes into her ken at all.

Lalitha was happy. She said so to Saroja, who didn't need telling. I am happy, she said, I feel like a dove on the wing, I could soar away, away like an eagle to the topmost peak of the sacred mountain. She trilled about the place. She flitted gracefully, creating new dance patterns. It was like sharing the house with some kind of bat or bird. Whatever has taken possession of the child? Aunt Alamelu grumbled aloud. My star, sang Lalitha, dear crusty aunt, my lucky stars are in the ascendant, they have me under their influence; and she danced with her aunt, hummed a few bars and made her step to it, it was ludicrous but Aunt Alamelu was melting, her eyes were tender as she patted Lalitha's cheek, asked what had got into the feckless creature and called on God to bless her.

*   *   *

WHEN the filming was done Mr. Gupta came to say goodbye.

For a whole hour before he was due Lalitha crouched in the courtyard, executing a *colam* pattern in saffron and white. The powder fell like ash through her fingers, it designed a dove on a trellis in a garden. The trellis was a common design, and so was the formal garden, but the dove was Lalitha's creation. Amma frowned when she saw it, it wasn't traditional, but she let it be because it was beautiful. Saroja was relieved; she had squatted next to Lalitha and helped block in the wings, anyhow she didn't want anything so pretty to be obliterated.

Mr. Gupta came in the car, which a team of two bullocks and a dozen men had heaved out of the bog. He was back in his two-tone shoes from which the monsoon had eventually parted him. His eyes were sad. I have come to take my leave, he said, which Saroja thought superfluous, that was so clearly the purpose of his visit. Please be seated, said Appa. He was formal, everyone was stiff and formal the way they had been in the beginning, it was as if the time between had never existed, only of course it had. Everyone had some mark to show for it, however small, even if it was outward like the clasp on Amma's shoulder. Mostly it was inward.

Thanks for everything, said Mr. Gupta. The same to you, said Lalitha, she was copying Miss Mendoza, who was good at such conversational ripostes. Well, I must be going, said Mr. Gupta. He shuffled his feet. He had taken off his shoes to enter the house and walked through into the courtyard in his socks. They were striped, pimento and tan, to contrast with the shoes, which Saroja guessed was the fashion, and hitched up in some mysterious way so that there wasn't a sign of a crease at the ankle. When Mr. Gupta shuffled his feet the dove got blurred, but no one seemed to notice except Saroja. She watched the socks getting powdered, and the dove disappearing, but you couldn't very well correct a guest even if he was a departing one.

Well, goodbye, said Mr. Gupta. Be seeing you, said Lalitha in her stylish manner. She was very bright, feverish about the eyes. Goodbye, said Devraj. Goodbye, said Saroja, she was the only one to bid him anything. Be seeing you, she thought of adding, but as she didn't think she would be seeing him again she refrained. She felt quite sorry about this. Devraj opened the car door for Mr. Gupta. They both got in and rattled off down the path, waving as they went. The path was badly rutted, worse after the monsoon than it had ever been. The car bounced like a ball as it went along, at times it seemed as if all four wheels left the ground, for quite a way you could hear Mr. Gupta's strident voice complaining. He had never got used to the village, clearly villages were not a part of the world of which he was a citizen.

Tears fell from Lalitha's eyes, she said it was to see her lovely dove destroyed. She knelt and brushed away the scuffed powder and drew again. This time it was an eagle, a golden eagle soaring over the plains. It's me, Lalitha told Saroja that night, when they were lying on their charpoys. She whispered, so that no one else could hear. What do you mean, asked Saroja, who liked to get things clear, have them explained. But Lalitha would not answer.

3

THERE WAS A kind of glory at school. It was pale, like
moonlight, a reflection of the sunlight that invested
Lalitha.

Was it exciting? asked Jaya. It must have been exciting having him call, she said, and wetted her lips and
invited Saroja to share her experience with the entire
class. Saroja thought back; she could think only of Mr.
Gupta moaning about the country and his two-tone
shoes which had stuck vividly in her mind. She said she
supposed it was. She made an effort and recalled the
hectic sensations of his first visit and said it had been
exciting. It was in the past tense, though; it was difficult
to imagine it actually happening in the same way that

it was difficult to imagine the river boiling up over its banks once it had shrunk to its narrow course. It was even more than that; something that was way out of their expectation, an out-of-the-blue happening.

How lucky some people are, said Jaya. She modified it slightly and said Some are and some aren't, and she sighed, she was like a budding Aunt Alamelu in Saroja's estimation though she was also her best friend. The girls sighed with Jaya, they knew whom she meant, even Nalini knew she was the target though she grew dimmer day by day as her head grew larger. It had become very big, it looked enormous because it was the only thing that grew, her body remained static. She looked like a gnome. Once a month she went to the clinic with her mother. Afterwards she stayed away from school for three days, it was a regular procedure. Jaya said they pumped the water out of her skull, she knew about such things from her uncle who was a compounder at the clinic, but Nalini said it was only a needle. People believed Jaya rather than Nalini, who had a soused brain, but Saroja preferred to go by what Nalini said, it was painful to think in terms of a pump.

One month Nalini went to the clinic and it wasn't enough, they transferred her to the hospital in town. Nalini's mother came back alone, they wouldn't let her ride in the ambulance. Besides, she had to pack all the things she would need for her stay, the hospital did not provide for relations, only for patients. Saroja accompanied Amma, who went to help her pack. That was the excuse, the reality was to take her the rice and dhal she would need to tide her over. Everyone contributed, it was quite usual for the families around to chip in if anyone was in trouble. Nalini's mother thanked them all, said she was grateful. She didn't look it, she only looked numb, which surprised Saroja since it had been coming a long time, Nalini's fate had been written on her forehead from the day she was born. When the rice and the dhal had been pooled there were sizable bundles. There was that, and the water jar and the cooking vessels and the *sigri* to cook on, and a pillow and a bedroll. It wasn't much, considering it was most of what she possessed, but Nalini's mother looked positively clobbered as she climbed up into the *jutka*. And no man to help her either, said Amma, and Saroja could tell she was visualizing herself without Appa, she was frantic for him though she would have masked the signs had he been present.

When they got back Amma bathed and put on clean clothes and went to pray at their shrine. The shrine was in the prayer room, next to the grain store. It was very small, just enough for two or perhaps three to sit and pray. There was a wooden platform a few inches high, on which were arranged God's pictures, all of them garlanded. During festivals and holy days the garlands were made of real flowers, roses and chrysanthemums and jasmine, but the rest of the time they were paper or pith. They gathered the dust alarmingly, Aunt and Amma were forever taking them off for dusting. In the center of the platform stood the *tulasi*, in a brass container. It was a sturdy plant, it had to be to survive in the tiny room which didn't have much light, although Appa did haul it in and out of the courtyard. It had a strong, delightful smell, in close weather it became intoxicating.

Amma's praying was a reverent mumbling, she copied it from the Sanskrit prayers intoned by the priests in the temple. She didn't know what it meant precisely. Hardly anyone did, not even Appa, who had a smattering of Sanskrit. It didn't matter, however, after a while it took hold of you, it was a background that helped you to slide into your own prayer, you got so deeply immersed in it you could not have said when you left the Sanskrit murmurings behind. One has to prepare before God can enter, Amma was fond of saying. Saroja felt something very like it must happen.

When her praying was finished Amma came out, called Lalitha and Saroja and gave them spoonfuls of consecrated milk. My daughters, she said, my beloved, my own flesh. There was a softness about her, she lingered with each in turn, you could tell from the flecks of fear in her tone she was casting them in the role of Nalini, herself taking the part of Nalini's mother, casting and retreating, she could not help herself. Now and then she sighed, said Poor woman, and Aunt Alamelu echoed her, said Poor woman, then branched off on another tack and said It's the best way for her, but Saroja was certain it wasn't, Nalini's mother had been content jogging along with her gnomelike daughter but soon she would have nothing.

Nalini was a long time dying.

Jaya said they were keeping her alive to carry out medical experiments on her. Saroja was sickened, she felt it was an outrage. She considered it some more and said Nalini's mother would never allow it, but Jaya said the poor had no choice, which Saroja knew was true, some things rang true and you could not dispute them.

It's a case of allowing them to experiment or being thrown out on the street, Jaya told Saroja, which so horrified her she consulted Appa.

Appa said he didn't know for sure. He wriggled and said he had heard stories, but there was no method of finding out because one was up against the medical establishment. It was very powerful, he said, it was dug right into society, and society was so poorly organized it didn't know what to do about it.

Amma was more forthright, she had experience of hospitals, where they had tinkered with her after the birth of the boys and before Lalitha. She had discharged herself and gone off, as she had done once before, to Varanasi. Physicians, she said, think they can do anything with their patients. Especially the Europeans, she said, they think they are gods, they have no religion, no ethic or scruple to restrain them though they trumpet they have which is nothing but codswallop. The head of the hospital was a European. Appa said one must take an overall view. One imbibes what is bad in the West as well as what is good, he said, there are no national frontiers. Do you mean our doctors are as arrogant as theirs? cried Amma in disbelief. They are the same clay, said Appa, one must face all possibilities.

The boys had come home together on leave, they schemed to make their holidays coincide and usually succeeded. They endorsed what was said, introduced other angles. Some doctors, they claimed, were the greediest members of society, their money-raking methods were a scandal, and Anand inched himself into the conversation despite Amma's off-putting presence and bracketed them with absentee landlords, who were pretty low in his estimation. The boys kept nodding. But for these physicians, they said, replete with contempt, everyone would have the treatment they needed, not just the poor for whom the government paid, and those rich enough to meet exorbitant medical bills, but everyone according to his need. In some countries they do, said Lalitha; she was smug, she had firsthand sources in Mr. Gupta and Miss Mendoza, felt she could take anyone on. Maybe, said the boys, who were better informed, who had gone through the university of life, according to Appa; maybe, but it has been wrought in the teeth of their opposition. It confused Saroja. In school they were told that medicine was a noble profession, that physicians were compassionate men whose vocation was the healing of the sick. And so they are, said Appa, it seemed to her he was in two minds about it. But they take some finding, said the boys.

Saroja went away where she could be on her own, to think about it. She had a place, where great rocks had tumbled down a hill, in geography they learned it had probably happened when Earth was being formed. The boulders were huge, strewn about the plain like a giant's playthings. They looked old and weathered, their undersides always felt cold and damp and sometimes grew a coating of moss, especially after the monsoon. Goats were drawn to the moss, rasped it off with their tongues, butting the boulders over if they could to gain free access. They were perverse creatures, left the pastures the goatherd found for them and hoofed it to these stony plains as if the devil were driving them. Moss was one love, their other craving was for the stark shrubs that flourished in these wastes. The plants had grayish-green buds you could pop with your fingers; when you pressed they burst into immediate flower, showing mauve centers stippled with milk that exuded. You had to be careful not to get the milk on your skin, it could raise up a rash, sometimes even blisters. Nothing happened to the goats; they gobbled the shrubs' crowns, it was a race if you wanted to pop the buds first.

The goats left trails of their droppings around the boulders and shrubs. The droppings were round and black, like small marbles, you learned it was the gut that shaped them. Jaya said it was her mother's womb that had shaped Nalini's peculiar skull. Later she admitted she was wrong; made it into a joke and invited them to laugh at her childish innocence, jeered at it herself. She was not innocent any more. She was knowing, but you couldn't be sure exactly how much she knew because she only let fall a little at a time, titbits that you found interesting, that led you on into hankering for further disclosures.

Saroja took her mind off Jaya, focused it instead on Nalini's plight, which was the object of her coming here. She hoped the experiments would not be too painful. She hoped intensely they wouldn't go on too long, but in the middle of this hope she got petrified in case she wanted Nalini to die quickly, which would tidy up her own feelings. It was so frightening she let out a shriek, it devastated a goat that had been peacefully browsing, it was extraordinary seeing the astonishment written so clearly on the bearded face. It made Saroja laugh despite herself. She held her sides and rocked, imagining someone else moved to corresponding laughter by her panics, an invisible presence, God who was invisible and omnipresent, who saw all and was intrigued and amused by human beings.

Saroja trailed back through the gloaming, it was dark when she got home. Amma scolded her sharply but it didn't affect her, she was clad in some kind of armor that deflected blows. Amma sighed and left off, divining her state. My youngest child, she said, sometimes I think she is the simplest, sometimes I cannot get through to her, I cannot understand her at all. What is there to understand? demanded Aunt Alamelu. She is only a child, it is not difficult to understand children, it is grown-ups who are devious mortals, why make a mystery out of nothing? But Amma was not to be convinced, she had reared children, she said, they were flesh of her flesh, whereas Aunt was only an onlooker. Sometimes she was quite short with her sister, blunt and sharp at the same time.

* * *

LALITHA reported Mr. Gupta's sayings. It filled in time while she waited for his summons to view the finished product as promised.

She said he believed in quality. She said he said they had a good deal to learn from the West, and she believed him absolutely. Saroja wondered if she was being devious, asked what particular learning she had in mind. Lots of things generally, Lalitha said, and her eyes were narrowing; his craft in particular, she said, the craft of film making, his work is outstanding. Better than that of other film makers? Saroja wanted to know; she had seen only a few films but she had enjoyed those she had seen. Simply no comparison, Lalitha said, they are crudities compared to his work, he has been trained in the West.

It got to be tedious, the way Lalitha kept on about Mr. Gupta. She has been dazzled by this man from another planet, said Aunt Alamelu, and even Appa did not rise to her defense. But Lalitha didn't need champions, she could look after herself, she did it better than ever when she and Mr. Gupta were linked. It is the quality of his work, she said, withering her aunt with an eyeful. It is that which is dazzling, which dazzles me. You will see, my day will dawn.

Her day dawned when Miss Mendoza came with a message.

Miss Mendoza had been relegated since Mr. Gupta, no one fussed over her as much as they had before his advent, but she bore him no grudge. The man is an artist, she said. It has taken him months, it shows how scrupulous he is, nothing slipshod about his method.

Do you mean it is finished? asked Lalitha.

Yes, and we are invited to a viewing, said Miss Mendoza, she was answering Lalitha but speaking sideways to Amma and Appa, whose permission would have to be given, watching them out of the corner of her eye. In the city, she said, it will be run through there, the film runs for twenty minutes but there is of course the traveling. I shall be glad, she said, her eyes were darting like arrows around Lalitha's head, to take charge of any girls who would like to go, naturally I shall be going myself since our school is featured so prominently.

Naturally, said Appa; he looked a bit dizzy, he had not calculated on Lalitha careering off with Miss Mendoza to the city, the farthest she had been away was to the town where the boys worked, it wasn't anywhere on the scale that the city was. Besides, she had gone with members of the family.

How long, he said, will the trip take? how much will it cost? His Adam's apple was bobbing, it moved the frayed edges of his round-neck shirt. A week, said Miss Mendoza. She spoke firmly. I do not believe in hustling, she said. One must rest and relax in order to obtain the maximum benefit from travel. It is barely a half-day's journey, Appa protested, his face had purpled at his own audacity. Nevertheless, Miss Mendoza told him, a week is the minimum to obtain optimum advantage, since one must allow for disturbance in one's internal clock. Which all of us carry, she said, tapping a point midway between her breasts, here. There was barely a dent, Saroja noticed, where her finger was prodding, it made her think of Amma's breasts which were so global there was a hollow like a well in between. She speculated on whether Miss Mendoza had any breasts at all, it was more interesting than the conversation which she suspected would not affect her one way or another, but a yelp from Appa set it flowing for her again. Fifty rupees! he was saying, he was boggling, he was stunned by the price of travel. *Please*, said Lalitha; she wrung her hands, she was a budding actress, but there was anguish under her acting, her brow was pearly with sweat.

Peanuts, said Miss Mendoza; you cannot expect to broaden the mind on peanuts. She was lofty, contemptuous of Appa, who was squirming, who had obviously made false representations about his resources. But there is a fund, she said, which exists for the purpose of furthering educational aims, which might be prepared to defray in part the expenses of an educational trip. Yes, yes, said Appa, I will apply, I would not stand in the way, never let it be said. . . . he was shivering with relief, gabbling. There is no need, said Miss Mendoza, I will do the necessary.

When she stood up she held herself straight, even straighter than usual, it crushed Appa. Afterwards he claimed it was the thought of applying for charity that had rendered thinking difficult for him, that in fact it had muzzled him. Amma said he had allowed himself to be intimidated, it was this that had wiped his memory clean as a slate. The truth was they had both forgotten that Deepavali was approaching. Miss Mendoza had not, but she was a Christian, the festival meant nothing to her. She worked the trip to coincide with the Hindu holiday, so she would be away from her school as little as possible, whereas for Appa and Amma it meant not having Lalitha on a special festival occasion.

* * *

How empty the house seems, said Appa.

He looked lost. He watched Saroja, who was filling little mud saucers with oil. He was nice to her, admired the wicks she had made and laid out ready in a row. Wicks are easy, said Saroja. She soaked one in oil and twisted it into place. She wished she could do something for Appa but she knew she could not, could not take the place of her missing sister, no human being could fill the place of another, the shape of the space was different.

When it was dark, a real black velvety darkness without streak or stripe of purple or indigo, she began lighting the wicks. Lalitha was not there to do her share. There were scores of wicks in saucers. She carried them out in pairs, dotted the ground around the house. Some she arranged on the verandah parapet; they glowed in a solemn row like owls' eyes, there was barely a breath of wind to distort them. The village was full of light, rings and ellipses according to the shapes of dwellings.

There was nothing around Manikkam's hut. The children were too unruly. One year they had run wild and upset the lamps, poor Manikkam's hut had gone up in flames. It was constructed of thatch and mud and a few bricks thrown in, but the bricks were *katcha*, not good quality like the bricks used for Appa's house. Highly inflammable, said Appa with disapproval. It took Manikkam four months to rebuild it, he had to do it in between reaping and plowing and sowing. The family were farmed out in various outhouses, two of the children had sheltered with Amma's buffalo. Manikkam said Never again. He would not allow the little oil lamps, which were cheap, and he could not afford firecrackers, which were not.

The children scrounged round, collected what neighbors gave them. As soon as it was dark they trooped off down to the river where families in like straits pooled their resources. Fireworks effects doubled in the water setting. There was a bonfire too. Anything went, it was a strange pile of rubbish, because nobody would burn good fuel or firewood.

In Saroja's house there were the little glimmering lamps and fireworks that Appa bought. This year he had bought hardly any, there had been the expenses of Lalitha's expedition. Anand came to the rescue. He was a gambler. When his luck was in he was generous with the money, it flowed from him as fast as he made it. He came home with a boxful of fireworks. It made a very fine display. He and Appa capered about lighting them, Amma and Aunt Alamelu stood watching, gave out little cries of admiration. Now and then they covered their ears at the louder explosions. Saroja was not like them, she loved the bangs, the louder the better. She handed her aunt a sparkler, which was safe and tame, the only thing she would handle. Aunt Alamelu held it as if it were a bomb, she made little exaggerated gestures of fright. Anand and Appa said it was the funniest thing in years, they split their sides at the sight. Amma joined in the laughter. Everyone tried hard but in the midst of it all something was missing, a piece had gone, the Lalitha-shaped piece was missing.

As soon as the fireworks were finished Saroja begged to be excused, hardly waited for an answer. She ran, she fled down to the river of which most nights she was deadly afraid. But not tonight. Tonight it was transformed, it was golden, it ran molten from the bonfires which the poor had lit along its banks. Around one she spotted her friends, the tribe that was Manikkam's, every single child down to the baby in arms, cavorting. Saroja linked arms with them, she shouted, she sang, she felt they were brothers and sisters who filled in the resounding hollows of her father's hearth.

Did you have to desert us too? Amma asked sadly on her return. On this night of all nights, Aunt Alamelu chipped in, when families ought to celebrate together. Saroja hung her head, she felt ashamed, but the glow of the bonfires still warmed her, she didn't regret having bolted as she had. Leave the child alone, commanded Appa. She is an individual, she has rights, are we to deny her her rights because she is a child? Yes, rights, said Aunt Alamelu. You have given your children their rights, brother, and what is the result? On Deepavali night we three old goats are left to prance round like kids for want of anything better—we, supposedly a joint family, a joint Hindu family, but where are the children and the children's children? Missing, brother, because we have flouted the teachings of our ancient scriptures and are now made to feel the pinch.

Appa was incensed. He danced in his rage, it was quite dramatic. Ancient scriptures, he cried, what ancient scriptures, you meddling old bag? Can you say which of them lays down that young men should rot upholding the joint family system? Is that what you had in your minuscule mind for my boys, that they should stagnate in this village where there is no outlet whatsoever for their energies and talents? Joint family! he said. He was breathing, he was bothered, you could feel his deep repulsion for curbs and compulsions, after all he had fought for freedom all his life. Saroja agreed with him, she longed to stand up and say she knew he was right, but there was a confusion which she could not resolve because she had been taught that peace flows from what is right, it was the first thing your elders impressed upon you, whereas upholding what was right had involved Appa in pain and turmoil.

Amma took Appa's side. She was pale and determined, spoke against herself, her flesh and grain. Saroja sensed the raspings, she had never realized before what Amma had gone through when the boys had left. It was our sons' decision, she said. They decided there was nothing for them in the village, are we to say they were wrong, should we have known contentment seeing them hanging around, unemployed loafers of whom we already have more than our share? As for children, where is the hurry? They will come in good time, as my own four did, and not a minute before! Anand sloped off, even before Amma had finished lambasting Aunt Alamelu. His cue for departure was when the conversation got to loafers and spongers, he knew from experience they would start on him next. He preferred, he claimed, taking to the wilderness to that. He invariably returned from it, though. Amma said he had found too cozy a pitch to turn it in lightly.

Aunt Alamelu had nowhere to slink to. She said it was the state her feet were in that foiled her. Saroja mulled it over, saw it wasn't that at all, it was her sex. Appa and Anand could stride off to the coffee shop, Manikkam had his bhang hideout, Bundi's liquor store was always crammed with men. Women had no bolt-holes. There was no escape for them, they had to stand where they were and take it. Saroja stood still and imagined it. Her heart was filled with panic, she could feel fear rising in a stream of endless bubbles and swelling and bursting inside her.

Whatever's the matter with the child? she heard Aunt Alamelu say. Nothing, replied Saroja. Nothing at all, she said, and ran outside and pretended she could see as clearly as if it were day the path that led to Chingleput's sweetshop which was her escape route.

For always, she said resolutely: always, even when I am a woman.

*　*　*

Miss Mendoza and her party which included Lalitha had celebrated Deepavali with Mr. Gupta in the big city. Lalitha told them about it. It was grand, she said, a really grand affair. Mr. Gupta had invited a hundred guests and they all sat on a balcony and watched fireworks set off by relays of servants. There had been a series of tableaux, she said, depicting scenes from the epics; the one she had been particularly impressed by had shown the demon king Ravanna being devastated by a barrage of catherine wheels. Aunt Alamelu gave a loud sniff. People like Mr. Gupta, she said, remembered to be Hindus only when it suited them, gave them the chance to indulge in pyrotechnics. Appa requested her to be quiet. He wanted to listen to his daughter. She had been away only a week but it could have been years the way he could not leave off looking at her.

You have got quite a bit thinner, he told her. Really? said Lalitha. She was offhand. She was used to adoration, not grateful for it as others would have been. Have some more curd, Appa urged. To please you, said Lalitha, and batted her lashes at him. Saroja deduced it must have become a habit, she had got so accustomed to using her eyes she had become indiscriminate. With food it was different, she was much more discriminating. Saroja was wolfing her share, but Lalitha nibbled delicately, picking at the dainties Amma had prepared. Amma had done so only at Appa's behest, saying that festive fare should be reserved for festivals, but he had overborne her, reminded her of the preparations she made when the boys were due home. Twice a year! Amma protested, but Appa was adamant, Lalitha's week had been like a six-month absence to him.

The women, said Lalitha, wore ravishing saris. The next time, she announced, I must have more clothes, it would be too shaming to appear again in that depressing ragbag I have. The next time! exclaimed Appa. He was goggling, like everyone else he had assumed Lalitha's week was a once-for-all event. Oh yes, said Lalitha. She was cool, her hands lay composed in her lap like lilies. Mr. Gupta has offered me a part in his next film and I have accepted. *You* have accepted, said Aunt Alamelu, since when do girls of good family—? Be quiet, said Appa, he lashed out at her, he had to do something because of his dread. This film, he said, that Mr. Gupta proposes, does he intend to make it soon, in the near future? That is his intention, said Lalitha primly. It is a question, she said, of finding the necessary backing, it is not easy in a philistine city which prefers to keep to rutted commercial paths.

Appa was looking hazy, it could have been Miss Mendoza speaking from the confusion written large on his face. Amma was downright bemused. Lalitha looked from one blank parent to the other, she elucidated for their benefit. Films are too expensive to make, she said, he has to raise the money before he can start, it's not easy. Films *coin* money! declared Amma. When your father and I went to see *Shakuntala* we had to wait two hours just to get in, the cinema was so crowded. Mr. Gupta does not make that kind of film, said Lalitha. What kind of film does he make, said Amma, *Shakuntala* was a fine film, you couldn't ask for better. He makes good films, said Lalitha patiently. He has no time for old-fashioned long-winded epics, she said, he is only interested in making artistic pictures, pictures of social realism.

Saroja tried to recall *Shakuntala*, to gauge its artistic merits, but it was so long ago she could not remember. She knew the story though; it was an edifying one and a favorite of Aunt Alamelu's, she would launch into it without ever anyone requesting a rendering. There was no cinema in their village, it was considered too small. There was one cinema to every three or four villages, the owner said otherwise it would not have been a paying proposition. He must have meant a gold mine, since every time one went the place was full, packed to overflowing, you paid even for standing room at the back. The nearest cinema to them was two villages away, it needed a lot of prodding and persuasion to get to it. Saroja had not been many times. She had seen *Rama and Sita* twice, and *Draupadi* twice, and *Shakuntala* once, and that was about her sum total. Lalitha had been more often. She was older, had other advantages.

How long, said Appa, before Mr. Gupta starts? Have you any idea? He was groping, fearful of making a false step that would drive her headlong into unknown territory. Not long, I hope, said Lalitha, it would be too gruesome, although as Mr. Gupta says it is part of one's life as an actress, it is the price exacted by one's Art. Are we to understand, inquired Amma pointblank, that you are an actress? Oh yes, said Lalitha, her lids came down like modest little hoods upon her cheeks. Mr. Gupta says I am a natural.

No one could be certain what was meant, although there were clues in her voice, her demeanor. Aunt Alamelu plunged, she was a rash woman, her secondary status did not always hold her, when brooked she tended not to remember it until it was too late. A natural, she cried, a natural what? In my day a natural was a simpleton, a creature without wits, surely that cannot have been what your Mr. Gupta meant? He meant a natural actress, said Lalitha. She rose, went outside and sluiced the crumbs of their festivities from the tips of her fingers, came back and stood in the doorway. She looked quite regal. Your day, dear Aunt, she said, is as dead as the dodo.

*   *   *

COME and talk, little sister, Lalitha invited. Saroja complied. They sat together on the charpoy which Lalitha had dragged out into the courtyard and Saroja felt very close to her sister sitting beside her in the starry darkness.

What was it like? asked Lalitha. Bleak, said Saroja, we

missed you. What was it like? she asked in turn. Heaven, said Lalitha. She sighed. It is my spiritual country, she said, it is my spiritual home. What is? asked Saroja. The city, said Lalitha, and my acting, it is all jumbled up in one bright parcel. How bright? asked Saroja. Do you think you will become a star? Who knows? said Lalitha softly. I would like to think so, she said, hugging Saroja tightly; I would very much like to think so.

*　*　*

In the morning there was school.

It was too dreary to think of, in the middle of all the excitement Lalitha had generated, but there it was, you could not dodge it. Saroja tried. She said she had a headache. Do you want to end up a dunce like me? Amma demanded. You manage well enough, said Saroja resentfully. You don't know with what difficulty, Amma replied grimly.

Saroja went and stood outside the bathroom, rapped on the door. Lalitha was inside, warbling. Miss Mendoza had given her the day off, which Saroja didn't consider fair. All the nice things seemed destined for Lalitha. If you don't hurry up I shall be late for school, she shouted, thudding on the panel. Lalitha came tripping out, freshly bathed and smelling of Amma's sandalwood. Who cares about school? she asked, high and mighty. She could afford to be, she would soon be leaving. I care, I have to, said Saroja furiously; you're the most selfish person I know. Tadpole, said Lalitha, you don't know many people, you know hardly anyone worth speaking of.

Saroja marched into the bathroom, speechless. All the closeness of the evening before had evaporated. She felt she hated her sister. There was an inch of water left in the *hunda*. Rather than wait for it to fill she squatted under the trickle coming from the tap and had a skimped, miserable bath. Aren't you ready yet? Amma called. I'm coming, I'm *coming!* snapped Saroja, wrestling with her clothes. There was a *davani* as well these days, it went on top of her blouse. She had to wear it, her breasts were sprouting. The *davani* was draped over them in gathers and folds, she supposed to stop them sticking out too much, calling attention to her burgeoning state.

Amma said it was for decorum. Saroja found it a thundering nuisance, especially mounted on her bike. The wispy ends trailed, got in the way of the spokes, her speed. Sometimes she wanted to whip it off, hurl it in the nearest ditch. It was Lalitha's anyway, a hand-down. Sometimes she fiercely wanted to suppress the swelling honey-beige buds that were the cause of her discomforts. Jaya was appalled to hear her. You don't know what you're saying, she said, she whispered, was knowing and slit-eyed as she displayed to Saroja. Her breasts were advanced by comparison, rounded and thrusting, whereas Saroja's were hardly more than swollen nipples. There's so much feeling in them, said Jaya. Her breasts were cupped in her hands, her thumbs were circling and circling the dark roundels in the middle.

It's ecstasy, can't you feel? said Jaya. You will when you're a woman.

Do you think I'm a child? said Saroja belligerently. I have feelings, you know. What sort of feelings? asked Jaya. She was tedious in her quest for such details. Saroja suspected she was not a natural, like Lalitha, it did not come to her by instinct, she had to fill in the blanks by asking. I cannot describe my feelings, she said, they are too complex. Jaya sniggered, made it clear she wasn't convinced. But they're nowhere as complex as Lalitha's, Saroja embroidered, Lalitha's feelings are incomparable.

Lalitha was her trump card. She had moved among the mighty, in a city, had sat on balconies with galaxies of film people and seen ladies in diaphanous saris which showed as much of their bodies as Manikkam's wife did in her slack moments, though it was that much more seductive on them.

Because of the way they carry themselves, Saroja told Jaya.

Because they start off being more beautiful, said Jaya, which made them giggle, Manikkam's wife was quite the ugliest woman around.

Lalitha is going to be a film star like these ladies, Saroja revealed, she could not keep it to herself any longer. When? asked Jaya, round-eyed. As soon as she hears, these things take time, she is waiting a summons, said Saroja. Jaya was impressed. All the girls were impressed, they flew round like sparrows, twittering. Even Miss Subramaniam came out of the restful aura that enclosed her, to inquire about Saroja's sister.

Saroja stopped off on her way home to tell Chingleput. He was making sugar necklaces that sold well in the temple, the beads were frosted sugar balls strung on intertwined silver and crimson thread.

A film star. Well, well, said Chingleput.

It is not an everyday thing, Saroja told him, most girls would give their eyes to be a film star. Well, said Chingleput, they are said to be well paid for their services, it isn't surprising they are required to give up so much. So much what? demanded Saroja. Eyes, and such, said Chingleput. Saroja ruminated. She crunched a sugar bead off the necklace he had given her to help her thinking. She thought of calling him envious, but that was manifestly impossible, he didn't even have a daughter. Don't worry, things have a way of working themselves out, said Chingleput.

Actually it wasn't Saroja's worry, it was Lalitha's. She fretted, waiting. No news is better than bad news, she said. She wound a string round her wrist, tied knots in it to mark the passing days. After thirty knots there was no space left on the string, she had to tie another one on. Perhaps this one will bring me luck, she said. She smiled, she rallied, told Saroja of the snow sherbets she had sipped sitting alongside Mr. Gupta and his guests. Rose-pink sherbets, she said, Himalayan snows and attar of roses. She described other luxuries. Carpets as thick as fur, she said, your feet sank in right up to the ankles. Saroja tried to visualize it, failed. And a freezer, said Lalitha, it was fantastic. Like Miss Mendoza's? asked Saroja. No comparison at all, said Lalitha, you simply can't talk about the two in the same breath. Saroja's imagination boggled again, she could not see how one refrigerator could be so superior to another.

Peasant, said Lalitha. She described the freezer; it was as big as a room, you could have walked into it if you had the desire.

*   *   *

Eat, said Aunt Alamelu.

I'm not hungry, said Lalitha, picking. You must force yourself, said her aunt, you mustn't outgrow your strength, a woman has many ordeals to face in the natural course of her life. I can't, said Lalitha, gave one of her pallid smiles; it's no good, I've tried. It's pathetic, said Aunt Alamelu. You look like a wraith, like one of those starving wretches that came over the border after the Partition. Your looks, she said, judiciously considering, would frighten a crow. *No!* said Lalitha. She was anguished, flew to her hand mirror, consulted it earnestly. Do I? she wailed. Do I look awful? You look fine, said Appa. A little bit thin, he said, he was wrung for his daughter, she was wrung for herself. Being beautiful was more trouble than it was worth, Saroja could not help concluding.

She expounded her theory to Lalitha. No, said Lalitha hollowly; it's worth all the trouble in the world. Her face was wan, there were bluish shadows like bruises under her eyes. Saroja's sympathy spurted up warmly again. It tended to dwindle when Lalitha was the focus of everyone's attention, but now the two of them were alone. I suppose it's the money holding him up, she said, money was the root cause she had discovered; it can't be very long now, can it? It could be any day, said Lalitha. Two months had gone by. Any hour, any minute, she stated. Her face grew radiant. He might come in person to summon me, she claimed.

Mr. Gupta is a busy man, said Appa. He slid the words in gingerly, past the guard Lalitha had put up. Of late she could not endure anyone but herself explaining away his silence. Yes, said Lalitha, he has a hundred things on his mind. She told them of the three telephones he had on his desk, one of which was colored red. Fancy that! said Aunt Alamelu. It's so primitive, Lalitha said, not being on the phone. It hampers one's career. It would have been simplicity itself for Mr. Gupta to have kept in touch, if only . . . Amma made no comment. Her face hinted she would have preferred Mr. Gupta forgotten. When Lalitha was absent she came out with it boldly. Better if he had never set foot, she said.

Lalitha was frequently absent. She went to the temple and made vows. She vowed away the presents he had given her, if only. Saroja knew from the pledge tabs she put on them, one by one a good many of the gifts Mr. Gupta had showered on her bore the telltale tabs.

Amma went on pilgrimages too. Saroja guessed her pledges would be for a contrary object, quite different to what Lalitha was wanting. She visualized the opposed prayers colliding, speculated on which of them would win. She wanted both of them to be successful, her riven parent and her sister who looked like a ghost, but clearly this was impossible.

If you wish hard enough, surely . . . ? said Lalitha.

It's the waiting, she said. Her eyes were full of hurt,

her body seemed brittle, you felt it might shatter if you touched it the least bit harshly.

When the heart gives up, said Lalitha of all people. She reminded Saroja of the little monkey they had rescued, which she had not thought about for years. Suddenly one day it had keeled over for no reason at all and died. It was healed, said Lalitha, but its heart didn't want to go on. Saroja grew uneasy. Your heart, she said, is it—are you—? My heart's in fine shape, said Lalitha.

In the morning she was gone.

She had walked to the next village and taken the bus into town. The bus driver told Appa, he had come along especially, considering it his duty. Appa was dignified, thanked the man for his trouble. He played it down, pretended he had known, but he had to have information. Where, he asked, had she gone on to from there? The bus driver spread his hands. From town there were so many routes—bus, train, long distance, short distance—she could have gone anywhere. Lalitha had said not a word as to her destination, merely picked up her case and got off his bus.

Miss Mendoza came. She came of her own accord, before Appa could summon her, which he had been saying he would do. They sat in the courtyard and wrangled, each pinning the blame on the other. Their voices carried, invaded the house, where Saroja had been incarcerated for protection. From Miss Mendoza's pernicious influence, it was intimated, which was deemed responsible for Lalitha's defection.

Poor Miss Mendoza did not look poisonous. Her face was pinched under the powder she had put on, her curls were wilting. Her status, which in Mr. Gupta's presence dwindled, was altogether gone. It enabled Appa to shout at her, to give vent to his pent-up feelings. You must know, he was shouting, you took her there, you must have some idea where she is! Miss Mendoza shifted in her chair, it was the one with the unraveled bottom, at one time they had been at pains to ensure she avoided it. Our trip was different, she said with dignity, totally different, Mr. Gupta had arranged special accommodation.

I do not wish to hear his name, said Amma. It is unavoidable, said Appa. He was ruthless about her foibles, reckless about his own. I will ruin him, he declared, I will sue your Mr. Gupta in the courts. It's not my Mr. Gupta, it's your daughter's doing, said brave Miss Mendoza. My daughter, I will not hear a word said, cried Appa, she is an innocent child, it is Mr. Gupta who has seduced her. Amma was silent, would not enter this area of the argument. We must not, said Miss Mendoza, jump to hasty conclusions. She looked tired, they all looked jaded from the drubbing they had given each other which had done no good. We must pool our resources, she said. Yes, said Appa. He was past his peak, the realities of the situation were worming in under his bluster.

I shall have to go down, he said, do what I can to find her. The bus leaves at nine o'clock, said Miss Mendoza. Her mouth looked like perished rubber, it was suddenly going in all directions, it had gone from her control. My best pupil, she wailed, Lalitha was our star, our pinnacle, there was no one to match our Lalitha. No one soothed her. Everyone was against Miss Mendoza because it was clear Lalitha would not have known where to go or how to cope if she had not blazed the fatal trail.

Her Lalitha, said Aunt Alamelu. She was indoors, obeying Appa's strict injunction to stay there. It is *our* Lalitha she has taken, it is entirely her doing. Saroja begged her to be fair. Aunt rounded on her. It's unfair to think anything else, she declared. That strutting pea-hen with her fancy notions, it was she put ideas into the poor child's head, where else did they spring from if not from her? Just see to what it has led, she and her may-pole capers! She had a long memory, had gone nosing down the years. Saroja could not follow all the twists. It seemed to her nevertheless that Miss Mendoza wasn't all that there was to it, Lalitha had had her own star to follow. Softly, step by step, she had left the village, like childhood, behind.

* * *

Appa caught the nine o'clock bus.

He was short of money. Lalitha had scooped up all she could find, left a note of apology tucked into his pocket case. Amma blamed Appa for leaving it lying around for all and sundry. Appa protested, said he had not expected his own daughter. He said he would have to foreclose on Manikkam, demand the return of that summer's loan, but Manikkam as usual was cleaned out, had been, he said, on the point of approaching Appa. Aunt Alamelu, snuffling, proposed a sale of her cooking vessels, which were her only wealth. Appa told her brusquely to pack up the histrionics. He would stop off on his way, borrow from the boys. On condition every single *paisa* is returned, said Amma. Appa claimed that was his intention, swore he would put the screw on Manikkam the moment he was back. He was gone a week. Amma and Aunt Alamelu carried on as if nothing had happened, but of course Manikkam knew. So did the whole of his crew, down to its smallest sentient member. They swarmed round Saroja whenever opportunity presented and demanded news of her sister. Opportunities seemed legion. Saroja echoed her aunt and called them a load of loafers, though her heart of hearts protested. Mind your own business, she shouted. She felt she understood exactly what Lalitha meant. There's no privacy for *anything*, she grumbled. Now don't *you* start, said Aunt. Amma said All the more reason for circumspection; she pointed out that they lived in a village. It set Saroja to pondering on its drawbacks, which she was not given to doing.

Appa came back scarred. In the course of a week there were furrows on his face which had never been there before. Saroja wondered if she had been missing and not his favored daughter if the furrows would have been as deep, as many as they were. She hated herself for the thought which had risen from the crawling ferment in her belly; even she knew its origin but knowing didn't help.

He'd gone everywhere, Appa said, he had scoured the city and drawn a blank. He took out a map to show them. It was criss-crossed with streets and dense with ticks which marked those he had taken. Up and down he had trudged, scrutinizing every female face in the hope, in what he knew was a hopeless quest. Saroja's rancor dissolved. She went with Appa every step of the way, felt his ache in her bones, the sore patch on his heel where the sandal had worn a hole. The sun had melted the tar, he told with distaste. In their village there were no tarred streets. Would *he* not reveal? inquired Amma; she was one-track in her thinking, kept him glued to the subject in hand. Mr. Gupta had been his first port of call but he wasn't available, explained Appa bleakly. Some of his fire came back. I'd have wrung the truth from him, he said, but he's flown, to America, for an indefinite period.

And then? Amma prodded. She wasn't sold on dramatics, no one was on another's but everyone indulged in his own from time to time by way of relief. Then he went to the police, said Appa, dejected. Going to the police on a mission like this was touching the bottom, but it was worse for him than most other people because of his battles with them during the independence struggle. In his youth, in the cities, he had felt their clubs on his back, his ribs had been cracked and had never properly mended. It was one reason for his forsaking big-city life: you had to be one hundred percent, he often declared, to take on a city. It was long ago but he still remembered, still never called policemen anything but uniformed thugs. Nevertheless he had swallowed his gall and gone to them, and had once again drawn blank.

Miss Mendoza came in the evening, after school. Aunt Alamelu saw her wobbling up the path, said Fancy Madam! and retired pointedly. Amma offered the barest courtesies: a chair, a glass of tea. She was not invited to enter. Have you any news? she inquired. Haven't you? said Amma accusingly, turning the question, implying it was up to the questioner to supply. No, said Miss Mendoza dolefully. She looked forlorn, her scrolls of hair were undone and dangling. My girls are usually—she said, none of them I am sure—I can vouch for their total loyalty. She was desperate, blew the undone curls off her forehead with abandon, like any village urchin. Loyalty is the least of one's concerns, said Amma. She was glittering, spiky, all the charity in her had been atomized.

Miss Mendoza went away, she came again, reported regularly for fresh doses of punishment. She's a glutton for it, said Anand, I wouldn't in her place. Saroja believed him, she knew he was a past master in the art of avoidance, especially when he had erred. Occasionally he did not realize when he had. His views and Amma's of what constituted error did not always coincide. It's the male/female thing, Anand was fond of saying, but the agility with which he slithered off made Saroja conclude his instinct kept him adequately informed, even when he didn't actually know.

Have you tried the YWCA? Miss Mendoza asked. She sucked her teeth, Anand said privately she was going to pieces. My daughter is a Hindu, said Amma. She was superior, towered over and crushed Miss Mendoza, who was a Christian and a convert at that. They provide hostels, a refuge for girls who are in any kind of trouble, persevered Miss Mendoza. No doubt, said Amma, Christian girls are frequently in need of the succor they offer. Miss Mendoza bent her head. She was patient, meek, implied she would suffer coals being heaped in the interests of her pupil. Perhaps Lalitha, she said, they take in girls of any denomination . . . perhaps she has found shelter . . . She offered the straw, Amma clutched it, she had to, but her hostility was irreducible. My husband will write, she promised grudgingly. I will write myself, said Miss Mendoza, some of her vigor had seeped back; to each and every branch, I shall not rest until Lalitha is restored to the bosom of her family.

Appa wrote. It was pathetic to see the eagerness with which he scanned the horizon for the postman. In reality it was an excuse. It wasn't a reply from the YWCA he watched for, he had scant belief in that. It was word from Lalitha that he craved. When she eventually wrote he could hardly contain himself. Amma had to slit open the envelope for him, his hands had become so incompetent.

It was a jaunty letter. Appa kept slapping his thighs and exclaiming as he read out bits. What a girl! he cried, and, Trust our Lalitha! She was well, she wrote, they were not to worry. She was, as a matter of fact, lodged in the lap of luxury. Mr. Gupta had arranged it all before he went away, not personally of course, he was too busy, but he had instructed his lieutenants. Lieutenants, mark that! exclaimed Appa. He was exhilarated, picked out bits from what she had written as if they were plums. A three-piece suite with satin cushions, an arbor covered in grapevines . . . I can picture it exactly, he claimed, I can see her sitting and writing as she describes in her letter.

Amma was silent throughout, she unsealed her lips only at the end to ask what would happen when Gupta returned. She demoted him, put nothing in front of his name; even mentioning it made the corners of her mouth flare downwards. She has to wait and see, said Appa. She says she has to be on the spot when they start casting, in such a competitive profession it's vital, it's no good her sitting miles away in a village, she has to be available. I take her point absolutely, he declared, he was quite carried away by his own advocacy. The point, which he had forgotten, was that no one cared a fig, not even he, about Lalitha becoming an actress, they preferred her career blasted so long as she came home.

No doubt, said Amma. She spoke dryly, squashed him flat by remarking that Lalitha had always excelled at embroidery, but Appa was resilient, he came back bouncing. She will survive, he said. Intact? asked Amma, and there was an interchange between them which Saroja did not miss, but could not quite interpret.

No one noticed that Lalitha had omitted to give her address.

They had to wait for her to communicate and she did not.

* * *

MANIKKAM came round for a loan. He did it to forestall Appa, who had yet to get back what he had previously lent. It's an outrage, Appa said. He attempted to roar but some of the verve had been taken from him since Lalitha. To tide me over, said Manikkam; my cow has died. His woes were so repetitive, so dreary, you wouldn't have felt anything but irritation except for seeing him in all his awesome misery. His bones showed. His presence was a breach of your peace, a blight upon your doorstep. Manikkam was aware. He left off his shirt, appeared in a loincloth deliberately. My children are starving, he said. He slapped his concave belly, which responded with hollow noises. How can they be, said Appa, when you're drawing government rations? It's not enough, said Manikkam. Because you're such a benighted manager, there's some kind of blight on your faculties, said Appa. His ire was rising. You should have lived in the era before we got our own government, he cried, then you'd really have had something to complain about! I'm not complaining, said Manikkam humbly, if it weren't for the children—You are, you are, you hideous old bag of bones, roared Appa. He was purple. He bent down and began rummaging in the trunk he kept under his charpoy. Here, he said in a nasty way, then he noticed Saroja, who was curious to see what was changing hands, and he ordered her out.

Saroja went. It was no use arguing when Appa was in this mood. She hung around the cactus hedge for Manikkam. What did you get? she asked. He looked glum. Nothing, he said. I *saw*, Saroja accused. Manikkam grew flustered. He had only his loincloth in which to hide the packet. It fell out of the folds and Saroja pounced. What is it? she said, smoothing the creases from the gossamer tube in her palm. It's nothing, said Manikkam, trying to snatch it back. Not till you tell, I can always ask Amma, Saroja threatened the nervous

skeleton. It's nothing, nothing for girls, cried Manikkam. He was obviously rattled, eyed her adamantine
jaw and capitulated. It's for men, he mumbled, it stops
babies, takes away the danger. It takes away the fun as
well, he said morosely, now don't go asking your
Amma, I have enough as it is on my plate. Saroja had
no intention of asking Amma; the sources of such information were not her parents, except what they let fall.
She handed the squashed thing back. She could deduce
a good deal from the shape, and by slotting together
what she already knew, but the method of it, the precise
detail of fitting and function of crumpled gossamer
evaded and tantalized her mind.

Saroja retreated with this new clue under her belt, sat
under the tamarind tree to consider. She draped the
gossamer over her father's jigger. She stuffed it up her
mother's aperture. The improbability was so extreme it
drove her to substitute Manikkam. Then Mr. Gupta
and Lalitha. It was coming easier now, it fitted, it
brought her to the verge of discovery. Her flesh shivered with a foretaste of knowledge. She heard her
mother calling. It penetrated her absorption, the sensations subsided. The images, on which discovery was
based, grew blurred, vanished.

What do you want? asked Saroja querulously.

What's wrong with all of you? countered Amma
crossly, do I have to shout myself hoarse each time a
meal is ready? She was already serving. Saroja sat down.
She toyed with her food. Appa was also toying, but he
had a purpose. He was arranging his helping of rice to
look as if part had been eaten. It was an impossible task.
The redistributed grains stubbornly resisted any sem-

143

blance of reduction. Eat, Brother, eat, urged Aunt. She believed in food. It was her panacea for affliction. In vengeful moods Amma told how her sister, to her shame, had put on weight after the death of her husband: she had grown so indecently fat she had hardly been able to attend the tenth-day obsequies.

What do you think I'm doing? asked Appa, chewing. He challenged her to dispute but Aunt was silent. They were all silent. The air was oppressive. It was Lalitha's invisible presence. It would have been better to have hauled her into view, spoken about her in company, but no one did. When you looked at Appa you felt you could not bear to, you left it to him. Mostly he did not. Sometimes he did, his wandering eye alighting on her belongings. There was enough scattered around: her beads, her bangles, the lacquered boxes he had bought her, Mr. Gupta's gifts, a trayful of scents and soaps. Lalitha had always had plenty, she had selected and taken with her only the best, but of course it wasn't the quality of the remnant that roused Appa, the merest rag was a subject for sad reflections.

Your father is moping, said Aunt Alamelu, specialist in self-evident sayings. Appa overheard her. I am not moping, he said. If I were it would be entirely natural, but, in fact, I am not. No one is blaming you, brother, gasped Aunt, who had not heard him come in. There is no reason to mope, said Appa. He transfixed her with an eye. It is merely a question of waiting, he said. Lalitha is furthering her career, she will return in her own good time.

But there were no letters brimful with details of her life and career that would have helped him along.

                              *   *   *

SCHOOL had its quota of thorns. The girls were avid for
news, they crowded Saroja and questioned her. Saroja
had nothing with which to appease them beyond that
one letter, from which the last rose petal had been
wrung. She regretted the lack of letters as much as
Appa, but she was better off in one respect. She could,
given courage, invent. Saroja nerved herself and began.
She told of Lalitha's life and imminent success. She
donned Lalitha's mantle and the detail cascaded, the
roses and jade, the camera crew who were stunned by
her sister's ability and beauty, the bowlfuls of iced lem-
onade. They could well have been true, she had no
means of telling one way or another.

    You're making it up, accused Jaya.

    Think what you like, said Saroja, offhand.

    I think she's let you down, said Jaya. There isn't any
news. There aren't any letters.

    Dozens, averred Saroja recklessly.

    One, said Jaya. Everyone knows.

    Dozens. No one knows, they come by special messen-
ger.

    Saroja waited anxiously. Jaya was rocked, she could
see, but she came back fighting.

    If there were, your father wouldn't look the way he
does, she said.

    My father's fine, said Lalitha.

    He's shot to pieces.

                                                    145

He's not.

Sick with worry. Your father's going potty over his missing daughter.

My father's fine, yelled Saroja. You just leave my father alone!

She got on her bike and rode home furiously. In the field where the shed was she spotted her father. He had a stick and was prodding at something in a patch of mire. She went over to see, in reality to carry out an inspection in the light of Jaya's strictures.

What is it? she said.

It's her bike, said Appa. His stick turned over clods, she saw the poor rusted spokes.

She was such a good cyclist, he said. Learned in a day, I remember.

No, said Saroja. Her chest felt tight.

It's as clear as yesterday, he said. I can see her skimming along this very path like a bird, she had such a good sense of balance.

She was rotten, said Saroja. She eyed her father. You're *potty*, she burst out.

Appa put down the stick. He considered Saroja.

You're right, he said. Silly of me, confusing you two. Of course you are the good one, you always have been, you're really quite an excellent bicyclist. In fact, he said handsomely, I'll go further and say you're the best in the district.

Saroja was restored. Her chest stopped hurting. She nodded casually, accepted his compliment, it wasn't vanity to do so if something were true.

The niggles came in the night. She could not sleep. She saw Appa as he had been in the field, bent, and his thin shirt billowing. The bones had registered without her knowing. They presented now, sharp, skeletal, clattered in front of her drawn eyelids. The padding of flesh was missing, was altogether melted about his rib cage. She mulled about the wastage, speculated whether it could be due to his state of mind.

In the morning, it was a Sunday, she trailed off to consult Manikkam.

Manikkam was standing in front of his hut, drying off in the sun. He had just finished bathing, had on the minimum. She studied him down to his codpiece. The bones were fearful, the state of his ribs worse than anything Appa could offer. It reassured Saroja. Nevertheless she asked, just to make certain. Do you think my father is potty? she said. Manikkam scratched his armpits, from which wet hair was hanging like banyan roots. Yes, like the rest of us, he said. No, seriously, said Saroja. I am being serious, said Manikkam. Well, perhaps less so than others, he conceded, though of course your father's got his troubles. Saroja nodded. She felt better. She would rather her father was sane, if sorrowful, than dotty, even if it secured him the measure of oblivion dottiness was reported to do. She wondered if Lalitha would agree. She missed her sister on occasions like these, not to mention the bubble and fizz that Lalitha created, there was always something fermenting when she was around.

In the afternoon she again made for Manikkam's. Home, these days, was not a place to be in. She scuffed her way along the rutted path down which Appa had actually imagined people could skim. The nearest anyone had come to skimming were Devraj and Mr. Gupta.

Their car had become airborne, like a bird, over brief stretches, but perhaps skimming wasn't the right word for that kind of motion. It had made Mr. Gupta hysterical, she remembered, he had bawled as he bounced.

At the hedge Saroja paused, and as there was no one to observe she picked up her skirt and took a flying leap over. It got her to Manikkam's a good two minutes quicker. The door was closed. The children deposited outside were hushed. She noticed they were the young ones, the older two were absent, they were the ones who usually ran errands.

What's up? asked Saroja.

Our mother, they answered.

Their mother was Saroja's good friend, fount of much knowledge. She tapped on the door, which was tied up with string. A voice with a hint of sepulcher in it replied, told her to keep out. Saroja asked why. The voice, which was Manikkam's, replied that there were things unfitting for her to see. A second voice, his wife's, disputed, maintained there would be no harm. Saroja squatted outside and drew designs in the dust while she waited for one or other to prevail. She suspected it would be Manikkam's wife. She was right. Manikkam came out. She says you can go in, he said. She says you're a sensible girl. He blinked, looked at her as if he were viewing her with new eyes. Saroja preened her feathers. Everyone knows that but you, she told him, underlined her victory with a saucy lift of her chin.

Inside it was different. She felt less confident. It was the smell, it menaced her nostrils. The root of it was blood. She could easily imagine bucking and rearing if she had been an animal, and her eyeballs swiveling to exhibit the whites. She stood by the door, in darkness from leaving the dazzling sun, trying to remember she was sensible.

It's all right, said Manikkam's wife. She was lying by the wall, her feet were up in a sling in which her infant usually slept. The raw warm salty smell came from her most strongly, it also rose from a bundle in the corner. It's nothing, she said to Saroja, nothing you shouldn't see, you're a woman too, aren't you, one of the tribe.

Saroja advanced. Her eyes adjusted to the gloom, she saw the smears on the bundle, on the rags on the floor. It's just a little blood, said Manikkam's wife. A woman gets used to it. All women. Heaven knows they ought, the amount that flows from them. Bloody sponges, they are, carry around this great soggy bag inside them ready to spout at the first opportunity. She let out a small moan. Saroja thought she looked horribly uncomfortable with her legs suspended. Are you comfortable? she asked cautiously. No, but one does not expect to be comfortable in my condition, said Manikkam's wife. You're not dying, are you? inquired Saroja anxiously. No, said Manikkam's wife, I've just lost a baby. She sounded quite calm. It horrified Saroja. She thought it was awful, losing one's baby. Her eyes began to prick, imagining the poor little expired baby done up in the sodden parcel, but Manikkam's wife said she wasn't to upset herself, it had been too small to feel anything. No bigger than my thumb, she said in exasperation, you wouldn't think, would you, it would take so much blood and bother to keep a little thing like that ticking?

Saroja went home. On the way in she hugged her

149

mother, who was sitting in the courtyard in the sunshine stripping corn off cobs. She was glad Amma wasn't in the position that Manikkam's wife was. Beneath the gladness were somber notes for the baby that wasn't. No bigger than a thumb: it was difficult to imagine. Saroja brought out the box in which lay her collection of treasures. Among them was the little cart Amma had given her a free hand in selecting, the tiny porcelain doll in a matchbox that the Sikh hawker had handed her with a smile, long ago when she had been a little girl. It had been a bribe, she realized now, to get her to leave him and her mother in peace, but she did not hold it against him. Nor against what he had given her, she could not transfer emotions. The doll continued to enchant her after she found out. It enchanted her still, it was so small, each tiny part so carefully modeled. Saroja pushed open the matchbox and gazed at the thumb-sized doll. It made her feel very sad for the little baby which had also been thumb-sized, but real, flesh and blood and perhaps even a real tiny skeleton.

4

Hot weather was upon them. Dust got in everything, however much you swept it out.

It got in Amma's hair, which was black and lustrous, gave it amber tones. It lay in peppery ridges under Saroja's fingernails. Chingleput's sweetmeats were gritty between one's molars. It made him groan. He was expert at accepting things, but he was a perfectionist where his skills were concerned. You're rich if you have just one, he told Saroja. You don't have to be a sun, rays in all directions, just one skill is sufficient to warm you. Saroja sat listening peacefully. She believed him. She liked his aura, which was calm, in contrast to the one at home, which was not so much frenzied as pet-

151

rified. She would have stayed longer with him, but restrictions had been imposed. I must go, she announced regretfully. Don't forget the mangoes, he called after her as she rode away. She liked the way he always made her welcome, but never fussed when she had to go. Comings and goings were equally easy with Chingleput.

Mangoes were ripening. Flocks of parrots settled in the trees and feasted. Amma congratulated herself. She had taken the first crop in for pickling before their arrival. The mangoes floated in brine. They were small and green, hard as marbles; saliva ran just looking at them, such was the power of salt and sour. The fruit on the trees were larger than fists, and softened by touches of gold. Sun-kissed, said Amma. She pressed her fingers to her lips, it was one of Lalitha's favored phrases. I wonder what that sister of yours is up to, she said, pasting gaiety over the slip. She's doing fine, said Saroja. It was her stock statement, she wasn't sure if she believed it from conviction or repetition. I'm sure she is, said Amma, gazing into distance down which Lalitha had vanished, though, she said, it would be nice to know for sure. Mmm, said Saroja, she made the syllable stony, to stop Amma going down paths that razed her.

Aunt Alamelu entered. Birds were stripping the trees, she said, she had been out scaring away the pests. She had chosen the hottest part of the day to do it in, the sun was a disc of white metal. Her soles were cracked, Aunt said, she could not endure to stand another moment on the burning earth. She sat down and massaged her ankles while she enumerated other plagues. Bandicoots in the grain store, she told them, next thing it would be the monkeys, it was time for the tribe to arrive. There is a season for everything, Amma said to stem the recital. Aunt said yes, and recalled that the marriage season would soon be upon them. Amma's face was pinched, she did not need reminding. In the marriage season mothers and daughters were closest, were on display, wore their best clothes and were invited and went to weddings when marriages were not being arranged within their own households. Last season Amma and Lalitha and Saroja had been part of the bustle. They had sallied out with flowers in their hair and wearing their prettiest, and on their return Amma had burned camphor in a silver ladle and circled the flame thrice around them to prevent the eye of envy ravaging her beautiful daughters.

But one always waited for the dust to settle.

Outside the dust was swirling. Through it Appa came bounding, waving a letter. From Lalitha, from Lalitha! he cried. He was choking with dust and emotion. He took a grip on himself. She's coming home tomorrow, he announced. Tomorrow, he repeated, then he was overcome again, he did a little jig in the courtyard with his slip of paper. Amma joined him. She was more stately, like a palm tree swayed by a buffoon wind. What does she say? she inquired in the interstices of his rejoicing, but Appa would not interrupt his rollicking to tell. In any case there couldn't have been much, since as far as Saroja could see there was only a single line of writing on the paper.

*　*　*

THE bus stopped in the next village. Appa and Saroja walked to the halt. Amma stayed at home, she planned a little celebration.

In the village Appa chartered a *jutka*. She will be tired, he said, it's a long drive, with three changes. They waited at the bus stop, which was sited in the shade of a banyan tree. The roots hung down like tresses. Children had tied the longer, stronger strands to form a hammock and were swinging on it to pass the time. No one knew exactly when the bus would come. It depended upon the connections, Appa said, but he also frowned and said the bus company ought to be able to maintain its schedule.

It was very hot. Saroja wished she had stayed at home where it was nice and cool but she also wanted to welcome her sister the moment she stepped off the bus. Waiting was tedious however. To stave off boredom she surveyed the people who were fussing and fuming like Appa, and those who had settled down to slumber. The sleepers were much the more numerous. They included the little *jutka* pony, which was asleep on its feet. Saroja yawned, fitted her back to the *jutka*'s knobbly hoop frame, fell into a reverie in which Lalitha was dominant, was clad in rose-pink silk, was descending like a queen from a car whose door Mr. Gupta, Devraj and Miss Mendoza were competing to hold open for her.

The bus roused her. It roused everybody, set the

crows cawing and the kites circling. It was some way off still, but the motor was thunderous. It's an old machine, said Appa; he judged from the sound, besides he had his city standards to compare by. Saroja could not tell if the bus was old or new, not even when it had rumbled to a stop, since every inch was smothered in dust. So were the passengers. You could tell they had had a rough ride from the way they were cowering under towels and shawls in which they had swathed themselves. In Saroja's opinion they looked ridiculous, exactly like rows of dusty cocoons except for one which stood out, which achieved grace despite inherent disadvantages. Lalitha! she shouted and ran, holding Appa's steamy hand and dragging him, to the boarding platform.

Lalitha descended with dignity. She had on cream-colored sandals and a plain voile sari (not rose-pink silk, Saroja noted with regret).Her hair was streaked with dust, like everyone else on the bus, and she looked very tired but it didn't detract from her prettiness.

Are you very tired? asked Appa. A bit, said Lalitha, stepping delicately behind Appa, who led the way. That old bone-shaker, she said with contempt, implied it was not her regular mode of conveyance. I have a *jutka*, said Appa, he sounded a little apprehensive, in case it wasn't up to his city-returned daughter's expectations, but Lalitha said That's fine. Just fine, she repeated, and her eyes lighted up in the old way, a brilliance that bowled over any who beheld.

In the *jutka* Appa plied Lalitha with questions, partly for his own benefit, partly for the benefit of the *jutka* driver, who could be trusted to spread the details. How was his friend Mr. Gupta, he inquired, and had Lalitha thanked him adequately for the luxuries he had lavished on her, and what further news of her career which was taking such excellent shape? Lalitha gave jaunty answers. Great, just great, she kept saying, everything was splendid, was going according to plan, she could not ask for better. Now and then she tucked back a curl, adjusted the folds of the voile, which kept slipping from the movement of the *jutka*, which made Appa ask the driver could he not manage a smoother ride, did he not see his daughter was unaccustomed to this rough country jolting?

The driver humored Appa, said he would do his best; it was obvious he was aiming for a handsome payment for the trip. In return Appa piled on the detail, made it clear Lalitha's absence had been authorized and approved and blessed by both parents. Are we to be stumbling blocks in the path of our children? he demanded. Saroja listened. She wondered if Appa had been carried away by his own eloquence, believed what he was saying: or if he was putting out what he wanted the village to believe, to scotch the rumors that had been circulating.

Appa, however, was less interesting than Lalitha.

Saroja considered her sister, thought she looked older, it was a matter of years rather than the months she had been away. Then she thought again, decided it wasn't a matter of aging at all but some kind of inner scoring like what had happened to her brothers. Lalitha caught her looking. Have I changed that much, become a stranger? she asked wistfully, the brightness of her manner was muted. Oh no, said Saroja. It's just that you look a bit different, she blurted. Bound to, bound to, said Appa, it's the city's sheen, there's no doubt at all about it, a city does add a certain luster. At this point the *jutka* driver turned round, his back was squashed against Appa's shoulder but he managed it, to confirm what had been said. True, true, he exclaimed, and told them about his nephew who lived in the city whose polish was such as to dazzle the entire family. The pony clopped on without his help; it knew the way, besides there was only one road to the village, just rough ground and fields on either side. It had blinkers on, in case a tractor happened to be working, but as there was only one among five villages this seemed a remote possibility. Saroja thought it a pity, there was so much hidden from it that would have delighted a pony's eye.

The rattle of the wheels alerted Amma. Sound traveled for miles across the countryside unless wedding bands were playing or funeral conches blowing, or when the monsoon struck. She had put on a clean sari and braided and coiled her hair and was waiting by the door with Aunt Alamelu upright on her cracked soles standing beside her peering out into the glare. Over the doorway a string of mango leaves had been hung to welcome Lalitha.

Saroja got out of the *jutka* first, having got in last, and waited for Lalitha, who suddenly seemed uncertain, seemed bereft, clung to the safety of the *jutka* with her pupils widening as if home was some kind of trap. Come on, said Saroja roughly, for she too felt the spear, feared the stark implausible threat posed by an ordinary dwelling which passed from her sister to her, transfixed her in the same intolerable way. Coming, said Lalitha docilely, and dropped her eyes, which had been too revealing, and the two of them went to meet their mother.

Inside it was better. Eating and drinking restored them, the atmosphere of homecoming asserted itself. Appa was in good form, he cracked jokes, gave wry accounts of his disastrous saga in the city and subtler ones of city slickers attempting to take the country bumpkin for a ride and coming unstuck in the process. He hadn't been bred there for nothing, he told them, chuckling: he spotted the jokers a mile off, city wiles were unlikely to topple a man who had imbibed them with his milk.

Lalitha contributed similar anecdotes. There was the man who had tried to sell her a ruby ring for a song, the ruby had been of a richness and depth to fool any-one but she had spotted the tinsel let into the metal under the glass. Then there was the woman proffering a lotion guaranteed to make her fair skin fairer—at ten rupees the bottle—as if, said Lalitha, the simplest crack-pot let alone herself could be induced to believe such nonsense, although she had to admit sales were brisk. One born every minute, said Appa, he applauded his daughter's acumen. Aunt Alamelu kept clucking, ex-claimed What a den! and, A proper thieves' kitchen!

Amma alone sat quiet. She let them run dry before she began, Saroja had to marvel at her control because she must have been bursting for exact information, all the talk so far had been at a general level. Mr. Gupta, she said. He's fine, just fine, Lalitha anticipated, but Amma drove on. Is he back? she said, does he know you have returned home? Has anything come of his film?

Has he been paying your expenses? If he hasn't who has? Her eyes were like gimlets, in that illuminating moment Saroja saw how closely she resembled her sister, her tender, comely Amma and poor crabbed Aunt could both bore through metal at a glance. Lalitha was taken off guard, she looked startled, but she recovered fast, clapped her hands over her ears and made a show of being overwhelmed. All these questions! she protested, there were shrill strains in her voice, her jaw was militant. Why, she said, it would take the whole night, and I'm simply too tired. Her shoulders drooped. Appa took her side, said the child was exhausted, to let the matter rest, but Amma said There's no time like the present and she waited, so Lalitha had no choice.

Mr. Gupta was back, she told them. He had been back a month. He had returned from America laden with presents, they had included a crate full of peaches. Saroja had never seen a peach except in pictures, she was curious to know how it tasted, if it was as luscious as it looked and Lalitha was eager to tell but Amma cut them both short. And the film? she inquired. As to that, Mr. Gupta had not been so fortunate, Lalitha admitted, the question of finance had yet to be resolved.

So no film, said Amma, she was so curt that Lalitha simply said yes, the monosyllable fell from her surprised lips like a pebble. So then what kept you, asked Amma, what went on for a whole month? She was flushed, she looked dangerous, you felt you would shrivel up if she so much as touched you. Lalitha shrank, but she came back fighting, the city had tempered her, the boys often said if there was one thing it did it toughened you, tanned your skin to leather so you were never as vulnerable as you had been. What went on, she repeated, she was speaking directly to Amma and Amma was staring right back, why, what do you think went on, are you putting yourself in my place?

Saroja looked away, she felt queasy. Long-ago words of Lalitha's drifted across her line of vision, it's her coming out in me, Lalitha had said, and had left Saroja picking at a scab, the edges of a mystery which was now within her grasp if she cared to. But she did not. She did not want to be rocked, she wanted to be as she was, stable, and the inviolate figures of Amma and Appa implanted in granite beside her. So she retreated. She focused her sights on the silvery trails one found in the morning, on the ground, it was one of her methods, and called up the little creamy creatures which retracted their horns when you touched, and applying the wand to herself curled into her own pearly, impervious capsule.

Whatever's the matter with the child? Aunt Alamelu began complaining. She hated mysteries, the glazed jellies that people presented in place of eyes which she could not penetrate. She's overtired, came Amma's voice, stripped of its barbs, and Appa, taking advantage of the situation, chimed in, saying it had been a tiring day for all of them and it was best to adjourn. Then they were rising, all of them on their feet, Lalitha yawning and Saroja swaying a little to keep up appearances although her mind was cut crystal, the respites she won for it were lifegiving but of a transient nature.

Sleep tight, little sweet, said Lalitha. It could have been like old times, though the old phrase had a new twist.

Saroja wanted to believe it was like old times, but she could not conjure up the necessary magic.

*　*　*

AUNT Alamelu was roasting coffee beans in a shallow pan over a charcoal brazier. The aroma filled the house. Lalitha came and leaned over Aunt, who was squatting, and made ecstatic noises. Heavenly, heavenly smell, she said, there's nothing in the whole city to touch it. Glad to hear it, said Aunt. She sniffed, she said she never thought to hear from madam's lips that their humble village could compete. Lalitha refused to be drawn. She sat beside Aunt and took the stiff palmyra fan from her and fanned the coals expertly, coaxing a glow but restraining the flames. I missed it, she said. Coffee? asked Aunt. Lots of things, said Lalitha, gazing into the bright coals in which entire patterns and pictures could be discerned as Saroja knew from experience.

But she could not sit and gaze like Lalitha.

I'm off, she announced. Where? asked Lalitha. School, said Saroja, which, she thought with resentment, seemed to be reserved for her. Aren't you going to start school again? she asked belligerently. Who can say? said Lalitha in a wondering voice. She sighed, the sound was so melancholy that no one pressed her, not even Amma.

The questions simmered. Sometimes they were popped. Lalitha answered with languor, as if she were not concerned, or they were beneath her notice. She developed arts, grew adept at side-stepping, at obliquities. As far as she could she kept out of Amma's way, went to see Miss Mendoza, went down to the river, which she said she found enthralling, spent hours in the buffalo shed for want of a better refuge. When cornered beyond hope of shielding by Appa she answered erratically, gave out a spate of details and descriptions of her life in the city. The details clashed. The realities did not fit. He was lavish, said Lalitha. I wanted for nothing. I had only to ask. How, when he was sitting in America? When he returned, naturally, said Lalitha, withering her aunt, her mother, her sister, her sister's aggravating classmates.

When he came back he showered me with luxuries, she said, marks of his favor because he has faith in me, he believes I have a brilliant future only nothing is achieved in a day, it all takes time.

How much time?

One must have patience, exercise one's skills, said Lalitha. But she no longer practiced her dancing. She sat around, sighing. He was wonderful, she said. He gave me his wallet, told me to help myself, there was a wad of notes inside as fat as my arm. Of course he knows I'll pay him back one day, he believes in me.

She had brought home no presents. Presents were the visible symbols of your success, it was commonly accepted right through the village. Even the boys, who were above such things, superior to conventions like Appa, were not empty-handed at homecomings.

Then why didn't you help yourself? inquired Aunt. Not even one new sari to show for your stay, and even the ones you took are in tatters.

Because I didn't *choose* to, flared Lalitha. Leave me alone will you? You're *hounding* me.

*   *   *

I‌t's the heat, said Lalitha.

It'll be school holidays soon, said Saroja.

There were electric fans in all the rooms, said Lalitha. With regulators, marked from 1 to 5, 5 was full on. I always had them on 5, I loved the blades whirring around at top speed though it created havoc with his papers.

Was he kind to you? asked Saroja gingerly.

So kind, so skilled, said Lalitha. There was a glow on her, in her voice, underneath her skin as if tapers were burning, it made you forget how thin she had become, how wan beneath the bloom which was the natural endowment of her age. Do you understand? she asked.

*   *   *

Do you know about facts? asked Lalitha.

She whispered, there was no need, their charpoys were out in the courtyard whereas Amma and Appa were sleeping within. Saroja lay rigid, she was outwardly still but her insides were turbulent. Do you know? said Lalitha, she seemed to be pleading, it was not like before when her voice ran like honey. About what? asked Saroja, who felt she was stifling, felt herself stiffening against her sister's desperation which was clawing at her through the questioning. About life, said Lalitha. Do you?

Saroja stared at the darkness. She forgot about the stars, which were her joy. She felt very dry, her eyeballs grated when she swiveled them in their sockets. I know about blood and birth, she said huskily. Do you? Then she rolled herself up, a prickly ball like a threatened animal with festoons of shawl round her because really she didn't want to hear, she wanted only to be spared Lalitha's probing.

But Lalitha would not let her be. She dragged off the swaddling. Her face hung over Saroja's like a mangled flower in the darkness. How do you know, she said to the exposed cringing visage of Saroja, how *much* do you know? Saroja squirmed, but she was pinned by the shoulders, Lalitha was crouched on her knees and was holding her down. I know from Manikkam's wife, she said. If you want to know why don't you ask her? She's had dozens of babies. I don't want to know about babies, said Lalitha harshly. She relaxed her grip, her hands rested lightly on Saroja's arms. Whatever made you think, poor sweet, that I did? she asked. Her voice was pure, and high, and sweet, and struck dreadful jarring notes on Saroja's ear, which was an instrument delicately attuned to pick up the slightest disharmony.

* * *

ON the last day of school the girls went a little mad with excitement.

Saroja watched them with a jaundiced eye, they seemed to her a lot of raving lunatics, she could not imagine herself taking part in such fatuous revelry although, she had to admit, she had reveled with the rest when the last term had ended. What's wrong with sourpuss? warbled Jaya as she bobbed past doing the prescribed jig. Nothing, said Saroja, I'm thinking, it would frizzle you up if I told you what I was thinking. Please yourself! said Jaya, and danced away.

Saroja thought about Nalini, she was in the mood for gloomy thoughts. Last term Nalini had joined in their end-of-term revels. After a while they had had to restrain her forcibly, her great bulbous head had wobbled so alarmingly on her stalklike neck. The way it was done, though, Nalini could never have guessed. Miss Subramaniam had wrapped her arms around her and half carried and half led her to the teachers' room and given her coconut milk to drink. There was coconut milk for all the girls, there was a shiny green pyramid of coconuts ready in the compound, but the teachers had made out it was a special treat for her. Nalini believed the story. She was dim. Sometimes, though, she made you wonder, said special treats were her diet because her time was short, which made you think twice about her endowments.

Jaya came jigging round on the second lap of the ritual. Wood apple, green apple, crab apple, custard apple, she flung at Saroja, panting. Dangle-dingle, idiots' jingle, Saroja flung back. She thought Jaya's ditty fatuous, more so even than her own. The only kinds of apple in the village were wood and custard, and they weren't really apples at all. Real apples came from Kulu, in the Vale of Kashmir, a place so distant and enchanted that none of them could even aspire to see it. Or they came from the hills, which were equally misty and legendary. Custard apples, on the other hand, grew everywhere. Anyone who had a bit of land planted one, the polished black pip split and sprouted as easily as pumpkin seed. Saroja loved the fruit, which were mushy and green, with quilted skins like velvety cushions. Inside each puff was a delectable substance, creamy and scented. Lalitha, who had eaten custard at Miss Mendoza's, said the taste was the same. Jaya made other, odious, comparisons. Saroja always shut her up when she began, she didn't want the fruit spoiled for her.

Jaya came bobbing round on the last lap leading the crocodile of girls. When they reached the second pillar of the corridor the ritual was over. Jaya flopped down beside Saroja, linked her arm through and asked to be friends. Saroja said it was her one desire. Her jaundice miraculously vanished, she felt like Jaya, as blithe as a bird. The two of them went arm in arm into the compound where Miss Subramaniam's bell was summoning them.

In Lalitha's school at the end of term Miss Mendoza handed out little books with blank colored pages in which you put a tick for each good deed you had done during the holidays. When school started again the girl with the most ticks was given a prize. One year Lalitha had won a prize, but it wasn't for good deeds, it was for the ticks she had scrawled in the book. She had forgotten about good deeds until the last day, then she simply sat down and penciled them in, they represented nothing. She never bothered about good deeds after that. The ease of substitution, she told Saroja, has been a revelation. Saroja thought Miss Mendoza must be simple, she could not quite see Miss Subramaniam allowing anything like that to get past her.

In Saroja's school they distributed tender coconut as a treat. The toddy-tapper brought them from the *tope* in which he worked, a great pile which he tipped out of his cart and arranged in a pyramid in the compound. When the girls and teachers were assembled he made crescent-shaped nicks in the nuts with his billhook for the milk to flow before splitting them into halves so you could scoop out the meat.

Some girls put the nick to their lips and drank straight from the coconut, which everyone conceded was the best way to do it, the milk took on an extra-special flavor coming directly from the palm to you like milk straight from the cow before it had been sloshed around in pails. But most were not so skilled, had to wait for jugs and tumblers to be filled, which being like middlemen robbed you of the best.

Tender coconut was starting point for their summer holiday. However hot the weather the milk was always cold, it cooled you down after all the exhilaration of breaking up. Jaya said it made life easier for the teach-

167

ers, they could make themselves heard delivering their speeches, then she added handsomely they weren't only doing themselves a good turn, there was another side to it since they paid out of their own pockets to stand their pupils a treat.

There was something about holidays, no doubt about it, that made you inclined to be virtuous and kindly.

* * *

SAROJA rocketed down the path full of joyous excitement that built up as she rode home.

She bounded indoors. It's holidays, she shouted. She swooped on her Amma and hugged her. She would have inflicted the same on her sister, only Lalitha did not look robust enough. She was smiling though. Was it a good show? she asked. It was fun, said Saroja, and described her day.

At the end we had tender coconut, she said. Lalitha's smile was wistful. Lucky thing, she said. You have it every holidays, said Appa, with an undercurrent. Saroja understood it wasn't to belittle her pleasure but to spare his elder daughter, who had missed out on the jollities, but she resented it all the same. It was lovely, she emphasized. The milk was like nectar, the pulp was like white jelly, it slipped down your throat, you didn't have to chew or anything. Was it, said Lalitha. She gave a little gasp, her face had greenish tinges. Are you all right? asked Appa solicitously. I'm okay, perfectly okay, chattered Lalitha. She clamped her jaws tight, but it didn't work; she started up, rushed outside. They heard her being sick. Saroja would not look at Appa, she guessed his message would be Now see what you've done. Instead, however, what she felt was the glances of the grown-ups colliding in regions somewhere above her head. There was a distinct draft.

Lalitha came back. She smelled of sick, though she had gargled and washed. She leaned against the doorpost. It's the heat, she said. No one accepted the explanation, you could feel it battering away desperately against their disbelief. There were fans in all the rooms in Mr. Gupta's house, said Lalitha. At his name a gust of formidable proportions swept through the room. It blasted them.

Lalitha felt the heat most. It must have seared her, being vulnerable. She attempted to speak, she couldn't. She swayed, she crumpled. Appa leapt to her aid. He picked her up, laid her on her charpoy. It must be the strain, all the work she's done and the damnable waiting, he said. The false notes rang wildly. Amma eyed him, it made him veer off on a different tack. She must go to the clinic, he cried, I will get a *jutka*. There's no clinic today, said Amma, it's only held once a week. Appa clutched his brow at the frustration. Amma disregarded the histrionics. Well, there's no hurry, we shall know soon enough, she said. She was dry, a bone whose marrow had been vaporized by some vengeful ray. She sent Appa away, it was a concern for women, and he was glad to go, he had the intellect but she had the granite chips which held them up, enabled them to function.

When he had gone she dragged it out of Lalitha that

169

she was late. How late, Amma wanted to know. Lalitha wasn't sure. She seemed to be past caring. She simply lay on the bed and let the tears flow, an endless stream from the wells of her sorrowing womanhood.

*　*　*

AMMA and Lalitha went to the clinic in a *jutka*. Appa procured it for them, advised them to nip in and out of the clinic smartly so no one would see them, but Amma wanted to know where should she take her sick child but to a clinic and where was the shame in that? In any case neither of them was in any state to be nippy, there was no spring left in Amma's step and Lalitha positively tottered.

Saroja and Aunt Alamelu stayed behind, got on with what had to be done in the house. After a while they could not, they could only wait, Appa outside and Saroja and Aunt indoors sitting side by side and listening for the sound of the cart and the anticipation was a little like the day of Lalitha's homecoming except that merriment was entirely absent.

Saroja thought about Jaya to cheer herself up, and about Chingleput, who had started a new line in ice-fruit. It was made of crushed ice and fruit syrup, and there was one special syrup distilled not from fruit but from rose petals which was the most delicious of all. Chingleput had given her a first taste, he often tried out new flavors on her, said he could trust her to give a true not a flattering verdict which was a hazard with friendships and free samples. When he saw her lick her lips he said he could tell he was on to a winner, smiled at her with his eyes, which were as clear as warm honey, and said she had a tongue like a rose leaf. Saroja's tongue was pink, not green, but she let it pass, she often let things pass now she was older, though her preference was still for worrying at them.

Chingleput made ice-fruit by pressing crushed ice round a stick and pouring syrup over. The shape which came up was not that of a fruit but of the ridges that rose between Chingleput's fingers. The ice-fruit looked like a knuckle-duster. The only place in the whole village where you could see a knuckle-duster was in Perumal the money-lender's. He had a pair on his desk, and the boys said they were for the use of the guard who took over at night. Even the boys, though, didn't know the name of the strange objects. Appa did. He had seen them used by the military during the independence risings, said steel knuckles masquerading as human had been the usual British hoodwink which had deceived no one except those who wished to be deceived.

Saroja shuddered to think of steel clunking on bone, she urged Chingleput to alter the shape of his ice-fruit but he had no molds other than his hands. In any case, he said, your generation, which is my best customer, is not crippled by memory and experience, you were born to freedom and light. He was right, because none of his customers ever objected to the shape of his ice-fruit, even Saroja desisted when ice and rose syrup were melting together in a heavenly combination on her tongue.

Saroja got so engrossed she forgot about Lalitha, she

171

would have forgotten her aunt as well but Aunt Alamelu, who harbored suspicions, kept jogging her to secure her attention. Are you listening? she said— nudge—and, Children should listen to their elders— jab. I am listening, said Saroja desperately, and the truth was she had to, she could not dodge everything though she would dearly have liked to because what Aunt Alamelu was saying in a variety of ways was that women were born to suffer, which Saroja did not want to believe being a woman herself, not to mention Lalitha.

Presently they heard the *jutka*. It must have been about four fields away but the sound carried clearly, the day was so still. Or perhaps the house was so hushed, the three of them doing nothing except with their thoughts which scurried around like mice, fearfully busy but silent inside their skulls. When the *jutka* drew near there was a clattering, whipstock drawn over the spokes of the wheels which was by way of announcement of imminent arrival. Appa poked his face in. They're coming, he said. He must have thought they were deaf. Perhaps it was just something to do. Saroja felt the craving herself but there was nothing she could think of to do except huddle in the doorway.

Amma climbed out first. Lalitha followed. It was not like the time she had descended like a queen from the bus, there was something lumpy, leaden about her movements. Both of them wore smiles, possibly for the jutka-wallah's benefit. Just a bit run-down, nothing serious, Amma announced, which was definitely for his benefit, she didn't normally speak so loudly. She opened the pill box she was carrying, displayed it to

Appa; Saroja could see large red tablets inside. Three of these daily, she'll be as right as rain, she said. Splendid, effused Appa. Well, let's hope so, said the *jutka* driver, climbing into his cart. Of course she will, Appa shouted after him jubilantly. There's no convincing these fellers, he said, shaking his head tolerantly as the *jutka* clattered away.

Amma looked at him. They are iron tablets, she said, and again Saroja felt that little scuffle of currents above her head as they all trooped in.

* * *

In Manikkam's hut there was only one room. If there was anything private going on they hustled the children out. If it was raining, the middle of the monsoon, they did not. In fact mostly they didn't bother because it was too much effort, the rowdier children hung around howling and hammering at the rickety hut until they were let in again, or they came over to Amma and Appa, which made for bad relations with Manikkam's best customer.

In Saroja's house there was the central room and smaller ones opening off it for grain storage and praying in and sleeping, but it came to the same thing anyway because everyone could hear what went on anywhere, there was no point in retreating to the smaller rooms, which weren't much bigger than cupboards and partitioned off only by curtains, so no one did. If you wanted to be private you had to go into the courtyard, which was open to all but at least you could see them coming; to be really private you had to go to the buffalo shed.

Lalitha had no liking for the buffalo shed but you could see she could have done with the shed from the longing glances she cast in its direction but no one was going to let her. They herded her in fact, like a precious heifer that had strayed, Appa in front and Aunt behind, and Amma holding her arm and propelling her forward. Saroja trailed after them. Her stomach was churning, she knew if you churned milk like that little globules of butter floated to the top and it made her wonder if fatty gobs were forming inside her belly, but more than that she wondered about the state of Lalitha's belly, which was even more harassed than her own.

Lalitha gave no sign. She sat among them and looked like a water lily. It made you feel coarse to look at her, all the lumpy qualities had subsided. Her beauty had returned, but in a different form: fined down and pale like the purest gold which the goldsmith said was good to look at but impossible to fashion, being too soft from an absence of dross.

No one took any notice of her. They talked round her and about her as if she weren't there but she was, a figurehead, a maypole round which they ran with their tangled ribbons. The ribbons were tatty and mournful, not a bright strand among them, the pattern was altogether woeful.

It has been confirmed, said Amma. Is it—? asked Appa. No question, said Amma. Ah-h-h! said Aunt Alamelu like an expiring animal. Appa bade her be

174

quiet but Aunt kept on with those wounded sounds. It began to be frightening, reminded Saroja of the soft cries Manikkam's wife had uttered, the bedraggled parcel in the corner. She could not connect Lalitha with such events, not even by calling up her imaginative powers, which were considerable. Is it a baby? she blurted. Are you some kind of simpleton? Appa wanted to know. Saroja forgave him, she knew he was upset, but she could feel it stinging. She told herself fiercely at least the simpleton hadn't got a baby inside her, which prevented the tears from spurting.

Amma was preoccupied, but she still noticed things. Why don't you leave her alone? she said. Why can't you leave her out, concentrate on the one that's in trouble? blazed Appa. Amma twisted her fingers together, her mouth was bitter. You have concentrated all right, she said, we can all see the result of the indulgences you have concentrated and lavished on one daughter.

God knows best, said Aunt. She was a rash woman. Amma and Appa stopped tearing at each other, went to work on her instead. Aunt Alamelu closed her eyes and rocked, she did it sitting, from the waist, like seaweed caught in a current but rooted in some soggy bed. Saroja suspected she had sealed off her hearing too because no matter what Amma and Appa threw at her she did not reply, did not rebut or refer to it even, merely kept on with what she was saying totally indifferent as to whether anyone was listening. God is good, she said, and, One must have faith in his boundless wisdom, and she told them the story of the little boy who was in reality God incarnate who had opened his mouth and revealed to astounded onlookers the world entire.

175

Appa sank into gloom, into silence before the advance of her thick, remorseless lava. He put his head in his hands. Amma's hands, which were laced in a basket, were supporting her forehead. When both were defeated Aunt Alamelu opened her eyes, focused them on a point above her brother-in-law's cranium and really began. Now you see, Brother, she said, where it has all led. Have I not said from the beginning no good would come of it? But who is there to heed an old woman, only when it is too late everyone comes knocking on her door.

No one is knocking, do you think if it were the last door, you old hag, have you gone clean out of your mind? cried Appa. He was electrified, had been taken by surprise so the words came out jumbled, made little sense, did not daunt Aunt, who had credos to expound that had been held back for years. Maypoles, she said, dancing around them and such Christian practices, is it a fitting pastime for our young Hindu maidens? And simpering with young men and flaunting themselves in films and such like, is there any propriety in it, no, it is shame-shame, totally contrary to the code of our Hindu decorum which has safeguarded the virtue of our youth for a thousand years. If it's gone on that long it's moldy, it stinks, it's high time it ended! shouted Appa. He had balled his fist, was thumping his open palm with it but Aunt carried on despite the ringing detonations. It is ended at our peril, Brother, she said, it is not for us puny denizens of this immoral age to question the wisdom of our ancient mentors.

She was in peril herself then. Appa sprang up, towered above her. His hand was raised. Our young people have a right to lead their own lives, he cried, are they to be deprived of their rights at the whim of mindless bigots like you? Aunt was dignified. She drew her sari over her head, which was threatened. You have given your children rights, Brother, she said, and they have come home to roost.

Appa would have struck her then, but Amma intervened. Do you want the whole village to hear? she cried. Can't you be calm? How can one think in this clamor? I am getting a headache.

Appa sat down. He was on his last legs, you could tell from the way his limbs buckled and let him down. Just get her away, for God's sake keep her away from me, he muttered, but Aunt had already gone, perhaps she guessed she had tried him too far, she had returned to the grain store. Now and then she rustled among the grain sacks, to remind of her presence, the good counsel she could provide if consulted but no one did. Saroja made to creep away too but Amma motioned her to stay. She divined that it was for her benefit, salutary, so that she could be armed against follies similar to Lalitha's, although this did not seem to her likely because she had not been cast in Lalitha's mold.

Amma's hands were still, usually they were occupied. Appa was stiff, his bones creaked when he moved. Lalitha was as quiet as the grave. Saroja stared at her, at that area of her which contained the baby, it seemed incredible that a tiny creature like it should cause so much bother, she remembered what Manikkam's wife had said and she entirely agreed. Lalitha must have felt the glance, she stirred, it was like a lever

177

releasing them all, there was a lot of shifting, Saroja was glad to stretch her limbs.

We must consider, said Amma, what is our best plan. Appa cleared his throat. The man ought to be horse-whipped, he said. It was one of his quaint sayings, a leftover from the British period, no one would horse-whip a man in India any more, not even a sepoy or a servant. It was also a last touch of bravura, a final flare which Amma quenched. We must discuss the matter with him, she said. Yes, said Appa, we must talk, it is the civilized thing to do . . . His eyes were misting. He felt in his pocket and drew out a crumpled sheath, this time he made no attempt to conceal it from his daughters. I educated the milkman, he said, but I couldn't do as much for my own child . . . she was innocent, and we let her go out as she was.

Lalitha raised her eyes. It was not his fault alone, it was mine as well, she let fall from bloodless lips. There is no fault, said Appa gently, at which there were strangled sounds from the grain store. No fault, he continued firmly, ignoring Aunt's anguish, unless it is with the world, it ticks like a cracked machine, comes up with a dirty wash whatever you put in it, it turns what is natural and magical into something sordid. His voice was warm, his eyes rested on Amma but she, flinty, upright, confronted by her own wounded flesh, would not respond to him, to this impractical dreamer as she had once called him in Saroja's hearing. It's a sin, she said, to bring an unwanted child into this world, cracked or otherwise. It's a sin to cause suffering to an unborn child, but what alternative—? Then she covered her face with her hands and wept.

178

Appa comforted her. He said pioneers always paid, they must think of their daughter as a pioneer. He patted her head, devised little schemes they might embark on which made little sense. Amma listened, she knew it was only to help her. Now and then she interrupted, dwelt on the scandal in the village, which had come uppermost now. Appa assured her there wouldn't be any. He had no sound reasons for his belief, rumors were already buzzing, they had been rife since Lalitha's escapade.

Listening to them, Saroja was torn between her parents; both were right, both were wrong. She wondered wildly why they couldn't solve the problem simply by the two of them marrying, Mr. Gupta and her sister, since his seed and her egg were already mated and fused in a baby. In her heart of hearts she knew why, the truth was that although both were Hindus, which was the important thing, their levels were different, not beyond the pale as she and Chingleput were, but unequal socially, which was almost as big an impediment.

It sicked her a little to think of it, because in her mind the baby had become paramount and she could see it had no future in what Appa and the boys called society as it was organized. It made her rebel. She plucked out the reality and anathematized it as her brothers did, but could not dent it, the reality had a dreadful persistence. So she passed it on, hoped devoutly, prayed with as much fervor as she could command that society be reorganized to make room for the baby.

Appa and Amma had all but run themselves dry, now they were reaching decisions. We must go to the city, said Appa; Anand can keep an eye on my affairs. I shall have to approach Perumal of course, travel is so expensive these days . . . And Saroja? murmured Amma, she was quick off the mark in case he reckoned the cost and cut out the younger daughter, which was clearly against her inclination. Ah yes, Saroja, said Appa. He cogitated. Saroja badly wanted not to be left behind, she said a prayer for herself while she listened to her heart thumping in the silence. Why, of course she must come with us, he said. Saroja let out an excited yelp, but it was eclipsed, swallowed up by Aunt, who had begun to shriek behind the grain-store curtain, the cotton was flapping with the might of her blasts.

Yes, take them both, she screeched, you are not a man, Brother, for half measures, it is not enough that one has been defiled, no, you will not be satisfied until you have delivered up two innocents for the city to devour.

I know what I'm doing, thundered Appa.

You're putting virgins in a whorehouse, shrieked Aunt.

It was so appalling that no one could go on; a raw and outraged silence fell.

*   *   *

SAROJA sounded out Chingleput, cautiously. He answered her straight. There are whores everywhere, he said. He shrugged dismissively. It's a way of earning a living. Especially in a city? Saroja probed. Perhaps, said Chingleput. There are more enticements in a city. To be a whore? Saroja asked. Who knows? Women have an entire battery of motives and incitements, said Chingleput, laughing. I'll tell you about the sea, he offered. Saroja accepted. There weren't many in the village who could talk about the sea, no one who could do it like Chingleput. When he spoke about it she could really imagine the unimaginable, she saw the fields of restless, rippling sapphire by sunlight, the leaping phosphorescence at night, the limitless sand which beyond belief was nothing but rock and the skeletons of sea creatures pulverized by the oceans.

It's magical, said Chingleput, in his faraway voice, in which Saroja detected accents, an ache, a shimmer of desire like her own buried in a subsoil of longing. I can hardly wait, she said. I don't suppose you'll get much more than a glimpse, said Chingleput. I don't see why not, argued Saroja. Well, there is your sister, he said.

But Saroja believed what she wanted to believe, which was that Lalitha would not, could not, monopolize the entire landscape.

* * *

THEY were going in a week. Meanwhile it was almost like old times.

Feel, said Lalitha.

Is there anything to feel? asked Saroja.

Maybe not, Lalitha admitted. She looked sideways at her sister. What day is it? she asked.

Two days to go, said Saroja.

181

One day, Saroja said. Lalitha was lying as if laid out. What is it? she asked her.

Nothing, said Lalitha. She opened her eyes. Nothing, little sweet, she said, and swung her legs to the floor.

Where are you going? asked Saroja. It was dusk. Amma and Appa had gone to the temple, one always did at the start of a journey. Aunt was slumbering.

Nowhere, said Lalitha. She was standing up. I'm going for a little walk, she said. She was walking along the path. Saroja stumbled after her. Where are you going? she called. Lalitha was walking quickly. You go back, she said roughly. No, I'll come too, I want to be with you, said Saroja. She was afraid, she didn't know why. Fear attacked her joints, rendered them clumsy. She knew the potholes by heart, but nevertheless she fell into them. Her mind was as disjointed as her limbs. Go back, said Lalitha, striding. She was a wraith in her pale clothes. Saroja was her shadow but not much of a shadow because the light was going, was almost gone, slivers of sun swam like frenzied goldfish in deepening inky pools.

When Lalitha took the fork Saroja knew. It led to the well where the woman walked in her dripping weeds, along the track where no one would walk by night.

She fought the knowledge. She ran up panting and placed herself in her sister's way to block her, she begged her to turn back, clung to her and besought her with the tears cascading down her face, but Lalitha would not. It's the suicide well, said Saroja. She named it, her teeth chattering, to try and exorcise the terror but it did not work, terror marched beside her step by step. I'm frightened, she gasped, she wailed, a long sighing wail that did not seem to be her own as she was dragged along in her sister's wake. I'm not, said Lalitha jerkily, I'm not afraid of ghosts, I'm not afraid of anything— Then why—? Only of facing him, she said, I cannot, I cannot. They blundered on. Saroja looked round wildly but there was nothing, no hut, no homestead, no human whom she could summon to their aid, only this dark plain over which they were borne which was infested with what she did not know but saw the loopy trails, the luminous plumes of sly presences that rose in the blackness and brushed against her eyeballs. Saroja prayed. She closed her eyes to conserve her strength, which could be drained by sights, and clung to her demented sister, and the two of them advanced, grappled together by their opposed and clashing resolves.

When they were close Saroja knew because of the bog that surrounded the well. It sucked at her feet, slithered over her instep and closed round her ankles. Her sandals were gone. She was floundering, trapped in slimy ooze that denied her a hold, a purchase. I'm falling, she shrieked. She fell, she was on her knees in the morass but lunged at her sister and held her, they were welded by mud and flesh into one.

Let go! cried Lalitha. I'll take you with me, she screamed, and fought like a demon. Saroja fought back. She was suddenly strong, she did not want to die, she was not going to die if she could help it. Her muscles responded. They were trim, in training from hauling and heaving at countless beasts from countless quagmires, whereas Lalitha's strength, which also came from her spirit, had little muscular backing.

It was only a question of time.

It was over. They lay on the crust of the bog, panting.

If the woman walked, as she had through the darks and depths of her childhood's phases, she would walk no more for Saroja. That, too, was over. She turned to her sister. Never again, she said: Promise. I promise, never again, said Lalitha.

*　*　*

WHEN they got back their parents were outside, searching. Amma was carrying an oil lamp, a wick in a saucer such as they lit only at Deepavali. Appa, armed with a hurricane lantern, was advancing warily over the hazardous pathway. What on earth—? he said when he saw them. Where—? How—?

Amma said nothing. She brought water for her daughters, who were caked in mud, stood in the oblong of light by the doorway while they crouched outside and washed the worst of it off. The silence rang in their ears like a muffled bell.

What happened? asked Appa, blundering up. Did you fall in the river?

The river was as dry as a bone. At this season you could see the cracks in the waterbed as every country-man knew. Saroja flew to his aid, to Lalitha's, to her own, she could not endure for the abyss to open again, not so soon after. The buffalo, she said, it strayed into a paddy field, it was up to its hocks . . . it was a struggle, she gasped, riven by memory, shivering and trembling while next to her Lalitha stood rigid, a stony, petrified column.

Aunt Alamelu ushered them in. Her cluck-clucking, the warm familiar interior, the pungent aroma of *sambrani* smoldering in a corner, pushed back the nightmare, introduced opportunities for pretending, for allowing the ordinary to resume. Appa castigated the buffalo, all buffaloes, especially the one he was fated to own. Amma scolded the girls, said this time they had really exceeded the limit, she advised them to pay close attention to what she was saying. Saroja attended. Lalitha listened with drooping eyelids, swore when challenged that not a word had escaped her, which seemed to Saroja dubious. Aunt made ginger *kasayam*. She called it an infallible elixir, it was her remedy for all manner of ills. The concoction came up steaming: crushed ginger root and sugar and spice infused in boiling water sent up strong, fragrant fumes. Aunt pounded the ginger root freshly each time, in a ponderous pestle and mortar, her eyes streaming from the sharp vapors, for she would have no truck with the ready-made kind, which was good neither for man nor beast, she said. The process took longer. It taught you to be patient.

Drink, said Aunt. Tears, snail trails of her dedication, glistened on her cheeks. Saroja drank gratefully, the powerful potion slid healing and burning down her throat. Over the rim of the bowl she watched Lalitha. Her sister looked normal; you would never have known. Under her eyelids, slyly, she glanced from face to face. All were normal, you would never have guessed what sizzled below. It filled her with awe that such astonishing powers of deception should lurk in the most humdrum, ordinary human frames.

5

SUGARCANE GREW, AS tall as a man, on either side of the road. When the wind blew the canes clashed with a sound like the rattling of sabers in a cinema saga. Ripe for cutting, said the passenger next to Saroja. They were not. The canes were an acid green and as thin as laths, you looked for a change in color and a girth of three fingers minimum before you cut. The passenger was a townsman. You spotted the townsmen from the remarks they came out with. Their turn would come later, when the country was left behind, but the countrymen were craftier, channeled their ignorance into civil questions, eschewed downright statements which would catch them out. You don't say! they exclaimed, and asked, humbly, Is that a fact? The bus was evenly divided between townspeople and country folk.

Rattling and honking the bus raced toward the city, its birthplace. It had been assembled there, part by shining part. Saroja knew because one of the boys had worked for a time in the factory where it was done. Nothing was shiny now, the bloom was off, except the knob of the gear much polished by the driver's palm. The country went leisurely by, you forgot you were hurtling along if you took your gaze off the road, extended it to take in the land. The hurtling was lovely, Saroja could not have enough of it, she bobbed up and down on the wooden seat and beat down her ballooning skirts as vigorously as the other women were doing. Now and again, though, she found it restful to look at the land, it linked with the orb enclosed within her, which rode with her wherever she went.

Paddy fields went by; paddy birds stalked among them, legs like stilts made of palest coral. Corn fields, the cobs wearing silk tassels of green and umber. Coconut groves, with huts clustered in the shade of the palms, tiny villages nowhere the size of their own. At one such they stopped, beside a tea stall. When the engine died your body ceased juddering, you felt there was something abnormal about being so still, it was like a new sensation. The driver swung round expertly and lowered himself backward onto the ground. The passengers tumbled out anyhow. They looked like dusty millers, everyone without exception was liberally coated, even eyelashes were not exempt.

Ten minutes, the driver said, surveying his flock. He tapped his wristwatch to emphasize the point; it had a luminous pink dial and was as big as a saucer. Appa glanced at his watch as well; it was nothing like as magnificent. Would you like some tea? he asked his family. Saroja nodded, she was quite parched. Lalitha made no answer. Her face had bilious tinges. Or a mango juice? asked Appa, spotting a crate full of bottles. Nothing, gasped Lalitha, her hand flew to her mouth. She fled a few yards to a cactus bush, they heard her retching.

Saroja drank her tea, feeling sorry for her sister. The sorrow wasn't enough to mar her pleasure in the journey. Appa consulted his watch. All set? he called. Ten minutes up! Lalitha emerged and rejoined them. That feels much better, she said with false cheer. Good, said Appa, and helped her into the bus. He shepherded Amma and Saroja in, and climbed up himself.

They were the only four passengers in their seats in the entire bus. Appa was frowning. He held up his watch and rapped the dial to show it was time to be off, but no one paid any attention. He bent forward and, to Saroja's horror, sounded the horn. It blasted everyone into silence, the cheerful humming around the tea stall instantly subsided. The driver, who had been holding forth, stopped in midsentence, revolved round slowly, looking for the culprit. Appa honked again; he was nothing if not brave. This time the driver put down his tumbler of tea, sauntered up with his hands in the pockets of his khaki shorts and leaned against the flank of his bus. What's the hurry, brother? he asked. About to have kittens or something?

Half an hour later they set off again. Lalitha had bundled herself right up to the eyebrows. Amma was unapproachable, an offended hedgehog. She rebuffed the women passengers with whom she had previously passed the time of day, stared fixedly out of the window. Appa was more robust. He had recovered his voice, chatted freely with his fellow passengers, accepted the fruit that they were passing round and passed some round himself. There were segments of orange, bananas, guavas, pomegranate, taken from rustling straw-lidded baskets.

Saroja was invited to share a pomegranate. The seeds poured into her cupped palm, lay there sparkling like jewels, stained the skin red. She crunched them up whole, seeds and pulp together. The seeds were gritty, but Aunt Alamelu maintained they were good for your bones. It also saved having to spit them out. Spitting and hawking, claimed Aunt, were the uncleanly habits of Christians who, she told them, shuddering, did not mind about spittle, thought nothing of using the same drinking cups. Miss Mendoza was a Christian but she did not spit, at least not blatantly. When she came to the pips in the grapes Amma had proffered her she lifted a spoon to her lips and blew them out with discreet little puffs, laying the spoon each time on the very edge of her plate. Saroja had watched closely, she had not seen anyone cope like this before. After a while Miss Mendoza desisted; they could hear the pips being ground between her teeth, her throaty swallowing. Soon she stopped eating grapes.

Saroja finished the last jeweled seed. She was thirsty, but she did not want to disturb Amma, who was asleep with the flask of water lodged in her lap. Instead she watched the road unrolling behind them, thought of

Chingleput, who had made this very same journey. But he had walked, not ridden in a bus. He had walked every step of the way, dragging his crippled foot. It suffused her with warm feelings thinking of him, his courage. At the same time it made her ache, she had to lean down and surreptitiously massage her foot. Her foot was a good shape, with a high arch and straight toes. Chingleput's foot twisted inward, his toes were all mashed together and had horny, misshapen nails. It was a wonder anyone could walk with that, but Chingleput wrapped sacking round it and managed. He managed very well.

Saroja dozed. She did not want to, journeys like this did not happen every day, but everyone else was dozing and it was catching. She slept, her head nodding and dipping uncomfortably, until she felt Amma's arm about her and she relaxed thankfully against the plump, soft flesh. When she woke it was midafternoon. The bus had stopped. All change, all change, the driver was shouting. Have we arrived? asked Saroja. She looked round and saw they couldn't possibly have, they seemed to be in the middle of nowhere. It's the bus halt, we get our connection here, explained Appa. He got up and began collecting his belongings together as others were doing.

The travelers, decanted from the bus onto the stony road, stood about waiting with their baskets and bundles spread around them. It was airless, very still. There was no sign of a bus. Where the spillage occurred a tea stall had been set up, but it wasn't much use as no one was manning it. People were getting peevish, they complained about the bus service, squinted up at the sun, which was at its zenith, and recounted cases of heat-stroke suffered by their relatives on this very spot. Appa looked very stern, said there was no doubt but that they had missed their connection, he had foreseen it happening which was why he had attempted to hurry them along. Those who had dallied over tea and talk looked guilty, even harassed, but a few brave souls spoke up, denied it was their responsibility and pinned the blame on the vanished bus driver. Appa got heated, then he cooled down. He did not intend to lose his temper, he told them, it was too hot for that, he would only opine that you couldn't run a country without a sense of time, or if you did there were penalties to pay such as missing vital connections. As he was speaking there was a distant rumbling and a bus hove into view.

The journey resumed. Saroja said to herself she wished it would never end, but the truth was she was a bit jolted, her seat was sore from bumping up and down on the wooden bench. She wondered about Lalitha, her heart went out to her sister, who had begun the journey feeling unwell, but when she turned round and looked she saw Lalitha was composed, the green tints had gone from her face. How are you? she asked. Fine, said Lalitha, are you enjoying the trip? She was smiling, there were dark rings under her eyes but the sparkle was back in them. Saroja thought with respect about her sister's qualities, she felt sure she could not have borne up the way Lalitha was doing, or gone off on this same long journey on her own, flinging herself at the unknown without so much as a basket of fruit or a single relative or friend to sustain her.

Well, are you? asked Lalitha. It's lovely, but I wish we

were there, it is a bit tiring, said Saroja. Cities are, said Lalitha.

There was no sign of a city, only the symptoms which Saroja recognized from descriptions of which there had been no lack in her life. The road was congested, they were no longer in sole ownership. Road users had multiplied tenfold, there were bicycles, buses, cars and carts to share with. The cars flashed past, by comparison the bus seemed to lumber along, its pretensions to high speed exposed.

The real dawdlers were the bullock carts, in the general race they hardly seemed to be moving. Passengers and drivers alike grew impatient, leaned out of windows and shouted and swore but you couldn't hurry the bullocks, they had their own pace and were not to be stampeded. Saroja's sympathy spurted strongly for the patient beasts, plodding along quite senselessly as far as they knew on this endless road, bearing the heavy yokes on their necks. In Miss Mendoza's school, which was Christian, they taught that animals were created for men, that God gave man dominion over beasts. It revolted Lalitha. She accepted a good deal but she could not accept that, she stuck to her own creed, which said each creation had its own right. Men used animals, of course, but you did it with circumspection, the injunction was upon you not to encroach on their integrity. There were divisions in Lalitha which stemmed from her school, made her part company from Saroja, whose school was differently rooted, but they came together in crucial matters like this, in basics she and Saroja and Amma and Appa and Aunt were of one mind.

The bullock carts went in convoy, seven, eight, ten

strung together in one long creaking cavalcade. They caused maximum irritation, you could not careen past them as the cars and buses wanted to do. Saroja had no such desire, she liked their measured pace, she did not mind trailing along behind the carts watching the bullocks' tails whisking, but she kept her thoughts to herself, not wanting to be called a peasant.

When it began to be dusk the convoys halted while the lanterns slung under the carts were lit. Some of them stopped where they were, right in the middle of the road, which set off fierce slanging matches between the bus drivers and carters. No consideration, no consideration whatever, pronounced Appa severely, the nearer they got to the city the more he took the side of city folk. Saroja thought there was the other side to it, which was the barrowloads of dust the buses raised and showered liberally upon the bullocks and carters in passing, but she didn't say this either because the inkling was hardening it didn't do to be countrified this close to a town, it was like a slur upon your capacities.

Town and country. The phrase resurrected the story retailed to her by Lalitha, who had got it from Miss Mendoza, about a town mouse and a country mouse. The way the story went, the town mouse visiting his country cousin had lamented the loss of his town comforts while enjoying what the country had to offer, while on a return visit it had been the other way round. The moral, as far as she could remember, was that there were snags in both life styles. Saroja was inclined to agree. As yet she had not experienced the life, but the styles were clearly different. She liked the noise, the activity, the market-day bustle that worked up each time they neared a town, and the lights strung along the streets like necklaces were altogether magical. On the other hand, she would not have cared to live as towns-people did, jammed together with neither pasture nor tillage to be seen nor spear of grass nor interstice of land, the natural world was altogether sunk under brick and cement, the entire horizon cluttered with buildings.

It grew worse, you wouldn't have thought it could but it did. The jumble of houses and hovels spread like a rash, slithered into each other and merged until there was one huge sprawling ugliness. At the height of this congestion, in the very middle of it, they stopped. They had reached the city, they were at the bus terminus which Appa said was in the city center.

Do we get off? asked Saroja. She regretted the question the moment it was out, nothing was more obvious than that it was the only thing to do. Appa, however, was too preoccupied to notice. He was urging them to hurry, he told them his one fear was that all the *jutkas* would be snaffled, leaving them stranded, since his knowledge of the city was no longer fresh, was rusty in fact, he could not guide them to their hotel as infallibly as he would once have been able.

While he spoke he stood by his seat, unaware he was blocking the other passengers until they told him. The way they did it you wouldn't have known they were the same people who had offered and accepted mangoes and pomegranates, they seemed to have lost all their manners. Appa jumped down. He stood guard over the belongings Amma was handing out, said his one fear was some city hoodlum would decamp with the lot. His fears multiplied, ate away his confidence. You wouldn't have suspected he was city-born.

Lalitha, on the other hand, was composure itself. She had been there twice before of course, but something more than the veneer of two visits invested her. I'll get a *jutka*, she said, you wait here. Appa left it to her. She has grit, he said, and even allowing for his customary panegyrics Saroja had to agree, she could not have coped as Lalitha was coping, she would have not known where to turn in the maelstrom of humanity through which Lalitha was breasting her nonchalant way. But then Lalitha was not, despite the accident of birth, as she took pains to tell you, a country girl: her soul, since the advent of Mr. Gupta, belonged to the city.

*　　*　　*

THEY were staying in a hotel which Anand had recommended.

No one thought much of Anand's recommendation but no one said so except Lalitha, who said it was a revelation. Of what, Amma was piqued into asking. Of how abysmal village standards can be, answered Lalitha, and she prowled around the room in which the four of them were incarcerated, pointing out flaws and faults which, she declared, amounted in toto to catastrophe. Amma was torn. Anand was the last person she wanted to champion, he was the inextricable thorn in her flesh. At the same time you could see she would have liked to flay Lalitha, concerning herself with such outward trifles at this disastrous time in her life. In the end she left it, said merely it would be wise to conserve their energies for the morning and set to opening their bedrolls and spreading their sleeping mats, necessary acts which encircled and finally disposed of her acrimony.

In the morning there were *idlies*, still wrapped in the muslin in which they had been steamed, dazzling white on bottle-green squares of banana leaf. Appa had bought them from the coffee shop opposite, two apiece. Saroja could have demolished the same again, but she didn't like to ask, she knew money was short. She blotted up the delicious floury crumbs left on her leaf with a careful finger, speculated on the day which was to be spent in tackling *him*. *He* and *him* were Mr. Gupta. No one seemed keen on naming the name: gone was the name-dropping era which had flourished, especially at school. You had brought it out airily then, dangled it like a medallion in front of the popping eyes of the girls. Mr. Gupta is Europe-trained. Mr. Gupta is making a film in which Lalitha will star. Uttering it now only made you feel queasy, you knew you should dismiss it if you could. Saroja did. She concentrated on the day itself, which had a life of its own. The day was fine. It was sunlit and clear, you could easily fancy there were joyful secrets sewn into its unseen, shimmering pockets.

You look happy, said Lalitha.

It's the smell, it's so lovely, said Saroja.

It wasn't a lie, not altogether. There was a smell, it drifted in from the compound, came from an old cork tree that had struggled up from the beaten earth. Cork flowers, said Lalitha, her eyes met her sister's, sharing a memory. Years ago there had been a cork tree on Appa's land, its starry white flowers carpeted the ground, gave off this sweet, piercing scent. If you broke off the stalk, blew down it in a certain way it made a sound like a tin trumpet. The boys had shown them how, they were still at home then, it was in the era, now misted over, before they had left their village.

Do you remember? asked Lalitha.

Of course, said Saroja. She darted out, she was single-minded, forgot it was the hotel compound not Appa's land until reminded by the curious stares of other residents but even that did not deter her. Here, she said, returning triumphant and laden and dropping the white stars in her sister's lap. Do you think it'll work? asked Lalitha. They puffed out their cheeks and blew together, split the quiet of the room with tinny, gratifying squeaks.

Appa looked at Saroja. Trust you, he said. Amma spread the blame equally, gave them a lecture on the need for decorum. Especially in cities, she said, the need was greatest there, men took advantage of the slightest lapse, the least fall in grace or modest behavior encouraged their lusts. Saroja got the impression of males prowling through the streets like wolves, on the lookout for girls like her sister and herself to seduce.

Of course they wouldn't know that Lalitha had already been seduced. Or would they? Saroja wondered furtively if there was some way men had of telling, perhaps from some mark visible only to them that you were, or the way you laid out your body for them. Or did they find out, inserting an exploring finger as Jaya had told how? Saroja felt herself blushing, the blood came up, her throat, the lobes of her ears were warm, were burning, she had to turn away in case Amma noticed. But Amma already had, not much escaped her, even less when all of you were cooped up in one room, nowhere to run to, no escape routes open. At least one of my children, she said, has the innocence to blush, which made Lalitha hang her head, made her flinch for her lost innocence which both of them knew was an indispensable dew and annointment for maidens.

Appa was waiting on the verandah outside. He always fled when Amma sparred with Lalitha, but this wasn't home, he couldn't get very far. The verandah ran the length of the rooms, of which there were eight or nine, it served them all, being a communal run for the residents. It had a parapet of fat little balusters, against which a half-dozen residents were leaning, though each took care to keep within his own rightful portion. Appa did the same, he paced up and down his own slice of verandah, eschewed fraternizing, which Amma had warned him against in case he let slip, she was really afraid of that, but he was friendly by nature, he could not refrain from sundry courteous peeps in their direction while he waited for his family.

It made Amma frown to hear him. She tightened her lips, implied all *her* talking would be done at *his* place. Are you ready? she asked her daughters. They were, they had been for quite some time, the strangeness of their sleeping quarters, the sound of the traffic thundering by, had roused them long before their accustomed hour.

Well, remember, said Amma. It was difficult to know which of her innumerable injunctions she meant, but they nodded solemnly, it was a solemn occasion, when she took time off from the distractions of the city Saroja could feel her spirits sinking, dragged down by the portentous nature of their mission.

Amma wore her country sandals. They were like Saroja's, had brown plaited thongs and bifurcated your toes at their natural break, big toe to one side, little siblings on the other. Lalitha had on what she called her town pair, which she had bought in this very city, out of the money she had taken without permission from Appa. They were made of a supple creamy leather, there was a latticework canopy that trapped all five toes, and a strap that encircled the ankle and stopped the sandals' soles flip-flapping against your own. Town or country, though, you got plastered with dust: Lalitha's feet were no better off than Saroja's as far as that went, even if they were more smartly shod.

* * *

In Mr. Gupta's house there was no dust. The floor gleamed. It was made of tiles, which were blue with gold flecks in them like the mica specks which made Rangu's River sparkle and dance on a sunny day. It's a heavenly blue, said Saroja, she whispered, she was not at ease in *his* house but the color insisted on comment. Aqua, corrected Lalitha, seawater blue. Amma shot them a glance, which reduced them to silence.

Silence, of the kind in which your thoughts were threshing and writhing, was not really silence at all. It

was distinctly bad for the nerves. Your body was crawling with nerves, roots, fibers, nerve endings, all of
which were making you twitch. It was the waiting, and
not knowing, that did it. Saroja bit her lips, hard. Pain
could take your mind off some things, divert it to
others, but Saroja's mind jibbed. It had abdicated its
main function, which was control, and watched the
turbulent antics of her body with sadistic pleasure. Her
parents, she observed, were in no better shape. They
were brittle in part, stiff as boards on the satiny chairs
on which servants had invited them to seat themselves,
and part of them jiggling, Amma plucking at the
fringed ends of her sari, Appa tugging at the skin of his
jaw, which was severely nicked from the overclose
shave he had given it that morning. Now and then he
glanced at his watch, he did not rap smartly on the dial
as he had done on the bus, he did it surreptitiously as
if he did not want the servants to note his impatience.

The servants made you uncomfortable. You could
tell they were looking you over, found you odd, although they kept well in the background. In the midst
of her discomfort Saroja felt a nugget of consolation,
felt glad there were servants: it confirmed what Lalitha
had said, which Jaya had disputed. When she got back,
she resolved, she would confront Jaya. Umpteen servants, she would say, reduce her to confusion with the
facts which upheld Lalitha, who needed every bit of
support that could be scraped together to counterweigh
the scandal of her pregnancy.

Pregnancy could be one thing, it could be quite another. The imbalances of this condition exercised
Saroja. If you were married and got pregnant everyone

was pleased except those unfortunate women who were barren. There were little ceremonies to call down blessings on you and when the baby was born everyone came round smiling bringing little presents. Even Manikkam's unwanted additions were welcomed, though his resources were nil, even by Appa, who bawled him out for his irresponsibility but never failed to stump up a gift or two.

If you weren't married and became pregnant the picture was quite different, it was altogether grim. You hushed it up as best you could and your baby, if ever it got born, had no future at all. Saroja thought it wrong: she often mulled about it, especially since her sister, and always reached the same conclusion. It was wrong, a crime against the baby, which was the same whether you were married or not, but she knew her elders like Aunt Alamelu who were the majority did not agree. It's the same the world over, Aunt claimed, but Appa disputed, asked how she knew. He said there were young people coming up who would refuse to crucify passion or the innocent fruits of passion. Fruits of unbridled lust, cried Aunt, she was beside herself. Of nature, said Appa. Then society will tame the beast! Aunt shouted. Nature is not beastly! Appa shouted back.

For all the shouting you knew. You sidled between and you knew then that all the rules and restrictions against which you had chafed since you were a little girl, all were designed, it was amply confirmed as you grew older, to stop you becoming pregnant until the marriage knot had been tied. It didn't work. There were dozens of unmarried girls with babies in the village. They would have been happy, the babies were darlings, but society wouldn't allow them to be, society the beastly tamer.

Not girls from families like ours, said Amma. These are low-class girls of low intelligence. She was wrong. Lalitha was none of these things but Lalitha was pregnant. From time to time there had been other girls like her too. Exceptions that prove the rule, claimed Amma. She stuck to her belief even after Lalitha, but she was less vocal. A family like theirs had produced a girl just like the others.

Saroja wrested herself away from this line of thinking, it offered little consolation. She stared at the pictures on *his* walls. They were different from the ones Amma put up, which were of Radha and Krishna, and Lakshmi, and Rama and Sita. Amma admired Sita, whom she did not resemble a great deal if you went by all that the sages had written about her. Sita was purity itself, she was devoted to Rama, her husband and god, would not have lifted her eyes to another. Amma was free with her looks, she stroked and caressed her own flesh, you could spot the seeds which had sprouted in Lalitha, her ways with her eyes and limbs, though Lalitha had added finesse of her own: but if Appa had taken to the wilderness (which was difficult to imagine, but Saroja finally succeeded) Amma would have followed him without a second thought. They bickered, over Anand and Aunt and Lalitha, shouted, were cold with each other more often than they were melting and tender, but Saroja knew Amma would have been bereft without Appa, and worse the other way round. She fell to wondering if her sister and Mr. Gupta were the same, bound and linked similarly, but it was hampering not having seen them together much. Imagination, of course, could fill in a good deal, but the kernel had to be there to begin with, the kernel which in this case had largely been formed in the city.

In the midst of this there were footsteps. It's him, said Appa, smoothing his hair. It wasn't. It was Devraj. Saroja! he said. It was the first thing he said. There were two tones to his voice, surprise and pleasure. Pleasure the uppermost. I did not expect to see you, he said. Appa rose, forestalled Saroja, who had been about to respond with answering pleasure. Mr. Gupta is expecting us, he said. I have an appointment . . . we have some urgent business to discuss. He was embarrassed, his Adam's apple chugged up and down, sharply.

Mr. Gupta has been detained, said Devraj.

An important appointment, said Devraj. His mouth was dry, he had to lick his lips to utter.

You learned at your mother's knee—you discovered it to be true for yourself later—that lies dried up the springs of saliva. A divine chemistry, it was said to be, a rejection, by that part of God which was in you, of pollutants of the spirit, which lies were. But Devraj wasn't lying on his own account, he was doing it for another. Saroja absolved him. She kept her eyes fixed on the seawater floor, from which his limbs rose like some ocean god's. They were clad in a foamy white dhoti. The molding, the power of those legs was visible through the muslin. As far as the knee, as far as eye could see. Eyelids down, that was the field of your roving eyeballs. Saroja lifted and leveled her lids but veiled her pupils, so that no one could tell where her gaze was wandering. Her heart was a hollow thudding chamber.

I understand, Devraj was saying.

My business is going to pot, stressed Appa. I have urgent affairs to attend to, I cannot hang about, you understand.

I understand, said Devraj.

Time, said Amma, significantly.

Time is crucial, said Appa. It is most urgent.

Next week, said Devraj.

Without fail, it is a vital matter, said Appa. His throat was working dreadfully.

Without fail, said Devraj.

He advanced, placed an arm around Appa's shoulders, which were juddering. When he raised his arm the sleeve fell away, gave a glimpse of the springy bush in the pit. Saroja felt herself judder like Appa. She hoped it was on her sister's account, but she could not dupe herself. At that moment she cared nothing about polluting her soul with a lie, but it simply would not come. She felt afraid. She was afraid of her feelings, of what he was doing to her. But he had done nothing, beyond pronouncing her name and one sentence.

Saroja opened her eyes, which had closed involuntarily. The others were standing. She jumped up too, knocking over a table in her haste. It was made of glass but it didn't break, she ascribed that to some saving miracle. Appa had on his long-suffering look, it had displaced the suffering. Devraj righted the fallen table. Not to worry, he said. It could have been for them generally, or just possibly for Saroja alone. I will not detain you further, then, Appa was saying. They were going. Saroja did not turn her head until they were safely past the gates, and then there was nothing to be seen but the compound wall which was studded with blue, green and tawny broken glass bottles.

The colors persisted, dancing in front of her eyes whether open or closed. They were the same as the colors that glinted from stars, green, blue and fiery. At home there were stars. You dragged your charpoy into the courtyard and lay watching them, you made up stories about the constellations, vied with Lalitha in the brilliance of your invention. You went on from there, topics were boundless, starlight induced them like bhang which unlocked Manikkam's lips from which poured endless, wondrous tales.

There were no stars to watch from the hotel room. The window was too small, set too low; the tiny lozenge of sky it gave you was imperforate, offered little opportunity. Saroja's deprived mind turned fractious. She longed to whisper to Lalitha, but she could not, there were four of them packed in the room. She returned to the lozenge, implanted a star to liven up the blank. After a little she could not be sure if the twinkling was real or imaginary. Sometimes bare sky yielded stars if you looked hard enough, they were there all the time, millions of them, more than enough for everyone born or to be born.

The star you were born under had to be in harmony with your husband's. If it were inimical the marriage was doomed. Actually it wouldn't come to that, you wouldn't have been allowed to marry in the first place unless you were headstrong, as Manikkam's wife said Lalitha was. Saroja wondered about Mr. Gupta's and

Lalitha's stars, if they were in harmony. Judging from the ructions she decided they could not possibly be. Whereas hers and Devraj's, she was convinced, were. Only you couldn't, of course, ask a man about his star. Such questions weren't put until there were intentions. There were absolutely none where Saroja and Devraj were concerned. No respectable intentions, which were tied up with marriage. The only kind there could possibly be between them was the kind between Mr. Gupta and Lalitha, which had landed them in such a dreadful mess. The sort you were warned against, told was disgusting, with Lachu held up to prove it. Lachu was disgusting. The sight of him jerking and grunting and ramming himself in full view returned to Saroja, sickened her. She tossed and turned, her body an alien creature full of strange, strong impulses beyond her control. She could not sleep. She hadn't slept a wink when it was time to wake up.

*   *   *

You were talking in your sleep last night, said Amma.

Saroja's heart rushed into her mouth. The taste was terrible. She had once seen a conjuror put a toad on his tongue, close his lips over it and make it vanish. She imagined the taste was the same, though it would be the feel as well which was involved. When Miss Mendoza worshipped she took God into her mouth. Lalitha said actually it was a wafer, it changed miraculously into a slice of God when placed on your tongue. Saroja rated this impossible, but Lalitha narrowed her eyes and said there are many ways of loving, and love was miraculous. This rang true to Saroja, but not as applied to Miss Mendoza.

In Miss Mendoza's house there was a picture of her God with his chest cut cruelly open. You could not see the chest because of the robes, but the heart was revealed. It was neat and trim and ruby-colored, not a bit like the raw hearts you saw in Muslim butcheries, or the organ that thudded with blood and emotion inside you, swelled and took up the whole of your rib cage so that you thought you would suffocate. The heart in the picture was meek and mild, it didn't foster your faith in miracles. There is such a thing as religious love, it is nearer to ecstasy, Lalitha said, all niminy-piminy like Miss Mendoza. Love is ecstasy, she said in her own natural tones. She had not said that for some time, it occurred to Saroja, in fact not for quite a long time.

Did something disturb you? probed Amma.

Yes. No. I just couldn't sleep, said Saroja, swallowing.

Neither could I, said Lalitha.

That is hardly surprising, said Amma.

Bats squeaking, interposed Appa, all night long.

Bat squeaks are inaudible to human ears, said Lalitha.

Well, I heard them, said Appa. He was ruffled, being unused to onslaughts from that quarter. He looked rough too, obviously had not slept well. When he rubbed his hand over his chin there was a rasping sound.

I'll get some tea, he said, then we can think what to do.

What is there to do except wait for his lordship? inquired Amma.

It's the waiting that wears one out, said Appa.

He wandered out for the tea. On the way back he paused to exchange greetings with fellow residents, it prolonged itself into a conversation. Appa's voice perked up, he was not good at enduring gloom. Trust your father, said Amma. The cat'll be out of the bag in no time, she prophesied grimly, and planned the remainder of the day to stall him.

They decided to go to the beach, partly at Saroja's suggestion, mainly because it was free. We're off to sample the sea air, it's good for the lungs, cried Appa, wrenching himself away from his newfound cronies. Yes, yes, excellent for the lungs, they chorused endorsement, glued to the verandah wall. Your father would make a wedding out of a funeral, Amma said sourly, marching on firmly with her daughters beside her, but Saroja would not condemn the ability wholesale, she was a bit fed up with the gloom, besides she felt funerals and Lalitha were best kept well apart.

The beach was everything Saroja had pictured and Chingleput had described. It was more. She could hardly believe it. She kicked off her sandals and raced along the sand, which spurted up in little warm fountains between her toes. Sea breeze was in her face, it smelled of brine, she had never smelled air as fresh as this before.

It's glorious, she called to Lalitha, who was catching up fast behind. Delectable, sang Lalitha, and reached out for Saroja. They clasped hands, sped down the sloping beach into the sea. Wavelets lapped round their ankles. It's cold! shrieked Saroja, but it wasn't, it was exhilarating, her limbs were tingling with pleasure. They waded in farther, bunching their skirts, to where the waves reared up greener, taller, curled and broke. When they retreated you could feel them towing you after them, and your toes dug into the sucking sands to keep you firm, and you discovered little highlands on which you were perched which had not been scoured away because you were implanted on top.

Saroja jumped off the highlands into the receding sea, but it turned in the blink of an eye, rushed back and swamped her before she could escape, screeching, up the soused slope. She splashed in the pools. The water fell back sparkling like crushed diamonds. Water baby! shouted Lalitha. Saroja agreed. She loved the sea. The sea was discovery, like nothing seen or described. It was also time remembered, an echo, a lost memory of something that ran in her veins.

They came out only because Amma was calling. The border of Lalitha's sari, the hem of Saroja's skirt, were sopping. They squeezed out the water, sat on the beach and spread out the folds to dry. I shall sing, Saroja said. She ran her tongue over her lips, which tasted salty, and sang a jolly, salty sea song Chingleput had taught her.

I wish I were you, said Lalitha.

Saroja stopped singing.

I too could be happy, said Lalitha.

Aren't you? asked Saroja.

Of course, said Lalitha, arranging damp pleats over the tiny hump of her baby. Come on, she said, time's up.

They heaved themselves up, rejoined their parents. Thought you were never coming, said Amma. She handed them the roast peas Appa had bought, each portion done up in a paper cone. The peas were still warm. They were buttery yellow with rustling brown skins which flaked off when you rubbed them between your fingers. The cones were generously filled, even for Saroja. She sat back replete. She weighted her ballooning skirts with sand and lay with her elbow supporting her. Small boys were sailing kites, the sky was streaked with twirly tails and shivering paper. At beach level vendors were selling little windmills of bright plastic. Saroja wished she was half her age, she would have liked to buy one but she did not want to be called childish. No such thoughts hindered Lalitha, she was already cajoling Appa. They selected a windmill together, laughing, inviting the vendor to laugh at them, which he did, stuck it in the sand and watched it whirring furiously in the wind.

When it was time to go Lalitha offered to take them back by a different route. On the way she pointed out the fashionable districts, made little detours to show them the expensive shops that rich people patronized. Saroja was fascinated, she was also a little awed by the prices charged, which seemed to her beyond anyone's competence. Lalitha said they were nothing, the really expensive items were those with no price tags on at all. Cost the earth, she said, she knew only because she had been taken to these very boutiques. Saroja believed her, she had seen the creamy sandals, but she did not envy her sister, she knew she would have felt thoroughly uncomfortable inside one of these splendid establishments.

It was none too comfortable walking through these

fashionable areas either. The place swarmed with limousines which cruised up and down, picking up and setting down women in smart clothes who eyed their little party, lifted carmine-tipped fingers to their lips and, she felt certain, tittered behind those polished ovals. Saroja had on her best outfit, green silk and a coin-spot scarf which she had thought were the height when she donned them, but somehow now they dwindled, the way the women eyed them she knew they were outlandish and give-away, positively shrieked of country. It made her feel awful, the way she had felt in Mr. Gupta's house under the sidelong scrutiny of the servants. She was sure these stylish ladies despised them, she conceded with every excuse because looking with their eyes she could see how they must appear, a homespun slab of ambling peasantry.

Excluding Lalitha, who had an air, cream sandals, and her beauty which outclassed that of all these city ladies.

Lalitha's beauty. You had had to lump it, live with it since you were born, but now it came into its own. Emboldened by association, Saroja lifted her head, stepped blithely again.

* * *

LONG before the week was up Appa was bosom friends with their two neighbors. Both of them were men, indeed most of the residents were men on their own. Appa said it was a hellish task finding somewhere to live in the city, people who could afford to gave up the struggle and lodged permanently in hotels.

He told how he had been in similar straits once. Amma said What about the family house, but Appa said it was after British Tommies had burned it down, and did she not recall him walking the streets up and down, up and down from dawn to midnight looking for shelter? Midnight to dawn more like it, said Amma, you were afraid of being nabbed in bed, you were too scared to sleep, but she said it gently because she admired Appa for what he had done for his country. Everyone who had was admired, especially by Amma's generation, which knew all the details. Saroja was hazy about the details, but she was aware Appa had been called a terrorist, which was the label the British pinned on patriots. It was difficult to picture Appa as a terrorist/patriot, you just gave him his due without argument.

Their right-hand neighbor had been a terrorist too, he and Appa fell on each other's necks when their pasts emerged. Unlike Appa he had irrefutable proof in the form of an official list of proscribed personnel on which his name appeared. He was fond of flourishing this document, which was so yellowed and frail with age it was a wonder it didn't fall to pieces when he flipped it open for display. There were holes all along the creases. His name, Shelvankar, was also partly holed, he had to fill in the blanks before you could read what it was. Holed or not it gave him status in the hotel, in the same way Appa and Anand and the dead Rangu had status in the village. Amma respected him, but she was afraid of what Appa might reveal to his newfound blood

brother when they took a turn together on the verandah, or leaned on the parapet and exchanged long,
charged confidences. Appa took to dramatic tiptoeing,
placed forefinger on mouth in token of his utter circumspection every time he went out to placate Amma, but
she remained unconvinced, did not hitch herself off the
hook until he was safely indoors again.

The neighbor on their left she did not respect at all.
This was a slim young man with black curly hair and
rather full lips whom Appa called son, or sometimes
sonny. Amma curled her lip when she heard. Son or
daughter, who can tell, she said, it is a case of which
guise is assumed for the masquerade. She dubbed him
Curly, said this would cover all eventualities. It puzzled
Saroja, she perceived submeanings but she could not
decipher them. She studied Curly, covertly, she didn't
want him to notice and be hurt if, as Amma hinted,
there was something peculiar about him, but there was
nothing very much that she could spot. Sometimes his
face looked a bit floury, as if he had rubbed powder on
it, sometimes his eyes seemed a little too brilliant, like
a woman's after putting on khol. Apart from this he
seemed quite ordinary to her, quite harmless in fact, for
instance he did not affect her at all in the way Devraj
did. Amma said he made her flesh creep. She was always polite to him, but she used her icy brand, it was
the summit of insult.

Lalitha told Saroja, under the cork tree, which was
the only place for such confidences, that Curly wore
women's clothes. Saris, she said, and blouses which he
stuffs up inside to give him boobs. Saroja said she
couldn't think why. Lalitha enlightened her, not very

213

much though. They're like that, she said. Curly's explanation sounded more reasonable. I'm an actor, he told them. He giggled. I'm an actress too, he said. Saroja's ears were flapping for more when Amma swooped out and bore them off. At night she tried to keep awake, Lalitha said it was the best time to peep out and catch Curly returning in full womanly glory. She could not stay awake. Lalitha's trouble was that she could not sleep.

Amma said she would go to a health center, get some tablets.

After, said Lalitha. After was after seeing Mr. Gupta, after doing with her baby whatever they were going to do with it.

Shall we all go? Appa wanted to know on the eve.

Amma said Yes. She mimed, made signs in the air because the door was open. Appa was thick, he didn't cotton on. Amma spelled out about exposure to corrupting influences, meaning Mendoza and Gupta: how once was plenty, she wasn't going to risk Saroja, not for anything. Curly overheard. He came up to Amma, he had a delicate, mincing way of walking. Ah, madam, he said. His eyes were melting, he looked really hurt. Ah, madam, you misjudge, I would not lay a finger on your daughter.

All the same, Saroja was not left behind. She went with the other three, made an unwanted fourth. She sat on the satiny chair next to her parents, who clearly did not know what was to be done with her even before Mr. Gupta put in an appearance. He was definitely appearing this time. The servant said so, his manner toward them was changed from the last occasion. Sahib is expecting you, he told them with a deferential air, and flicked a duster over the chairs they were to sit on, which he hadn't done before.

Mr. Gupta came in briskly. He looked glum even while greeting them, his lips split to show his gums, but you could tell what a struggle it had been. He had kept the appointment, he said, but his time was strictly limited. He bent his glance on Saroja and his gloom thickened. Surely not in front of the child? he said, and snapped his fingers. Devraj appeared. If you will come this way, he said to Saroja, who was burning with humiliation on several counts. Where? said Amma, bristling. On the balcony, said Devraj, he was taken aback by her ferocity. It's just off here, he explained. Amma inclined her head, she was quite regal.

Saroja followed Devraj. He had on a shirt of Madras checks with short sleeves and an open collar. Mr. Gupta was wearing an orange silk shirt with long sleeves and diamond cuff links. He looked exceedingly hot in it. Devraj looked cool. His shirt billowed in the breeze on the balcony. Will you have a fruit cordial? he asked. Saroja recalled Miss Mendoza with gratitude. That will be nice, she replied. She hoped he would bring her the cordial himself, but instead he sent a servant. Saroja detected Amma's influence in this, she felt he would have liked to return but feared her baleful strictures. Besides he had to hover, be ready to answer peremptory calls. No doubt Mr. Gupta paid him to dance attendance on him, appear when he snapped his fingers. Saroja hated Mr. Gupta.

Not much love was lost by her parents either, judging from the sounds. Saroja sipped her cordial and listened to the carrying voices. When the wind was right they came over so clearly they might have been in the same room.

Appa opened the proceedings, said what a terrible shock it had been to them, it had cast a shadow over their entire lives. Mr. Gupta said he understood, he understood perfectly; he sounded nervous, as if on guard against admitting anything. His daughter's life was in ruins, Appa continued. His voice quavered, then it picked up, rose accusingly. Her whole future had lain before his fair and lovely daughter, he said; with her talent and looks it had been a great future to which they had all looked forward, now all was reduced to ashes. Mr. Gupta said it was a great pity, a great pity. Amma inquired if that was all he had to say. She was in her iron mood, Saroja could visualize strong men—even Mr. Gupta—quailing before her. What else could he say, what did she expect him to say? Mr. Gupta wanted to know. Amma said he had found plenty to say in the era when he was flattering her and turning her head as a preliminary to enticing her into his clutches. Mr. Gupta gave a gasp. Amma told him he was a first-rate actor. Mr. Gupta said he wasn't acting, he was truly flabbergasted. He inquired who it was that had seized Lalitha bodily and put her on that bus. Lalitha interposed, said it had been of her own will and volition. Amma said significantly one knew all about that kind of thing. Mr. Gupta asked if she meant he was some kind of Svengali. Clearly no one knew what he meant, silence fell briefly.

Saroja looked round the balcony, she had been too engrossed to do so before. She supposed this was where

Lalitha had sat and watched the lavish display of Deepavali fireworks. A hundred guests, Lalitha had said, it must have been a mistake, you couldn't have packed anything like that number in, not with the utmost squashing. She looked for the vine-covered arbor Lalitha had described, but she could see nothing resembling it from where she was, she assumed it must be in another part of the grounds. There was a single vine, growing up a trellis from a pot in a corner of the balcony. It had small bunches of grapes clinging to it, but the grapes were green and shriveled, instead of a bloom they were coated with a grayish city dust. Saroja felt no urge to sample one, the way she was tempted to when she looked at Manikkam's crop. In a good year, when he was less idle than usual and had hoed and cultivated the stony ground to a rich tilth, grapes hung from his vines in thick clusters, each one rounded to bursting and a bloom like dew on it, it was all you could do not to keep popping grapes into your mouth. Appa repaid Manikkam for all the popping you did, he did it gladly, any sign of prosperity in Manikkam made him fall about with gratitude because it took some of the load off his shoulders.

Devraj came out. Are you all right? he asked. Saroja wondered why she should not be, it was Lalitha who was the subject of concern. Then she thought it could be an excuse to enjoy her company. She dismissed the thought at once, poured scorn on the idea of her company being enjoyable, but already she was hot and cold, she was sure it showed in her face. I took the opportunity, said Devraj, your mother being preoccupied. He smiled, it made him look quite handsome. Usually his brow was furrowed with Mr. Gupta's problems. Saroja wanted to smile back, she wanted to go further and stroke his hair, which had bluish lights in the black, but she remembered Amma's injunctions, she thought with despair if only he hadn't mentioned her name she would have forgotten, she would have responded warmly to his overtures.

But now it was too late. Mr. Gupta was calling, in that peremptory voice she loathed. Devraj was going. I'll take your glass, he said. His hand touched hers. It gave her a shock, she felt she was on fire. When he took his hand away she had the absurd feeling that her skin was rising up to maintain the contact, it couldn't bear to let him go. It reminded her of an experiment in school, iron filings had jumped up like little frenzied men and glued themselves to a magnetized rod. She quelled the feeling instantly, it was too preposterous, but the fire inside refused to die. She wondered if this was what Lalitha had felt like, if it was the cause of her opening herself to *him*, allowing him to put the seed of the baby inside her. It was the only explanation for a girl to be so careless. It was also a frightening thought, made her speculate on whether she, too, was cast in the wanton mold Aunt Alamelu had described; but the thought would not root. What rooted itself was the suspicion that it wasn't necessary to be cast in Lalitha's mold or any mold, the urge was implanted deep and indestructibly in every human being.

Saroja wrenched her mind off these tracks which were making her dizzy, sought to restore her equilibrium by returning her attention to what was going on. She had to strain her ears to hear. After the earlier rumpus it was surprising, but when she listened she realized Amma was out of the fray, her contributions which had stoked up the flames were missing, had been overcome by her emotions which she partly expressed and partly stifled in one or two low sobs. Appa and Mr. Gupta, taking advantage, were indulging themselves man-to-man. What is one to do? Appa was saying. The pass in which one finds oneself. . . . To which Mr. Gupta agreed, he said he could not agree more, the situation was a damnable one. He sounded quite sorrowful but he wasn't desperate the way Lalitha was, it was his baby but of course he wasn't carrying it. Amma, recovering from her temporary weakness, pointed this out. The sorrows of womankind, she said, but she wasn't prepared for him not to share them. Mr. Gupta came back fighting, said a great deal in a distraught fashion. The gist of it was that Lalitha had flung herself at him, he had never been so pestered in his life. Appa reminded him he was referring to his daughter, an innocent and well-brought-up young girl. Mr. Gupta inquired coarsely what she was doing in his studio then, flapping her lashes and issuing invitations to all and sundry.

It made Appa furious, he had never been able to bear the least harsh word against Lalitha. He asked in a terrible voice if Mr. Gupta was implying his daughter was a wanton, if he was would he so state before witnesses. He called loudly for Devraj. Mr. Gupta told Devraj to go back. He said he would only say that Lalitha was a natural.

Saroja remembered he had told Lalitha she was a natural soon after they first met. She had interpreted it variously—a natural dancer, a natural actress, a natural woman. Or had he meant a natural harlot?

Amma was haunted by the same question, she pursued Mr. Gupta, drove him into corners and would not let go, her own peace of mind seemed involved in extracting an answer. Mr. Gupta capitulated, finally.

Lalitha is a woman with the natural desires of a woman, he said. His voice was very hoarse.

Of which you took advantage, Appa accused.

I am not made of stone, said Mr. Gupta, huskily.

Saroja felt quite sorry for him then, the way she had felt for the Sikh hawker. She understood that he too had feelings, could be hurt as much as anyone else. When she thought that he became real to her, ceased to be an elevated being who sat on satin chairs and walked on aqua floors and turned into an ordinary man who knew about suffering, who was suffering if his voice was anything to go by.

All of them, in fact, in varying degree, were suffering. Saroja's sole hope and prayer was that it could be ended quickly, she closed her eyes while she addressed God and sent up an anguished plea. When she opened them Lalitha was standing in front of her. They sent me out, she said, they're settling it all without me. She was like burned-out wood, only just holding her shape. Saroja sprang out of her chair, thrust it forward to receive the cindery figure before it could crumble.

Perhaps it's best having it all settled for one, she said.

Of course, said Lalitha.

They found nothing more to say to each other. The two of them, who had never lacked for words, were stumped for communication. Presently Devraj was sent to summon them and he too was mute, locked in as they were, the three of them made a joyless, wordless trio. Nor were the others much better. Appa and Amma were utterly subdued, and only Mr. Gupta, perhaps from having the onus on him, found the ability to speak. Everything will be taken care of, I will arrange everything, he said. He blew his nose, avoided everyone's eye, especially Lalitha's. It will all be taken care of, he repeated himself.

They were going. The usual courtesies were missing, were not missed. Except for Devraj, who deserted Mr. Gupta to escort them to the door. Saroja wondered if she would ever see him again. She thought not. Her heart was one huge clenched fist of pain. I hope we shall meet again, said Devraj. He said it cunningly, making out he meant all of them but Saroja knew he meant only herself. I hope so, she took it on her to reply. Her voice was so ordinary it was miraculous. Amma, nevertheless, flashed her a glance. I hope so, Saroja repeated defiantly. Since it was the last time she was immune to those flashes of lightning.

When they were outside, past the gates and on the road, she turned for a last look. Devraj was looking too, standing gazing by the door. He smiled, he waved. Saroja longed to run back, fling herself into his arms and tell him she cared although she knew it was hopeless. Instead she followed her parents, which was the proper thing to do. The improper thing was to fling yourself at a man, and she knew what came of that, Lalitha was living evidence. Lalitha, Lalitha. It seemed to Saroja as if her sister was destined to shape the stream of her life.

6

It was a time of secrets.

What is happening? asked Saroja fretfully.

Nothing, yet, said Lalitha.

What is *going* to happen?

Everything will be taken care of, replied Lalitha.

She, Amma, Appa, had latched on to this phrase which Mr. Gupta had spawned, brought it out like a bulwark behind which they took cover from Saroja. Jointly. Side-stepping her sister, which was the normal alliance, Lalitha was joined up with Amma and Appa. Saroja knew why, it made her resentful. It was because they were initiates, the three of them. They knew about union, and frenzy, and the ejection and admission of seed in which was shrouded the creation of life: the minute, exact detail of it was kept from her.

They knew, she suspected, what was to come.

The thing that was opaque to her was plain to them but they were not telling Saroja, who was virgin. Saroja the virgin who could not know about life, to whom they were not letting on.

You're ashamed. You're *afraid*, said Saroja bluntly. What of? asked Lalitha.

Saroja retreated. She was not sure. It was too murderous to name. She was afraid that to name it would bring it into being. Word made flesh. Flesh forming about the skeleton crouched with the trinity behind the bulwark, inviting it to step out in bloody rags. Saroja shivered. She longed for Chingleput, who might have taken down the skeleton for her inspection, divested it of its power. Or Jaya, from whose welter of information you could pick out one or two factual nuggets. Or best of all, Manikkam's wife, who told you, thought nothing of hitching up her clothes to demonstrate in the flesh if you asked. You never felt afraid of asking her. She was never afraid of imparting information. Aunt Alamelu called her a dangerous woman, said time would reveal all, no need to resort to an ignorant peasant. Saroja could not wait for the revelations of time. She wanted to know now. If she knew, she was convinced, she would feel better. She felt awful. There were cramps in her stomach.

Not too good, little flower? asked Curly. He spoke like an ass, but his eyes were concerned.

Before she could answer, eagle-eyed Amma was calling her in.

Madam, your daughter's a worry-guts, called Curly from the verandah. It made Amma's face harden. You certainly pick them, she said.

223

In Saroja's view Amma was becoming like her sister. Her soft, lovely, doe-eyed Amma turning into crabbed Aunt? Saroja threw out the idea, crept to her mother for warmth. Tentatively, so she could back out, pretend to some other motive if her move was rejected. But Amma enfolded her. Poor child, she said, it must be awful for you. Is there anything you would like to do? she asked. Shall we go to the beach? asked Saroja despairingly. At a time like this? began Amma. She looked at Saroja and checked herself. Well, we'll see, we must ask Appa, she said.

Appa was out on a secret errand.

Saroja knew. She had seen him puzzling over the slip of paper Mr. Gupta had handed him on which an address was written. Finally he had had to ask Shelvankar to direct him.

When he came back he was fierce. Is it arranged? asked Amma. Appa looked at Saroja big-ears. There is no privacy in this place for anything, he grumbled. It might have been the shade of Lalitha complaining. Lalitha, though, was not complaining. She was not with them, she had abdicated. The way she was she might have been a zombie.

Never mind her, said Amma sharply, have you been able to or not? It's no go, said Appa, all I got was a lecture on medical ethics. He made gestures, rubbed forefinger and thumb together. It's a case of that, he said with disgust, lectures for those who haven't the stuff, action for those who do. He swore. Amma begged him not to sound off like a Tommy. She said every man had his price. Appa said too true, but the price the medico had wanted was scandalous, way above what Gupta had provided him with. He sank into gloom, said he supposed he would have to approach Gupta again. Amma said he need feel no compunction on that score, it was all *his* doing, he had introduced them to tragedy and could not expect to escape unscathed. She needled Appa until he took himself off.

Amma had things to do too. Secrecy made her shifty, she would not tell them anything. She contemplated her daughters doubtfully, asked if she could trust them to behave themselves while she was out. Saroja said coldly, Yes. Amma relented. She said she wasn't thinking of them so much, it was others she couldn't trust. She meant Curly. Saroja wondered what had got into her mother to think so harshly of him. She thought Curly completely harmless.

What do you think? she asked her sister.

I don't seem able to think about anything, said Lalitha. She drooped, there were great black hollows under her eyes. Let's go out, said Saroja. Just for a little while, a little fresh air, she wheedled. They went out, stood by the cork tree that yielded fresh memories. The boys had carved the cork into tiny boat shapes, attached paper sails and launched them on Rangu's river. They had made boats for their sisters, the four of them raced on the riverbank alongside their dizzy craft. The sails got sodden and fell off but the boats never sank, you saw them bobbing and dipping long after your legs gave out.

Do you remember? asked Saroja. Of course, said Lalitha. She smiled, there was a pale life there, under the deadwood. We were all children then, she said. It's strange to think, began Saroja. I'm not going to, I don't seem able, said Lalitha roughly. A light breeze whipped her hair, sent flowers drifting down off the tree. Butterflies hovered, drawn by the scent; alighted, palpitating; settled, folded their wings like praying hands. They were easy to trap.

This one's a Jezebel, said Lalitha. She knew, in her school there was a glass case full of butterflies, with labels, and pins driven through their bodies. She pounced, her hands were a cage, her fingers were dusted with the golden pollen of imprisoned wings. They call it a Common Jezebel, she said, like me. I'm called many things too, said Curly. Are you averse to my company, little flower? he asked. Saroja was jolted, she hadn't heard him padding up, but she wasn't averse, if anything she was intrigued. What names? she asked. Just names, said Curly, like your saintly mother calls me. She doesn't call you anything, said Saroja, feeling very hot and guilty. If she did, what matter? asked Curly. He pinched his nostrils together with thumb and forefinger, splayed the other three out in a fan. Foul air, he said nasally, and giggled. One doesn't *have* to smell it.

Amma came back, she was bulging with parcels. Saroja looked at her with slanted eyes. What are you staring at? challenged Amma, trying to dispose of her burdens. She was guilty, Saroja could tell, her nose had become expert at sniffing out guilt, it led her to poke around the parcels. A few things for Lalitha, said badgered Amma, leave them alone, will you?

Late evening Appa returned, the two of them conferred. There was no cork tree let-out for them, they had to confer in the room, in the very middle because Amma believed Curly had his ear to the wall, which was thin. At the end Lalitha was drawn into their council. Saroja was left outside the ring. In the village if a man was suspected of wrongdoing they drew a circle around him, summoned the priest. If he was innocent he merely stepped out of it, if he wasn't he couldn't. It was only a circle in chalk, but he was incapable, it might have been the ramparts of a fort the helplessness that seized him, you could see him sweating and agonizing inside it.

Saroja wasn't sure, now, if she wanted to be inside or outside their ring of knowledge. She suspected both states were bad, but she felt being perched on the periphery as she was was downright devilish.

At night she dreamed.

It was more the turmoil of her mind that slid into a dream, but it was sweeter, went further, went too far and turned into a nightmare. She was home, lying in the shade of the tamarind tree, watching the bright blue sky through criss-crossed fingers. Devraj appeared. She was not in the least surprised to see him, he and the country went well together. I followed you, he said. I knew you would, she replied. He lay down beside her and started to caress her. She allowed him to, she discovered she had no sense of shame in revealing, in yielding the shyest, most guarded recesses of her body to him. Each caress was like a passing flame. The sensations were exquisite, were mounting, she could not bear them but she wanted more, she begged him to pierce her entirely and give her peace. I will, he cried, and lunged. Lalitha appeared. She was naked, her belly was enormous but she didn't seem to mind. Her eyes were shining, rainwet, diamonds hung on the lashes. It's so lovely, she said, there's nothing like it when they spill their seed. Saroja burst into tears. She twisted herself away from Devraj, his sucking, clinging, spilling body. You're killing me, he cried. You're killing my baby, Saroja shouted at him. She woke. She was alone in the room. There was an almond-milk moisture between her legs, her flesh was swollen and quivering. She wiped herself dry and got up, convinced she must still be dreaming, but in fact Amma and Lalitha were gone. Their sleeping mats were rolled up and disposed neatly against the wall.

Appa was on the verandah, discoursing with Shelvankar. When she emerged he looked furtive, she guessed he had been blabbing but what about exactly she did not know. Your mother's gone out, he told her. He swallowed and added, with Lalitha. I know, said Saroja. Appa looked relieved, but the relief was momentary, her presence was a constraint on him. Shall I get you some coffee? he asked, and bolted without waiting for an answer.

Saroja drank her coffee. She was still a little unstrung from the night, and thinking about Lalitha, and Lalitha again. She lambasted her sister, so malevolently that she grew a little afraid, called back the words and cleansed out her mouth by reciting God's name.

Toward noon Appa came in bearing rice and dhal, curds in a pot. The rice was saffron flavored, studded with peas and cashew nuts. It looked tempting but she could not eat. Appa made no comment, he was in the same predicament. His face was haggard. They picked at the rice in silence. The silence was oppressive, it was intolerable but neither of them seemed able to break it. Appa made an effort. Are you enjoying your trip to the city? he asked. So-so, said Saroja. It was one of Lalitha's sophisticated sayings which she·had brought back with her to the village. It finished the two of them. As soon as he could Appa fled. He had his crony to go to. Saroja had no one, except the banned Curly. She defied the ban, tapped on the wall, on his door, but he was out. She resigned herself to her thoughts, which were discordant and sickly.

Twilight came. Crimson and orange streamers shot across the sky in an extravagant display. It was the dust that did it, she had been told, the more the better. Saroja could well believe it. The city was full of dust, its sunsets were full of splendor.

The colors faded quickly, drained back into the sky. Dusk fell. Bats came out, described arabesques in the sludgy light that was left. Once as a small child, she had been afraid of them, but not after Chingleput caught one, showed her the small furry frightened creature bonded to those huge wings.

The bats were after the butterflies, which were dying, whose day was over. They fluttered their wings feebly, were seized, were finished. The gauzy wings spiraled down, unattached, aimless without their host. It was tragic to see but the bats were happy, it was their hour. Everything had its hour. Everyone too. It made her wonder when hers was due, it definitely wasn't the present.

Saroja slid off the parapet, sat on the verandah steps; abandoned that and went inside but that was no better. She was afflicted. She wished Amma was back, and again she did not. She did not want to know. She walked up and down the room, which was cramped and in bad repair. There were patches of mold, cracks in the walls which Lalitha had fussed over. Lalitha who demanded beauty and perfection out of life, who was herself so exquisitely fashioned. But it gave you no claims, none at all, no guarantees whatsoever.

Saroja flung herself down on her mat, buried her face in the pillow. Somewhere within her she carried the sphere of quiet: it was always there, it waited for you, but you could not always enter, the more frenzied you were the harder it got, you could only stand back and marvel at the ease with which, at one time, you had been able to step into it. Saroja waited, she submitted and held herself back, her being advanced, was clasped to the orb, it began to dissolve and enter its heritage.

Saroja, said Amma.

Yes, said Saroja reluctantly.

You must have been asleep, poor child, Amma said. Come and lie down, she said to Lalitha.

Then all was bustle and flurry, but it took place in semi-silence, in the semi-darkness, it was like watching a shadow play, or a film in the village cinema when the voltage was falling. Amma flitted about in the gloom, arrangements were on her mind, she pulled and shifted and unrolled, picked things up and put them down, making her dispositions. She seemed dedicated to whispers, the only sound came from her bangles, the gold and glass clashed as she worked, as she did things for Lalitha, who lay with her eyes closed, like felled timber. She looked half dead. Is she all right? asked Saroja. Her bowels had turned to water. Hush, said Amma. She put her hand over the light switch to forestall Saroja, who hated the darkness that denied her. I can't see her properly, I want to see she's all right, she begged. Lalitha opened her eyes. I'm fine, she said. Her voice was clear and metallic. I'm just fine, it's him that's a bloody pulp.

* * *

Appa spent the night on the verandah, where Amma
had tossed his bedroll. She let him in, shivering, at
dawn. He had not slept much, he said, ascribed it to the
dew. His eyes slid about, avoiding, there was hardly
anywhere they could rest without painful reminders.
Saroja could not bear to look either, the room was cluttered with the contents of the parcels, now disclosed,
diapers and binders and rolls of cotton wool that Amma
had bought, with which she had staunched Lalitha's
wound.

Amma said she felt for Appa, she hadn't slept much
either. Her eyes were swollen. She went out and bathed
them, came back saying That's better, but it wasn't.
Nothing ever would be, Saroja felt. Is there anything
you want? Appa asked. He looked half dead too. I think
we have everything, said Amma, wearily, but gently,
you could tell she would have done anything to spare
him but there was nothing she could do. We must leave
soon, she said. As soon as—said Appa, and got stuck.
The worst thing for him was he could not communicate
about or with his beloved daughter.

* * *

On the third day Lalitha was up and about. She looked
ugly, the lily quality was gone. Her skin was coarse,

gave the impression of lumps lying just under the surface. The bump in her belly was still there, it made Saroja speculate. Lalitha caught her looking. It's gone, she said, it's left a little swelling. Do you mean the baby's gone, asked Saroja; her heart was hammering. Of course, said Lalitha, didn't you know it was planned, you're not that simple? I suppose I did, said Saroja wretchedly, only I didn't know exactly, I still don't know—You still don't know? said Lalitha. She eyed her sister.

Do you want to? she asked, harshly.

Yes, said Saroja, huskily.

They sucked him out, said Lalitha, bit by bit. He came out in pieces. I could feel him going, though they said I wouldn't feel anything. He wouldn't have filled a tumbler, except for the fluid. It took ten minutes. She paused, she was hideously dry. If I hadn't wanted him it might have been different, she said, an unwanted child is better off unborn. But I did want him, I wanted him most when he was going, those last ten minutes of his life.

It's horrible, I don't want to hear, Saroja burst out.

Why not, said Lalitha, you're a woman, aren't you? You aren't going to slide through life untouched, you don't think?

Not like this, Saroja gasped.

Like what, like me? asked Lalitha. Well, maybe not. But you want to know, you want to know the detail of it to help you along.

Didn't you? asked Saroja. She mouthed, she could not utter.

All I know is it's horrible, said Lalitha, but more

horrible to have gone through with it, there would have been no place for him. She licked her blistered lips. It isn't fair, she said. You'd think there was some other way, wouldn't you? To keep a child if you wanted to, whether you were married or not? But there isn't, no way at all.

If there had been— said Saroja.

Too late, said Lalitha. She smiled, she glittered, there was the sharpness of daggers about her. The thing to remember, my sweet, is never to cry over spilt milk.

I'm not, said Saroja. Her eyes were brimming.

Over men or babies, said Lalitha. I'm telling you now because I shan't be able to tell you later.

Why not, said Saroja, a great fear stirring.

Because it's too raw to go over, said Lalitha.

Saroja went away, leaving her sister alone under the cork tree. Her stomach was knotted with grief for the baby that had been done away with. Through the red membranes of her eyelids the scraps of her knowledge meshed together, she saw the gaping hole between Lalitha's legs through which they had drawn him, she saw the whole raw picture. It's society, she heard herself mumbling. It's the way society is organized, she heard her brothers say. Saroja agreed. After all the years of semi-comprehension she took up her stand solidly alongside them and flayed the system. Then she turned on herself, savaged the woman in her who had suspected, who had all but known all the time but had gone along with what had been hatching.

You're only a child, how can you understand? said Amma. She had come back from the temple, had gone there to pray but it had brought her no comfort. It's the

233

same the world over, she said with pity, there's no room for the children of sin. Open your eyes, she begged. Saroja opened her eyes, she saw with clarity, she saw her mother's blotched face, her own was spongy with unshed tears. The sin is not to make room for them, she said bluntly. The sin is to conceive, said Amma. It is so quickly done, so easy to do . . . yet who would have thought? She sat down, clasped her hands round her knees and rocked. Your sister wandered too far, she said wearily, she was lured outside the code of our community and is paying the penalty, that is all.

* * *

By the end of the week Lalitha was jaunty again. She swung her hips as she walked. She chaffed Appa, demanding to know what doldrums he was in. She washed her hair, borrowed a hand mirror from Curly to set tendrils curling around her face.

What are you doing? asked Amma. She was like quartz.

What do you think I'm doing, said Lalitha, I'm making myself look respectable, isn't that what you want?

What I want is best left out of account, said Amma, it's your life, it's what *you* want to make of it.

Oh no, said Lalitha, it's what *you* want, I know, I've graduated.

Appa was gaunt with distress. He hated conflict between Amma and Lalitha, since coming to the city it had acquired deadly undertones. Besides, Lalitha's recovery had revitalized him, he didn't want to go under again. We've all been under some strain, he said. It wasn't a brilliant beginning, he stopped, cast around, his eyes lit upon Saroja, he used her to leaven the appalling atmosphere. Have you seen all you want to see of the city? he asked. Yes, said Saroja. What they had seen was on the one outing, could have been counted on the fingers of one hand. We ought to be going home soon, said Appa. He dared to lift his eyes to Lalitha. As soon as you're fit, he said. I'm fit all right, said Lalitha, she was like flint, looked straight back at him and he had to lower his eyes. I'm fit for anything now, it's over and done with, isn't it? Yes, well, said Appa. We'll go in a day or two, he declared. I can't wait, said Saroja passionately.

*   *   *

I can't wait to get home, Saroja told Curly.

Now that they've scraped out your sister there's nothing to keep you, is there? said Curly.

Nothing, said Saroja. Who told you? she asked.

All of you. It stuck out a mile in spite of your sainted mother's efforts, said Curly. I shall be desolate, he told her, when you're gone, little flower, a hole will be left in my life.

It will mend soon enough, said Saroja. She was cruel, she didn't know why. Then she softened toward him, despite Amma's suspicions he had done her no wrong, at times he had lightened her load. I shall miss you, she

235

said. And I shall miss you, said Curly. He eyed her, his eyes were rimmed with khol, which Amma had remarked on with loathing. You take me as I am, and that's a rare thing.

I must go, said Saroja. She didn't have to, except that Amma, in the distance, was looming. We are leaving tomorrow, she said.

I shall look out for you in the morning before you go, said Curly.

* * *

In the morning Lalitha was gone.

This time she had taken nothing with her, not even a rupee was missing. Her bedroll was stacked against the wall. She had scrawled a note, left it tucked in her bedding. It said she couldn't face going back to the village: it stifled her, her talents, her ambition. She intended to stay in the city where she belonged. She could look after herself. They weren't to search for her, which in any case would be a waste of time because they would never find her.

Where does one begin to search? asked Appa. He was bewildered and frantic in turn.

There is a time of darkness, said Amma. She folded her hands, sat very still, sat cross-legged on the mat she had spread. It is the night of anguish which comes to most people in their lifetime. It will pass.

If it doesn't, cried Appa. We must find her. Get up, get up, he urged her.

It's a big city, said Amma, unmoving.

236

We must search, Appa insisted.

They searched. They took Saroja with them because they were afraid of losing her too, because they were afraid of leaving her alone, because they were afraid of each other's company, their fears escalated and mangled them.

They went to the beach. Amma said it was like inviting knives but it was worse for Saroja, who remembered the sucking sands, scanned the serene emerald of the sea beyond where the waves broke, and wondered. They returned through the fashionable quarters where the boutiques were, where Lalitha might be. She was not. A bell rang in Appa's mind and they made their way to the YWCA, which took in girls in need, of any denomination. Was Lalitha in need, was she a Christian? the lady in charge inquired. She was a Christian, hard-faced, you could spot the Christians in a crowd from the hardness of their faces, perhaps it was the rigor of their religion. Appa said Lalitha was certainly in need of help, but she wasn't a Christian. The lady told him it made no difference, they never turned away any girl in need, but Lalitha hadn't applied. It comforted Appa, he hadn't seen the notice which said Hostel Full. He said his daughter might still apply, clung to the hope although Amma said it was the last place she would make for. Gupta's was another last place, according to Amma, but Appa turned obstinate, said they could leave no stone upturned and went on his own when she refused to accompany him.

Saroja and Amma fended for themselves. The market, said Amma, it's the kind of place your sister. . . . They knew this main central market existed, Shelvankar had told them, but they didn't know where. They had to ask a dozen people the way. Getting anyone to stop long enough to answer was one problem, following their directions another. The streets and bazaars all looked alike, people jostled you when you paused to get your bearings, fumed impatiently when you didn't get out of their way quickly enough.

Saroja trailed after Amma. Sometimes she took the lead. Somehow, eventually, they found the market. It was a market for everything, fruit, flowers, vegetables, meat and grain. Saroja didn't think it at all likely Lalitha would be found in this sprawling, noisy hive, but she held her peace. They squelched through the narrow alleys, over slimy, rotting vegetables and crushed flower petals. Saroja slipped on a sucked mango stone, fell against a fruit stall. Can't you look where you're going? said Amma. She picked up the fallen fruit, rebuilt the demolished pyramid. Imprecations fell fast and free from the stall-holder's lips. A snarling race, these city folk, said Amma, loudly. Country baboons, the stall-holder gave back in crescendo. They moved on, Saroja nursing her arm, which had been grazed and was bleeding a little. You'll *never* find Lalitha in a place like this, she said savagely. Where *will* I find her? asked Amma.

Appa was waiting at the rendezvous they had arranged. He had been to Gupta's, had drawn a blank, had been waiting a long time. Wherever have you been? he asked querulously. Amma was too tired to speak. We got lost, said Saroja. Did you see— she began. I saw no one except that footling assistant of Gupta's, said Appa tetchily. Did he say anything? Saroja persevered. She wondered why she did, anything between them was over, would have been finally severed by departure, which only Lalitha delayed; but she could not help herself, the longing welled up. Not a word, said Appa.

It was too late to do more. They went back, to the one room which oscillated wildly between a haven and a prison cell with bars.

Next day they set out again, early, before the sun got up, got vicious and broiled the city.

And the next day, and the next.

They walked everywhere. They had to go carefully, husband their resources, said Appa, buses were expensive at three fares a time. He looked harassed, counted his money each morning before they set out. His sandals were fraying, he did a great deal more walking around than Amma and Saroja. He told them that at times he felt he was going round in circles. Sometimes he did not know where next to aim for. Neither did Amma. They conferred. Saroja stood waiting in the sun, mute as if she had suffered a stroke, her coin-spot scarf, which was sadly worn, wound round her blistering head and shoulders.

The temple, said Amma, it's not likely but . . . Highly unlikely, said Appa, it's not at all the kind of place. . . . The trouble was neither of them had any idea what kind of place Lalitha would head for. She was outside their scope, she had catapulted herself outside the orbit of her community, they had nothing to go by.

But anything was better than nothing.

They went to the temple at feeding time. At least it's one free meal, Lalitha knows that, said Amma, anguished. They scanned the line of poor, to whom rice was being doled out. There was no one in the least like

Lalitha, no well-dressed, well-brought-up young girls like her at all, nor did you expect there would be because naturally they would all be safely at home with their families.

Your sister is isolate, said Amma. Her anger surfaced. Made isolate by that Western punk Gupta, she said, curse the day he and his ways crossed our threshold.

At night Amma spoke in her sleep. Every night. It disturbed Saroja. Lying awake in the dark, she hoped devoutly the ravings of her mother would be wafted through the ether to harass Mr. Gupta, deprive him of peace as they had been stripped of theirs. She doubted it, she did not set any great store in the power of her wishes and wants. Prayer was another matter, but you could not implore malign issues of divinity. Malevolence belonged to another domain, you entered it at your peril, asked your evil host for an evil outcome out of the demented strength of your passion. People like them would not enter such malignant terrain at all, not even at the end of their tether. Saroja hoped Amma was not at the end of her tether. She prayed, one's parents were a suitable subject for prayer.

In the mornings she inspected her mother closely. Amma appeared utterly normal. What passed for normality here would have seemed the direst symptoms of disturbance at home. Saroja brooded on the relativity of standards, she longed for the immutable pattern of her life to resume in place of the chaotic flux induced by the city.

What is it? asked Amma.

Nothing. I was thinking about school, said Saroja.

It was the last thing, really. She hadn't thought about

school since the last day, it had lost all relevance. She thought about it now, slowly plaiting her hair: what would she say to the girls when she got back, about the city, about Lalitha, who had made this awesome choice, gone off to face the world on her own.

Don't be long, said Amma.

Saroja finished her plait, tied the end with a scrap of Lalitha's ribbon. She put on her blouse and scarf. The coin-spot was in ruins, too delicate for city climate, continuous use. Her sandals were in equally poor shape, only marginally better than Appa's. She eyed Lalitha's, not the creamy pair in which she had walked away, but her second-best ones. Yes, why not? She has no use for them, said Amma. When Saroja wriggled her toes in she felt the screw of paper threaded under the broad strap of the toe loop. She waited until Amma had turned away, palmed it adroitly.

Are you ready? asked Amma.

In a minute, said Saroja.

She whisked into the bathroom, unscrewed the note after bolting the door.

Stay if you want to, no one can stop you, Lalitha had written.

Saroja stood very still, clasping the paper. She couldn't think of anything worse than to stay on in the city. There was nothing she wanted more. The sleeve of the Madras check shirt brushed against her cheek, seducing, the bait in the trap cunningly, sweetly concealed.

Saroja, Saroja, Amma was calling. Saroja tore the note into little pieces, sluiced them away. Paper messages, Madras checks, were nothing to her, could never be anything. I'm *coming!* she called back furiously.

* * *

THAT day was reserved for the hospital. It was Appa's idea. In case, he said, his voice was pitiful. Amma was back to iron. Do you mean the morgue? she asked. Appa recoiled. No, he gasped, I mean if she's been in an accident—The police would have been notified, said Amma. I'll go there then, said Appa. He hated the thought of going to them, but he had no option.

Police stations were not the sort of place women went to, except in a body for the protection of their children. Saroja and Amma waited outside. They stood under a neem tree for the shade but there wasn't much of it, the tree was stunted with only a straggly growth of leaves. Saroja sat down, despite Amma she plumped down right in the dust, among the squashed and scattered acid-green berries. Mind it doesn't get on your skirt, said Amma. Saroja was past caring. It was very hot. It was also the wedding season, she remembered, she could hear marriage music. The procession passed quite close. The bride was a girl of Lalitha's age, but nowhere as pretty. Her little heart-shaped face was half buried in flower garlands. Her mother sat behind her, in the same carriage. She was wearing a red brocade sari. Now and then she leaned forward proprietarilly, patted a stray strand of her daughter's hair into place. Lucky woman, said Amma. Her face was wistful, had shed its hard indentations.

242

The day wore on. The light was bleached, fell white and burning on their backs. Dust eddied up in little swirls, as if the earth were gasping. Appa came out. Not a sign, no news, he said. It's a long time to wait for no news, said Amma. Where next? I can't think, I'm coming to the end of my resources, said Appa. He turned to Saroja. You're her generation, he appealed to her, in Lalitha's place where would you go? I'd go straight home, said Saroja passionately. Is that the best you can do? said Appa. He subdued his irritation and pleaded with her. Please try, he begged. Saroja could not. She was conscious only of her aching haunches, and the pain in her breast, and the dizziness that stalked her as they tramped through the stifling, bewildering, terrible streets of this hideous maze.

She hated the city.

She didn't belong to it, she wanted to go away and never come back.

She wanted to go home. At home there were fields to rest your eyes on, colors that changed with the seasons. The tender green of new crops, the tawny shades of harvest, the tints of freshly turned earth, you could have told the week and the month of the year by these alone. You knew each grove, each acre, each homestead on it, who owned them, and the owners of the names. You knew every pathway. No one could ever be lost, not by trying. The wells, the fields, each had its name: the well beside the water meadow, the well by the banyan, the field next to the mill. You always knew where you were. You knew who you were.

The city took it all away from you. You were one in a hundred, in a thousand, you were no longer you, you might have been an amoeba. You drifted, amoebalike,

243

through the baffling streets, wondering where you were, what business you had. What on earth, people echoed your doubts, eyebrows arched, faces pained, in their moments of enforced awareness of your existence. You knew what you were doing on earth, all right, but it grew blurred here in the city. You couldn't answer, in any case your lips were sealed. You stood, buffeted, like a tree in a storm, like some stubborn tedious obstruction people implied, their looks, their sighs, their jabbing elbows were eloquent. Then you walked on, counting, plotting your way to the second crossroad at the third intersection, which was the way the city was laid out, and the carts threw up stones which were sharp under shrinking country soles, and by midday the tar on the roads was melting.

I'm tired, said Saroja, halting.

It's time we went home, said Amma.

I've run out of cash, said Appa. He jingled the coppers in his pocket. Gupta said any time for return expenses, he said bitterly, I shall have to call on him.

It'll save us a trip, it's on the way back to the hotel, said Appa.

No, said Saroja violently.

Yes, why not, we may as well get it over and done with, said Amma.

*   *   *

Saroja was on the balcony again. Appa and Amma and Gupta were inside, haggling.

It was like some hallucination. It was the same. The

grapes still grew in the corner, the dusty blight on them.

Devraj came in. I'm so sorry, he said, about your sister, about everything.

Saroja sat silent. Her lips were withered, dead yellowed leaves.

Are you angry with me? he asked. Is it something I've done? I wouldn't for the world, I care too much.

He came close. He touched her.

Please, he said.

Saroja leapt up. Her flesh was molten. She knew what he was asking. She knew where it ended. She had dragged her bloated gravid sister out of the bog, she had seen the bloody pulp of the baby.

Take your hands off me, she cried, and Aunt Alamelu of all people loomed up, put words she was fighting for into her mouth. What do you take me for, she screamed, a virgin in your whorehouse?

She couldn't stop screaming. They couldn't stop her. They put her in a taxi and all the way back those rasping sounds kept bursting out of her throat, for the life of her she couldn't throttle them back.

*   *   *

AMMA packed her things, Appa's, Saroja's and Lalitha's. She wept, quietly, when she came to Lalitha's belongings, it was like seeing the wax fall from a wasting candle, those silent drops.

At the terminal Appa handed up all the bundles he had handed down, not so long ago, on this very spot.

This time he did not bother to count them. The jokes he cracked were feeble, verged on derangement considering the hollow creature that uttered them. Those who noticed, recoiled: pasted a grin on their faces and shot off at speed as far as they could from the doomed family. Appa did not care. He was past caring for anything.

So was Saroja. She sat by herself on a seat at the very end of the bus. Her thoughts were quiet, at last, in contrast to the feverish clamor of the crowd. Her eyes were puffy, she watched through slits the bustling scene around, feeling cut off, utterly remote. Amma clambered in, sat next to her. How are you? she asked. She looked calm but she wasn't, she was chewed up, her lips were ragged and her eyes kept shifting, Saroja could tell her mother would have been better off if her surviving daughter had been strapped into her seat. So she made a great effort for Amma's sake, hauled herself out of her indifference. I'm all right, she said, I'll be all right when we're home.

Then she discovered it was true. Her core, which was numb, was beginning to feel, the icy encrustations were flaking away and whirling off into space, the process accelerated as they drew away from the city. Saroja sat up. Her eyes and her mind began chiming together, resuming a positive functioning. She began to take in things, it was no longer a case of watching a pointless kaleidoscope slide past, the unconnected pieces had meaning after all. I'm coming alive, she said to herself, cautiously. It seemed quite a feat. She would not allow it to intoxicate, however, permitted only the barest traces of contentment as she watched the macadam landscape retreating.

246

Those roads, those loopy roads. How they had un-strung you, your sense of direction and destination! And the bricks and concrete wherever you turned, however far you walked, their drabness like a blight on your soul. And the bicycle hordes, all whooshing tires and flashing spokes as they bore down on you, hell-bent. She and Amma had rushed for shelter, Saroja remembered, before they learned to take it in their stride, saunter on unconcerned like the rest of the crowd. She smiled. Already it was memory. Soon the cyclists would come in a different mold: village-brand, with time to wave as they passed by, without shrill double bells on their handlebars.

Soon there would be land: not the patches that passed for it in the town but great swathes and acres of land; and clear, uncluttered skylines. Saroja sat forward, hugging her knees. She saw cane fields go by, and after their second halt corn and paddy. There was hardly any traffic, a bus or two like the one they were in, a few bullock carts. The bullocks had bright brass caps to the tips of their horns, it was a country custom, reminded her they were well out of the city. In the city bullocks' horns were sel-dom adorned, she recalled. She hadn't noticed at the time, though she had noticed that men took the place of bullocks, which was rare in the village, har-nessed themselves up like beasts and dragged their carts through the streets.

Like Chingleput, who had shaken the dust of the city off his feet, but had not rid himself of its customs.

Chingleput, whom she would soon be seeing. It was soothing to think of him. Saroja settled herself to it and something like peace washed over her. She was asleep when they arrived.

* * *

THEY were home.

Aunt Alamelu was standing in the doorway, waiting to receive them.

She chose it, it's her life, said Appa.

I know, I had your letter, said Aunt.

Well, let's go in, said Amma.

Inside the house everything was the same, that was the astonishing part. Saroja wandered around, touching, feeling, she felt she had been away for years, simultaneously she felt she had not been away at all. She peered into their little prayer room. The shrine had been freshly tended, looked the way it had the last time she had seen it. In the grain store the sacks were still bulging, one woman's eating had made little inroad. She went into the courtyard. It had been swept and watered to lay the dust, felt cool to her feet and smelled deliciously of wet earth. In the center Aunt had drawn a wavery *colam*, the only hint of festivity to mark their homecoming: not doves, like Lalitha's, Aunt had no visions or wings to inspire her, it was an honest effort of loops and dots.

Saroja moved on, to the path that led to the shed and the fields beyond, down which—yesterday, a lifetime ago—she had sped on her bike. She wondered where it was, where Aunt—who disapproved—had stashed it. It had not been in the house. Lalitha's bike, the rusted remnants, were lying in the churned-up mud by the shed. She unlatched the door. Against the wall was her bicycle, sharing the shed with the buffalo. Both were in fine fettle, both clamored for attention. The buffalo won, it had lustrous, irresistible eyes and a formidable bellow. She caressed the animal, it would be in her sole care now, promised to look after it from that day on. The bicycle's day was tomorrow. That too was a promise, she made it to herself.

* * *

In the morning Amma said: Where are you off to?

Saroja was canny. She knew what would come if she told. She knew it all, wanted no half-baked, half-veiled exhortations.

I'm going to see Jaya, she said.

* * *

Chingleput was waiting for her. He knew she was back, the whole village knew. He had prepared her favorite sweet. It melted on Saroja's tongue.

I tasted nothing to touch it the whole time we were in the city, she said.

You've come back empty, what have you done with your heart? asked Chingleput.

The incomparable sweetness on Saroja's tongue was tinctured with the bitterness of aloes, infiltrated by seawater salt.

Don't cry, said Chingleput. A good deal is changing, you can go back if you want to.

How can I, it isn't possible, said Saroja, sobbing, but intrigued.

When you're a little older, if you still want to, said Chingleput. Your whole life is in front of you. He clasped her. His organ was hard, was nuzzling her body. Don't be afraid, I'm a man, I can't help it, said Chingleput.

Saroja wasn't afraid. She knew too much, she had gone through too much to be afraid of anything. But she knew she wasn't for him, she would never be. So she drew away from him. She got up and mounted her bike. She could hardly see for the tears that were cascading down her face, she couldn't have told for whom they were falling, for her, or Chingleput, or for what was ended. After a while she didn't try. She thought instead of when she was older, felt the wind in her face and the tears drying as she skimmed down the path that led past the fields to the house.